GEEK GIRL

Holly Smale is a debut author. Clumsy, a bit geeky and somewhat shy, she spent the majority of her teenage years hiding in the changing room toilets. She was unexpectedly spotted by a top London modelling agency at the age of fifteen and spent the following two years falling over on catwalks, going bright red and breaking things she couldn't afford to replace. By the time Holly had graduated from Bristol University with a BA in English Literature and an MA in Shakespeare she had given up modelling and set herself on the path to becoming a writer. Holly is now a fully fledged author and blogger and is currently writing the sequel to *Geek Girl*.

For my grandad. My favourite geek.

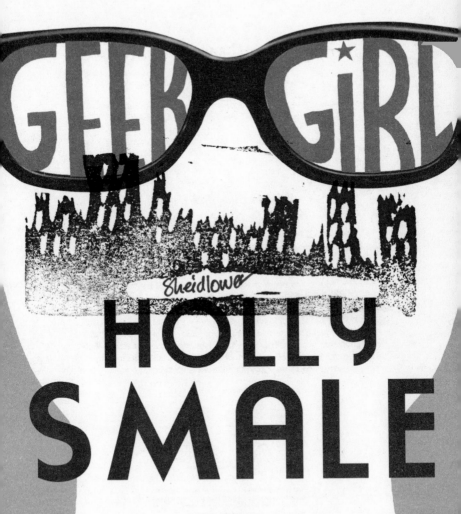

GEEK GIRL

Sheidlowe

HOLLY SMALE

HarperCollins *Children's Books*

First published in paperback in Great Britain
by HarperCollins *Children's Books* in 2013
HarperCollins *Children's Books* is a division of HarperCollins*Publishers* Ltd,
77-85 Fulham Palace Road, Hammersmith, London, W6 8JB.

The HarperCollins website address is: www.harpercollins.co.uk

1

Copyright © Holly Smale 2013

ISBN 978-0-00-748944-2

Printed and bound in England by Clays Ltd, St Ives plc

geek/giːk/h noun informal, chiefly N. Amer.

1 an unfashionable or socially inept person.

2 an obsessive enthusiast.

3 a person who feels the need to look up the word 'geek' in the dictionary.

DERIVATIVES *geeky* adjective.

ORIGIN from the related English dialect word *geck* 'fool'.

I

My name is Harriet Manners, and I am a geek.

I know I'm a geek because I've just looked it up in the *Oxford English Dictionary*. I drew a little tick next to all the symptoms I recognise, and I appear to have them all. Which – and I should be perfectly honest here – hasn't come as an enormous surprise. The fact that I have an *Oxford English Dictionary* on my bedside table anyway should have been one clue. That I keep a Natural History Museum pencil and ruler next to it so that I can neatly underline interesting entries should have been another.

Oh, and then there's the word **GEEK**, drawn in red marker pen on the outside pocket of my school satchel. That was done yesterday.

I didn't do it, obviously. If I *did* decide to deface my own property, I'd choose a poignant line from a really good book, or an interesting fact not many people know. And I definitely wouldn't do it in red. I'd do it in

black, or blue, or perhaps green. I'm not a big fan of the colour red, even if it *is* the longest wavelength of light discernible by the human eye.

To be absolutely candid with you, I don't actually know *who* decided to write on my bag – although I have my suspicions – but I can tell you that their writing is almost illegible. They clearly weren't listening during our English lesson last week when we were told that handwriting is a very important Expression of the Self. Which is quite lucky because if I can just find a similar shade of pen, I might be able to slip in the letter *R* in between *G* and *E*. I can pretend that it's a reference to my interest in ancient history and feta cheese.

I prefer Cheddar, but nobody has to know that.

Anyway, the point is: as my satchel, the anonymous vandal and the *Oxford English Dictionary* appear to agree with each other, I can only conclude that I am, in fact, a geek.

Did you know that in the old days the word 'geek' was used to describe a carnival performer who bit the head off a live chicken or snake or bat as part of their stage act?

Exactly. Only a geek would know a thing like that.

I think it's what they call ironic.

2

Now that you know who I am, you're going to want to know where I am and what I'm doing, right? Character, action and location: that's what makes a story. I read it in a book called *What Makes a Story*, written by a man who hasn't got any stories at the moment, but knows exactly how he'll tell them when he eventually does.

So.

It's currently December, I'm in bed – tucked under about fourteen covers – and I'm not doing anything at all apart from getting warmer by the second. In fact, I don't want to alarm you or anything, but I think I might be really sick. My hands are clammy, my stomach's churning and I'm *significantly* paler than I was ten minutes ago. Plus, there's what can only be described as a sort of... *rash* on my face. Little red spots scattered at totally random and not at *all* symmetrical points on my cheeks and forehead. With a big one on my chin. And one just next to my left ear.

I take another look in the little hand-held mirror on my bedside table, and then sigh as loudly as I can. There's no doubt about it: I'm clearly very ill. It would be wrong to risk spreading this dangerous infection to other, possibly less hardy, immune systems. I shall just have to battle through this illness alone.

All day. Without going anywhere at all.

Sniffling, I shuffle under my duvets a little further and look at my clock on the opposite wall (it's very clever: all the numbers are painted at the bottom as if they've just fallen down, although this does mean that when I'm in a hurry, I have to sort of guess what the time is). Then I close my eyes and mentally count:

10, 9, 8, 7, 6, 5, 4, 3, 2...

At which point, absolutely on cue as always, the door opens and the room explodes: hair and handbag and coat and arms everywhere. Like a sort of girl bomb. And there, as if by very punctual magic, is Nat.

Nat – for the record – is my Best Friend, and we are so utterly in tune that it's like we have one brain, divided into two pieces at birth. Or (more likely) two brains, entwined shortly afterwards. Although we didn't meet until we were five years old, so obviously I'm speaking *metaphorically* or we'd both be dead.

What I'm trying to say is: we're close. We're

harmonised. We're one and the same. We're like a perfect stream of consciousness, with never a cross word between us. We work with perfect, unquestioning synergy. Like two dolphins that jump at exactly the same time and pass the ball to each other at Sea World.

Anyway. Nat takes one step into the room, looks at me, and then stops and puts her hands on her hips.

"Good morning," I croak from under the covers, and then I start coughing violently. Human coughs release air at roughly 60mph, and without being vain, I'd like to think that mine reaches 65mph or 70mph minimum.

"Don't even *think* about it," Nat snaps.

I stop coughing and look at her with my roundest, most confused eyes. "Hmmm?" I say innocently. And then I start coughing again.

"I mean it. Don't even think about thinking about it."

I have *no* idea what she's talking about. The fever must be making my brain swell.

"Nat," I say feebly, closing my eyes and pressing my hand against my head. I'm a shell of the person I used to be. A husk. "I have bad news." I open one eye and take a peek round the room. Nat still has her hands on her hips.

"Let me guess," she says in a dry voice. "You're sick."

I give a weak but courageous smile: the sort Jane gives Lizzie in *Pride and Prejudice* when she's bedridden with a really bad cold, but is being very brave about it. "You know me so well," I say affectionately. "It's like we have one mind, Nat."

"And you're out of it if you think I'm not about to drag you out of bed by your feet." Nat takes a few steps towards me. "Also, I want my lipstick back," she adds.

I clear my throat. "Lipstick?"

"The one you've dotted all over your face."

I open my mouth and then shut it again. "It's not lipstick," I say in a small voice. "It's a dangerous infection."

"Then your dangerous infection is glittery, Harriet, and just so happens to match my new shoes perfectly."

I shift a little bit further down the bed so that only my eyes are visible. "Infections are very advanced these days," I say with as much dignity as I can muster. "They are sometimes extremely light-reflective."

"Featuring small flecks of gold?"

I raise my chin defiantly. "Sometimes."

Nat's nose twitches and she rolls her eyes. "Right.

And your face is producing white talcum powder, is it?"

I sniff quickly. Oh, *sugar cookies.* "It's important to keep sick people dry," I say as airily as I can. "Dampness can allow bacteria to develop."

Nat sighs again. "Get out of bed, Harriet."

"But—"

"Get out of bed."

"Nat, I…"

"Out. Now."

I look down at the duvets in a panic. "But I'm not ready! I'm in my pyjamas!" I'm going to give it one last desperate shot. "Nat," I say, changing tack and using my most serious, profound voice. "You don't understand. How will you feel if you're wrong? How will you *live* with yourself? I might be *dying*."

"Actually, you're right," Nat agrees, taking another two steps towards me. "You are. I'm literally seconds away from killing you, Harriet Manners. And if that happens, I'll live with myself just fine. Now get out of bed, you little faker."

And, before I can protect myself, Nat lunges suddenly towards me and tugs the covers away.

There's a long silence.

"Oh, *Harriet*," Nat eventually says in a sad and

simultaneously triumphant voice.

Because I'm lying in bed, fully dressed, with my shoes on. And in one hand is a box of talcum powder; in the other is a bright red lipstick.

3

OK, so I lied a little bit.

Twice, actually.

Nat and I are not in perfect harmony at all. We're definitely close, and we definitely spend all of our time together, and we definitely adore each other very much, but there are *moments* now we've almost grown up where our interests and passions divide a teensy bit.

Or – you know – a lot.

It doesn't stop us being inseparable, obviously. We're Best Friends because we frequently make each other laugh, so much so that I once made orange juice come out of her nose (on to her mum's white rug – we stopped laughing pretty shortly afterwards). And also because I remember when she peed on the ballet-room floor, aged six, and she is the only person in the entire world who knows I still have a dinosaur poster taped to the inside of my wardrobe.

But over the last few years, there have definitely been *minuscule* points where our desires and needs

have… conflicted a little bit. Which is why I *may* have said I was a little bit sicker than I actually felt this morning, which was: not much.

Or at all, actually. I feel great.

And why Nat is a bit snappy with me as we run towards the school coach as fast as my legs will carry me.

"You know," Nat sighs as she waits for me to catch up for the twelfth time. "I watched that *stupid* documentary on the Russian Revolution for you last week, and it was about four hundred hours long. The least you can do is participate in an Educational Opportunity to See Textiles from an Intimate and Consumer Perspective with me."

"*Shopping*," I puff, holding my sides together so they don't fall apart. "It's called shopping."

"That's not what's written on the leaflet. It's a school trip: there has to be *something* educational about it."

"No," I huff. "There isn't." Nat pauses again so that I can try and catch up. "It's just shopping."

To be fair, I think I have a point. We're going to The Clothes Show Live, in Birmingham. So-called – presumably – because they show clothes to you. Live. In Birmingham. And let you buy them. And take them home with you afterwards.

Which is otherwise known as *shopping*.

"It'll be fun," Nat says from a few metres ahead of me. "They've got everything there, Harriet. Everything anyone could possibly ever want."

"Really?" I say in the most sarcastic voice I can find, considering that I'm now running so fast that my breath is starting to squeak. "Do they have a triceratops skull?"

"…No."

"Do they have a life-size model of the first airborne plane?"

"…Probably not."

"And do they have a John Donne manuscript, with little white gloves so that you can actually touch it?"

Nat thinks about it. "I think it's unlikely they have that," she admits.

"Then they don't have *everything* I want, do they?"

We reach the coach steps and I can barely breathe. I don't understand it: we've both run the same distance, and we've both expended the same energy. I'm an entire centimetre shorter than Nat so I have less mass to move, at the same speed (on average). We both have exactly the same amount of PE lessons. And yet – despite the laws of physics – I'm huffing and purple, and Nat's only slightly glowing and still capable of breathing out of her nose.

Sometimes science makes no sense at all.

Nat starts rapping in a panic on the bus door. We're late – thanks to my excellent acting skills – and it looks like the class might be about to leave without us. "Harriet," Nat snaps, turning to look at me as the doors start making sucking noises, as if they're kissing. "Tsar Nicholas II was overthrown by Lenin in 1917."

I blink in surprise. "Yes," I say. "He was."

"And do you think I want to know that? It's not even on our exam syllabus. I *never* had to know that. So now it's your turn to pick up a few pairs of shoes and make *ooh* and *aah* sounds for me because Jo ate prawns and she's allergic to prawns and she got sick and couldn't come and I'm not sitting on a bus on my own for five hours. OK?"

Nat takes a deep breath and I look at my hands in shame. I am a selfish, selfish person. I am also a very sparkly person: my hands are covered in gold glitter.

"OK," I say in a small voice. "I'm sorry, Nat."

"You're forgiven." The coach doors finally slide open. "Now get on this bus and pretend for one little day that you have the teeniest, tiniest smidgen of interest in fashion."

"All right," I say, my voice getting even smaller.

Because – in case you haven't worked this out by now – here's the key thing that really divides Nat and me:

I don't.

4

So, before we get on the bus, you might want to know a little more about me.

You might not, obviously. You might be thinking, *Just get on with it, Harriet, because I haven't got all day*, which is what Annabel says all the time. Adults rarely have all day, from what I can tell. However, if – like me – you read cereal boxes at the breakfast table and shampoo bottles in the bath and bus timetables when you already know what bus you're getting, here's a little more information:

1. My mother is dead. That's usually the bit where people look awkward and start talking about how rainy the sky looks, but she died when I was three days old so missing her is a bit like loving a character from a book. The only stories I have of her belong to other people.

2. I have a stepmother, Annabel. She married Dad when I was seven, she's alive and she works as a lawyer. (You would not believe the amount of arguments my parents have over those two facts. "I am living," Annabel will scream. "You're a lawyer," Dad will shout back. "Who are you kidding?")

3. Dad's In Advertising. ("Not in adverts," Annabel always points out when they have dinner parties. "I write them," Dad replies in frustration. "I'm as In Advertising as you can get."
    "Apart from actors," Annabel says under her breath, at which point Dad stomps off to the kitchen to get another bottle of beer.)

4. I'm an only child. Thanks to my parents, I am destined to a life of never having anyone to squabble with in the back seat of the car.

5. Nat isn't just my Best Friend. She gave herself this title, even though I told her it was a bit unnecessary: she's also my Only Friend. This might be because I have a tendency to correct

people's grammar and tell them facts they're not interested in.

6.   And put things in lists. Like this one.

7.   Nat and I met ten years ago when we were five, which makes us fifteen. I know you could have worked that out by yourself, but I can't assume people like doing equations in their heads just because I do.

8.   Nat is beautiful. When we were young, adults would put a hand under her chin and say, "She's going to break hearts, this one," as if she couldn't hear them and wasn't deciding when would be the best time to start.

9.   I am not. My impact on hearts is like an earthquake happening on the other side of the world: if I'm lucky, I can hope for a teacup tinkling in its saucer. And even then it's a bit of a surprise and everybody talks about it for days afterwards.

Other things will probably filter through in stages

– like the fact that I only eat toast in triangles because it means there are no soggy edges, and my favourite book is the first half of *Great Expectations* and the last half of *Wuthering Heights* – but you don't need to know them right now. In fact, arguably, you never need to know them. The last book Dad bought me had a gun on the front cover.

Anyway, the final defining fact that I may already have mentioned in passing is:

10.   I don't like fashion.

I never really have, and I can't imagine I ever will.

I got away with it until I was about ten. Under that age, non-uniform didn't really exist: we were either in our school uniform, or our pyjamas, or our swimming costumes, or dressed like angels or sheep for the school nativity. We had to go and get an outfit especially for non-uniform days.

Then teenagehood hit like a big pink glittery sledgehammer. Suddenly there were rules and breaking them *mattered*. Skirt lengths and trouser shapes and eye-shadow shades and heel heights and knowing how long you could go without wearing mascara before people accused you of being a lesbian.

Suddenly the world was divided into the right and the horribly, horribly wrong. And the people stuck between, who for the life of them couldn't tell the difference. People who wore white socks and black shoes; who liked having hair on their legs because it was fluffy at night-time. People who really missed the sheep outfit, and secretly wanted to wear it to school even when it wasn't Christmas.

People like me.

If there had been *consistent* rules, I'd have done my best to keep up. Made some sort of pie chart or line graph and then resentfully applied the basics. But fashion's not like that: it's a slippery old fish. You try to grab it round the neck and it slides out of your grip and shoots off in another direction, and every desperate grab towards it makes you look even more stupid. Until you're sliding around on the floor, everybody is laughing at you and the fish has shot under the table.

So – to put it simply – I gave up. Brains have only got so much they can absorb, so I decided I didn't have space. I'd rather know that hummingbirds can't walk, or that one teaspoon of a neutron star weighs billions of tonnes, or that bluebirds can't see the colour blue.

Nat, however, went the other way. And suddenly the sheep and the angel – who hung out quite happily in the fields of Bethlehem together – didn't have as much in common any more.

We're still Best Friends. She's still the girl who lost her first baby tooth in my apple, and I'm still the girl who stuck one of her sunflower seeds up my nose in primary school and couldn't get it out again. But sometimes, every now and then, the gap between us gets so big it feels like one of us is going to slip through.

Something tells me that today that person is going to be me.

5

Anyway.

What all this means is: I'm not thrilled to be here. I've stopped whining, but let's just say I'm not spinning round and round in circles, farting at intervals, like my dog Hugo does when he's excited. In fact, I did two years of doing woodwork *specifically* so I didn't have to come on this textiles trip. Two years of accidentally sanding down my thumbs and cringing to the sound of metal on metal, purely to get out of today. And then Jo eats prawns and does a little vomiting and *BAM*: here I am.

The first step on to the coach is uneventful, just one step, directly behind Nat's. The second step is slightly less successful. The coach starts before we've sat down and I'm thrown sideways, in the process kicking a nice fluffy green bag the way I've never, ever managed to kick a football in my entire life.

"Moron," Chloe hisses as she retrieves it.

"I'm n-n-not," I stutter, cheeks lighting up. "A

moron only has an IQ of between 50 and 69. I think mine's a little higher than that."

And then it all goes wrong. On the third step, the driver sees a family of ducks on the road, hits the brakes and sends me flying towards the end of the bus. I instinctively grab whatever will protect me from slamming my face on the floor. A headrest, a shoulder, an armrest, a seat.

Somebody's knee.

"Ugh," a voice shouts in total disgust, "she's *touching me*."

And there – staring at me as if she just sicked me up – is Alexa.

6

People Who Hate Harriet Manners
1. Alexa Roberts

Alexa. My nemesis, my adversary, my opponent, my arch-enemy. Whatever you want to call somebody who hates your guts.

I've known her three days longer than I've known Nat and I've yet to work out what her problem is. I can only conclude that her feelings towards me are very similar to what I've read about love: passionate, random, inexplicable and totally uncontrollable. She can't help hating me any more than Heathcliff could help loving Cathy. It's simply written in the stars. Which would be quite sweet if she wasn't such a cow all of the time.

And I wasn't totally terrified of her.

I stare at Alexa in total shock. I'm still clinging to her tight-covered leg like a frightened baby monkey clinging on to a tree. "Let _go_," she snaps. "Oh my _God_."

28

I scrabble away, trying desperately to stand up. There are approximately 13,914,291,404 legs in the world – over half of them in trousers – and I had to grab *this* one?

"Ugh," she says loudly to anybody who will listen. "Do you think I might have caught something? Oh, God, I can already feel it starting…" She cowers in her seat. "No…The *light*… It *hurts*… I can feel myself changing… Suddenly I want to do my homework… It's too late!" She puts her hands over her face and then pulls them away, crosses her eyes, protrudes her teeth and pulls the ugliest expression I've ever seen on public transport. "Nooooooo! I've caught it! I'm… I'm… I'm a geeeeeeeeeeeeek!"

People start sniggering and from somewhere on the left I can hear a little ripple of applause. Alexa bows a couple of times, pulls a face at me and then goes back to reading her magazine.

My cheeks are flushed, my hands are shaking. My eyes are starting to prickle. All the normal responses to ritual humiliation. The thing I want to make really clear right now is that I don't mind *being* a geek. *Being* a geek is fine. It's unimpressive, sure, but it's pretty unobtrusive. I could be a geek all day long, as long as people left me alone.

The thing is: they don't.

"*Seriously*," Nat snaps in a loud voice from a few metres in front of me. "Did you sniff wet paint as a child or something, Alexa?"

Alexa rolls her eyes. "Barbie *talks*. Run away and play with your shoes, Natalie. This has nothing to do with you."

I'm trying desperately to think of something clever to say. Something biting, poignant, incisive, deeply wounding. Something that will give Alexa just an ounce of the hurt she gives me on an almost daily basis.

"You suck," I say in the tiniest voice I've ever heard.

Yeah, I think. *That should do it.* And then I hold my chin up as high as I can get it, walk the rest of the way down the aisle and sink into the seat next to Nat before my knees give way.

I'm in my seat for about three seconds when the morning promptly decides to get worse. I barely have time to open my crossword book first.

"Harriet!" a delighted voice says, and a little pale face pops over the back of the seat in front of me. "You're here! You're really, actually, actually *here*!" As if I'm Father Christmas and he's a six-year-old whose chimney I've just climbed down.

"Yes, Toby," I say reluctantly. "I'm here." And then I turn to scowl at Nat.

It's Toby Pilgrim.

Toby "my knees buckle when I run" Pilgrim. Toby "I bring my own Bunsen burner to school" Pilgrim. Toby "I wear bicycle clips on my trousers *and I don't even have a bike*" Pilgrim. Nat should have told me he'd be here.

I'm now following my own stalker to Birmingham.

7

Imagine you're a polar bear and you find yourself in the middle of a rainforest. There are flying squirrels, and monkeys, and bright green frogs, and you have no idea how you got there or what you're supposed to do next. You're lonely, you're lost, you're frightened and all you know – for absolute certain – is that you shouldn't be there.

Now imagine you find *another* polar bear. You're so happy to see another polar bear – *any* polar bear – that it doesn't matter what kind it is. You follow that polar bear around, just because it's not a monkey. Or a flying squirrel. Because it's the only thing that makes it OK to be a polar bear in the middle of a rainforest.

Well, that's how it is with Toby. One geek, incoherently happy to find another geek in the middle of a world full of normal people. Thrilled to discover that there is someone else like him. It's not me he wants. It's my social standing. Or lack thereof.

And let me get something straight: I'm not going

32

to have a romance with someone just because they're made out of the same stuff as me. *No.* I'd rather be on my own. Or – you know – in unrequited love with a parrot. Or one of those little lemurs with the stripy tails.

"Harriet!" Toby says again and a little bit of bogey starts dripping from his nose. He promptly wipes it on his jumper sleeve and beams at me. "I can't believe you came!"

I glare at Nat and she grins, winks and goes back to reading her magazine. I am not feeling very *harmonised* with her at the moment, if I'm being totally honest. In fact, I sort of feel like hitting her over the head with my crossword puzzle.

"Yes," I say, trying to edge away. "Apparently I had to."

"But isn't this just wonderful?" he gasps, clambering up on to his knees in his unbridled enthusiasm. I notice that his T-shirt says THERE'S NO PLACE LIKE **127.0.0.1.** "Of all the buses in all the towns in all the world, you walk on to mine. Can you see what I did there? It's a quote from *Casablanca*, except that I replaced the words *gin joints* with *bus* and the word *into* with *on to*."

"You did, yes."

Nat makes a snuffle of amusement and I subtly pinch her leg.

"Do you know what I learnt this morning, Harriet? I learnt that the phrase *rule of thumb* came from a time when a man was only legally allowed to beat his wife with something the width of his own thumb. I can lend you the book, although there's a pizza stain on page 143 which you might have to read round."

"Erm. Right. Thanks." I nod knowingly and then lift my book so that Toby realises the conversation is over.

He doesn't.

"*And*," he continues, holding it down so he can see me properly. "You know the most *unbelievable* thing?"

It's funny, when Toby behaves like this, I can suddenly see why I'm so annoying.

"Well, did you know that…" The coach swerves slightly into the middle lane. Toby swallows. "That…" he continues and licks his lips. The coach swerves back into the slow lane. "That—" Toby's face goes abruptly green and he clears his throat. "I don't want you to think I'm easily distracted, Harriet," he finally continues in a little voice, "but I'm suddenly not feeling so well. I don't take too kindly to vehicles, particularly the ones that move. Do you remember the ride-on lawnmower in Year One?"

I look at him in horror and Nat immediately stops smirking. "Oh, no," she says in a dark voice. "No, *no*." Nat obviously remembers it too.

"Harriet," Toby continues, licking his lips again and going an even stranger colour. "I think we might need to stop the bus."

"*Toby*," Nat snaps in a low, warning voice. "Breathe in through your nose and out through your—"

But it's too late. The coach makes one more sudden movement and – as if in slow motion – Toby gives me one look of pure apology.

And vomits all over my lap.

8

In case you were wondering, that's what Toby did on the ride-on lawnmower in Year One too. Except this time he manages to broaden his horizons in the most literal sense and hit Nat too.

She's not happy about it. I mean, I'm not happy about it either. I don't relish being hit by the contents of other people's digestive tracts. But Nat's *really* not happy about it.

She's so unhappy about it that when the coach finally pulls up to The Clothes Show at the NEC, Birmingham – two and a half hours later – she's *still* shouting at him. And Toby's telling both of us how much better he feels now because, "Isn't it funny how it feels OK when all the vomit's gone?"

"I don't *believe* this," Nat is still snapping, stomping across the carpark. We're both now wearing PE kit: luckily two of the boys had football practice straight after the trip, so – after a lot of whining – Miss Fletcher managed to convince them to lend us their kit. We're wearing orange football shirts, green football shorts and white knee socks.

I quite like it. It's making me feel quite sporty. Nat, on the other hand, isn't so keen. We were forced to keep our shoes on, and – while my trainers look quite normal – Nat's red high heels... don't.

"Do you *know* how long it took me to choose my outfit this morning?" she's yelling at Toby as we approach the front doors.

Toby contemplates this like it's not a rhetorical question. "Twenty minutes?" he offers. Nat's face goes slightly puce. "Thirty?" Nat's jawline starts flexing. "An hour and a half?"

"*A really long time!*" she shouts. "A really, *really* long time!" Nat looks down at herself. "I had a brand-new dress and *leggings from American Apparel,* Toby. Do you know how much they cost? I was wearing *Prada perfume.*" She picks up a piece of green nylon between her fingers. "*And now I'm wearing a boy's football kit and I smell of sick!*"

I pat her arm as comfortingly as I can.

"At least my vomit was sort of chocolatey," Toby says cheerfully. "I had Coco Pops for breakfast."

Nat grits her teeth.

"Anyway," Toby continues blithely, "I think you look awesome. You both match. It's super trendy."

Nat scrunches her mouth up, clenches her fists and furrows her brow right in the centre. It's like watching somebody shake a bottle of fizzy drink without taking the lid off. "Toby," she says in a low hiss. "Go. *Now.*"

"OK," Toby agrees. "Anywhere in particular?"

"*Anywhere*. Just *go. NOW.*"

"Toby," I say in a low voice, taking him by the arm. I'm really, genuinely scared for his safety. "I think maybe you should go inside." I look at Nat. "As quickly as possible," I add.

"Ah." Toby contemplates this for a few seconds and then nods. "Ah. I see. Then I shall see you both anon."

And – giving me what looks disturbingly like an attempt at a wink over his shoulder – he skips off through the swing doors.

When he's gone and I know that Nat can't rip his head off and feed it to a large flock of pigeons, I turn to her.

"Nat," I say, chewing on a fingernail anxiously. "It's not that bad. Honestly. We smell fine. And if you put my coat on over the top, nobody will see what you're wearing. It's longer than yours."

"You don't get it," Nat says and suddenly the anger

pops: she just sounds miserable. "You just don't *get* it."

I think Nat underestimates my powers of empathy. Which is a shame because I am a very empathetic person. *Em*pathetic. Not *pathetic*.

"Sure I do," I say in a reassuring voice. "You don't like football. I get that."

"It's not that. Today was *really important,* Harriet. I *really* needed to look good."

I stare at her blankly. After a few seconds, Nat rolls her eyes and hits herself on the forehead in frustration. "*They're* in there."

I stare at the revolving doors. "*Who's* in there?" I whisper in terror. I think about it for a few seconds. "Vampires?"

"*Vampires.*" Nat looks at me in consternation. "You have got to start reading proper books."

I don't know what she's talking about. Just because I own a lot of books about things that don't actually exist in real life in no way indicates that I'm not connected to the real world. I totally am.

Nat takes a deep breath. "I put the prawns in Jo's dinner," she says, avoiding my eyes.

I stare at her. "Nat! Why would you do that?"

"Because I need you today," she says in a tiny voice.

"I need you for support. *They're* in there." And she looks again at the doors and swallows.

"*Who?*"

"Model agents, Harriet," Nat says as if I'm an idiot. "Lots and lots of model agents."

"Oh," I say stupidly, and then think about it. "*Ohhhhhhhh.*"

And I finally understand what I'm doing here.

9

We were seven when Nat decided that she wanted to be a model.

"Gosh," somebody's mum said at a school disco. "Natalie. You're getting gorgeous. Maybe you could be a model when you grow up."

I paused from filling my party dress pockets with chocolate cake and jelly sweets. "A model of what?" I asked curiously. And then my greedy little hand went out to grab a mini jam roll. "I have a model airplane," I added proudly.

The mum gave me the look that I was already used to by then.

"A model," she explained, looking at Nat, "is a girl or a boy who gets paid ridiculous quantities of money to wear clothes they don't own and have their photo taken." I looked at Nat and already I could see her eyes starting to glow: the seed of the dream being planted. "Just hope you grow tall and thin," the mum added bitterly, "because if you

41

ask me, they all look like aliens."

At which point Nat put her chocolate cake down and spent the rest of the night sitting on the floor, with me pulling on her feet to make her legs longer.

And I spent the rest of the night talking about space travel.

It's finally here.

Eight years of buying *Vogue* and not eating pudding (Nat, not me: I eat hers) and we've finally made it to the very edge of Nat's destiny. I feel a bit like Sam in *The Lord of the Rings*, just before Frodo throws the ring into the fires of Mount Doom. Except in a more positive, magical way. With slightly less hairy feet.

Nat doesn't look as excited as I thought she would. She looks terrified and as stiff as a board standing, totally still, in the middle of the NEC entrance. She's staring at the crowd as if it's a pond full of fish and she's a really hungry cat, and – honestly – I'm not even sure she's breathing. I'm tempted to put my head on her chest just to check.

The thing is: she's doing it all wrong.

I know a lot about stories and magic – thanks to reading loads of books and also belonging to a forum on the internet – and the most basic rule is that *it has to come as a surprise*. Nobody hopped into a wardrobe to find Narnia; they hopped in, thinking it was just a wardrobe. They didn't climb up the Faraway Tree, knowing it was a Faraway Tree; they thought it was just a really big tree. Harry Potter thought he was a normal boy; Mary Poppins was supposed to be a regular nanny.

It's the first and only rule. *Magic comes when you're not looking for it.*

But Nat's looking for it, and the harder she looks, the less likely it is to turn up. She's scaring the fashion magic off with her knowing, waiting vibes.

"Come on," I say, trying to distract her by pulling at her (or technically *my*) coat sleeve. I need to get her to think about something else so that the magic can do its thing. "Let's just go and shop, OK?"

"Mmm."

I don't think she can even hear me any more. "Look!" I say enthusiastically, pulling her to the nearest stall. "Nat, look! Handbags! Shoes! Hair bobbles!"

Nat gives me a distracted glance. "You're dragging my coat on the floor."

"Oh." I bundle it back under my arm and start tugging Nat towards the next stall.

"What do you think?" I say, picking up a small blue sequined hat and plopping it on my head. When we were little, we'd spend hours and hours in department stores, trying on different hats and pretending we were going to a royal wedding.

"Uh-huh." Nat gets a little bit more tense and looks over her shoulder.

"Come on, what about this one?" I pick up a large floppy hat covered in big pink flowers and put it on. "Look." I wiggle my bottom at her.

Nat abruptly whips round. "Oh my God," she whispers and it takes me a few seconds to realise that it has nothing at all to do with my bottom.

"Have you seen one?"

"I think so!" She looks again. "Yes, I think I can definitely see an agent!"

I peer into the crowd, but I can't see anything. They must be like fairies: you can only see them when they want you to.

"Stay right here, Harriet," Nat whispers urgently. She starts moving into the crowds. "Don't move a muscle. I'll be back in a second."

Now I'm confused. "But..." This makes no sense. "Don't you need me with you?" I call after her. "Isn't that why I'm here? For support?"

"*In spirit will do just fine, Harriet,*" Nat shouts back. "Love you!"

And then she disappears completely.

10

Is she kidding me? *In spirit?*

I could have done *in spirit* quite happily from my bedroom, thank you very much. I could have texted Nat support from my own fake deathbed. I pick up another hat crossly. Next time Nat wants me to go shopping, I am *so* throwing myself down the stairs.

"Excuse me?" a voice interrupts, and when I turn around, there's a lady staring at me with a deep crease between her eyebrows. "Can you read?"

"Umm," I reply in surprise. "Yes. Very well, actually. My reading age is over twenty. But thank you for asking."

"Really? Can you read that sign there? Read it out loud."

Poor lady. Maybe she didn't go to all of her English lessons at school. "Of course," I say in a friendly and – I hope – not patronising tone. Not everyone benefits equally from a full education system. "It says, *Don't Touch The Hats.*"

There's a pause and then I realise that she probably doesn't have a literacy problem after all. "Oh," I add as her meaning sinks in.

"That's a hat," she says pointing to the one in my hand. "And that's a hat." She points to the one on my head. "And you're touching them *all over*."

I quickly put the one in my hand back on the stall and grab the one on my head. "Sorry. It's, erm, very…" What? How would you describe a hat? "*Hatty*," I improvise, and then I pat it and put it back on the stall. At which point my chewed nail snags on a flower.

We both watch as the flower separates itself from the hat and throws itself on the floor, like a little child having a hissy fit. And then – as if in slow motion – what was clearly just one piece of thread breaks and, one by one, every other flower on the ribbon follows it.

Oh, sugar cookies.

"That's a very interesting design concept," I say after clearing my throat awkwardly a couple of times and starting to back away. "Self-detaching flowers? It's very modern."

"*They're not self-detaching*," Hat Lady says in a low, angry voice, staring at the pile on the floor. "*You detached them*." And then she points at a felt-tip sign that says *You Break It You Buy It,* followed by the most inappropriately placed smiley face I have ever seen in my entire life. "And now you're going to have to pay for it."

God. She sounds a little bit like someone from the Italian Mafia. Maybe the Italian Mafia has a hat section.

"You know," I say, backing away a little bit faster. "You are very lucky that hat didn't kill me. I could have choked on one of those flowers and died. The playwright Tennessee Williams died from choking on a bottle cap. *Then* how would you have felt?"

"I'll take a cheque or debit card details."

I take a few more steps backwards and she follows. "Tell you what," I say in the most lawyer-y, Annabel-like voice I can find. "How about *I* forget that you tried to kill me if *you* forget that I broke your hat? How does that sound?"

"Pay for the hat," she says, taking another step towards me.

"No."

"Pay for the hat."

"*I can't.*"

"Pay for the h—"

At which point fate or karma or the universe or a God who doesn't like me very much steps in. And sends me flying bottom-first into the rest of her stall.

$$\underline{\textbf{II}}$$

People Who Hate Harriet Manners
Alexa Roberts
Hat Lady
Owners of stalls 24D 24E 24F 24G 24H

I try to blame Nat's coat dangling on the floor, but Hat Lady is having none of it. There is a lot of squeaking: mine, mostly, followed by hers. And then the crowd gets suddenly bigger.

Apparently I haven't just knocked over the hat table. Her stall has dominoed into the stall next to it, which has dominoed into the stall next to *that*, and before I know what's happening there are six stalls, strewn creatively over the floor, with me lying in a heap in the middle. It's the fault of those silly fake partitions, in my opinion. They just aren't stable enough.

Clearly, neither am I.

"*This is why I didn't want you to touch the hats,*" Hat Lady is screaming at me as I struggle to get up.

49

Every time I put my hand down, something crunches. And not in a good-crunch kind of way. In a hand-through-hat kind of way. "You've ruined *everything*!"

From my position on the floor I can see that the tables have crushed at least seven hats, and another three have been hit by the jug of water on one of the now tipped-over chairs. Along with the sign. Another four hats have shoe-shaped dents in them and footprints on the brim. I'm sitting on at least three.

OK, she has a point.

"I'm sorry," I'm saying over and over again (*crunch, crunch, crunch*). Everywhere I look are the faces of people who don't seem to like me very much. "I'm *really* sorry. I'll pay for it. I'll pay for *all* of it."

I have no idea how, but I suspect it's going to involve a lot of car washing and about six hundred years' worth of groundings.

"*It's not enough*," the woman yells. "*This is my biggest sale day of the year! I need to attract a client base!*"

I look around briefly. From the size of the crowd, she's definitely attracted something.

"I'm sorry," I say again, with my face flaming – because I really, truly, honestly am – and I'm just about to burst into guilty tears when a man wearing a fluorescent yellow jacket and a jaunty black hat leans forward and grabs hold of my hand.

"I'm afraid you're going to have to come with me," he says firmly. Then he looks at Hat Lady. "Don't worry, Sugar," he adds. "She's going to pay for the hats. I'll make sure of it personally." And he starts leading me away from the carnage.

I gape at him, totally speechless.

So far today, I have nearly died of my own fake illness, fallen over – three times – been shouted at, humiliated, vomited on, abandoned and I've managed to trash an entire section of an indoor market. And now, just at the point where I thought it was impossible for things to get worse...

I've just been arrested.

12

This is what happens when I'm forced to go out in public.

"I didn't do it!" I gasp as the man pulls me through the crowds. He's holding my hand and – I have to be honest with you – I'm not sure he's allowed. I think it might be against the law or something. "I mean," I clarify, "I *did* do it. But I didn't mean to. I'm just..." How can I put it? "Socially disadvantaged."

And – just so you know – that's what I'm going to plead in court as well.

"Cherub-cheeks, that sounds so *fun*," the man says over his shoulder in a high voice that doesn't seem to fit him properly. "Society is *tedious*, don't you think? *Sooo* much better to be pushed out of it."

What did he just call me?

"I haven't been pushed out of it," I tell him indignantly. "I just don't seem to be able to get in it in the first place. Anyway," I add as firmly as I can, "you should know I'm only fifteen." *Too young to go to jail,*

I want to add, but I don't want to give him any ideas.

"Fifteen? *Perfectomondo*, my little Sugar-kitten. So much potential for free publicity."

The blood drains from my cheeks. *Free publicity?* Oh, God, he's going to use me as a warning to other underage wannabe hat vandals.

"Before you take me anywhere," I say quickly, "I need to find my best friend. She's not going to know where I've gone."

He stops walking and swivels round with his spare hand on his hip.

"Mini-treetop, once I have a photo of you, you can go wherever the tiddlywinks you like." And then he tinkles with laughter.

I freeze. "A photo?"

"Well, *yes*, my little Peach-melba. I could draw a picture, but Head Office thought that was *ever* so unfunny last time." He giggles and pushes me away with a limp wrist. "Oh," he adds casually. "I'm Wilbur, by the way. That's *bur* not *iam*. From Infinity Models."

My knees abruptly buckle, but Wilbur-not-iam keeps tugging as if I'm on wheels. Suddenly I know how Toby feels when he tries to do the high jump.

Infinity Models?

No.

No, no, no, *no*.

No no no no no no NONONONONO.

"Oh, it has just been a *mare* this morning," Wilbur continues as if he's not dragging me bodily across the floor.

"But *w-w-why*?" I finally managed to stutter.

"Oh, you know, total chaos. The Birmingham Clothes Show: highlight of the fashion year etcetera etcetera. Well, apart from London Fashion Week, obviously. And Milan. And New York. And Paris. Actually, it's quite far down the list, but hey, it's still a *blast*."

I can't really feel my mouth. "N-n-not why is it busy. Why would you want *my* photo?"

"Oh, Baby-baby Panda," he says over his shoulder. "You're, like, so *tomorrow* you're next Wednesday. No, you're the Thursday after. Do you know what I mean?"

I stare at him with my mouth slightly open. I think it's safe to say that the answer to that question is no. "But—"

"And I am *loving* this look," he interrupts, pointing at the football kit. "So new. So fresh. So unusual. *Inspired.*"

"My jeans had sick on them," I blurt out in disbelief.

"*My Jeans Had Sick On Them. I love it.* Such an imagination! *Darling*-foot—" and here Wilbur pauses so that he can pull me through a particularly dense crowd of really angry-looking girls – "I think you might be about to make my career, my little Pot of Tigers."

One of the girls behind me mutters in confusion: "Hey, she's *ginger*."

(She's wrong, by the way: I'm not. I am *strawberry blonde*.)

"I don't underst—"

"All will become clear shortly," Wilbur reassures me. "Maybe. Maybe not, actually, but hey, clarity is *so* overrated." He pushes me against the wall. "Now stand there and look gorgeous."

What? I don't even know how to *start* attempting that.

"But—" I say again.

Wilbur takes a Polaroid picture, shakes it and puts it on the table. "Now turn to the side?"

I stare at him, still frozen in shock. None of this is making sense. He tuts and gently pushes my shoulders round so I'm facing the other wall, and then takes another photo.

"*Wilbur*—" I turn to frantically search the crowd for Nat's dark head, but I can't see anything.

"Baby-pudding," Wilbur interrupts, "you know you look *just* like a treefrog? Darling, you could climb up a tree with no help at all and I wouldn't be shocked in the slightest."

I pause and stare at him with my mouth open. Did he just say I look like something with suckers on its feet? Then my mind clears. *Focus*, Harriet. For God's sake, *focus*.

"I have to go," I explain urgently as Wilbur twists me round and takes a final photo. "I have to get out of here. I have to—"

But I can see Nat heading straight towards us. And I know two things for certain:

1. The magic has gone horribly wrong.
2. Nat is going to kill me.

13

Hiding under the table probably isn't the best impromptu decision I've ever made, but it's the only one I can think of. Which is a problem.

First of all, because Wilbur knows I'm here. He just saw me drop to my knees and crawl away. Second, because the table cloth doesn't quite reach the floor. And third, because there's already somebody else under here.

"Hi," the person under the table says, and then he offers me a piece of chewing gum.

There are times in my life when the synapses in my brain move quite fast. For example, during English exams I've normally completed the essay with plenty of time to doodle little relevant pictures in the margin in the hope that it gets me extra points. However, there are other times when those synapses don't do anything at all. They just sit there in confused silence, shrugging at me.

This is one of them.

I stare at the chewing gum in shock and then blink at the boy who's holding it. He's so good-looking, it feels like my brain has collapsed and my skull is about to fold in on itself. Which is actually not as unpleasant a sensation as you might think.

"Well?" the boy says, leaning back against the wall and looking at me with his eyelids lowered. "Do you want the gum or not?"

He's about my age and he looks like a dark lion. He has large black curls that point in every direction and slanted eyes and a wide mouth that curves up at the edges. He's so beautiful that all I can hear in my head is a high-pitched white noise like a recently switched-off television.

It takes an interaction of seventy-two different muscles to produce human speech, and right now not a single one of them is working. I open and shut my mouth a few times, like a goldfish.

"I can see," he continues in a lazy accent that doesn't seem to be English, "that it's an extremely important decision and you need to think about it carefully. So I'll give you a few more seconds to weigh up the pros and cons."

He has really sharp canine teeth, and when he says Fs, they catch on his bottom lip. There's a mole under his left eye and he smells sort of green, like… grass. Or vegetables. Or maybe lime sweets.

One of his curls is sticking up at the back, like a little duck tail. And I've just realised that I'm still staring at him, and he's still looking at me, and he's still waiting for me to answer him. I quickly trawl my mind for an appropriate response.

"Chewing gum is banned in Singapore," I whisper. "Completely banned." And then I blink twice. It's probably not the best introductory statement I've ever opened with.

His eyes shoot wide open. "Are we in Singapore? How long have I been asleep? How fast does this table move?"

Nice one, Harriet.

"No," I whisper back, my cheeks already hot, "we're still in Birmingham. I'm just making the point that if we *were* in Singapore, we could be arrested for even having chewing gum in our possession."

Stop talking, Harriet.

"Is that so?"

"Yes," I gulp. "Luckily we're not in Singapore, so you're safe."

"Well, thank God for UK legislation," he says, leaning his head against the wall again. His mouth

59

twitches. And then there's a long silence while he closes his eyes and I go red all over and try to work out whether it's possible to make a worse first impression.

It's not.

"I'm Harriet Manners," I admit finally and then I put my hand out to shake his, realise it's sweaty with nerves, swoop it back in and pretend I'm scratching my knee instead.

"Hello, Harriet Manners," Lion Boy says and all I can think is: *I know there's something outside the table that I'm supposed to be running away from, but I can't quite remember what it is.*

"Erm…" *Think, Harriet. Think of something normal to say.* "Have you been here long?"

"About half an hour."

"Why?"

"I'm hiding from Wilbur. He's using me as bait. He keeps chucking me into the crowd to see how many pretty girls I can come back with."

"Like a maggot?"

He laughs. "Yes. Pretty much exactly like a maggot."

"And have you… caught anything?"

"I'm not sure yet," he says, opening one eye and looking straight at me. "It's too early to say."

"Oh." I glance briefly at my watch. "It's not that

early," I inform him. "Actually, it's nearly lunchtime."

The boy looks at my watch – which has a knife, fork and spoon instead of hands – raises an eyebrow and stares at me hard for a few seconds. His nose wiggles a little bit. And then – clearly fascinated by the mesmerising first impression I've made – he closes his eyes again.

With Lion Boy apparently unconscious, I suddenly feel a great need to ask him all sorts of questions. I want to know *everything*. For instance, what is his accent and where is he from? If I get a world map out of my bag, can he point to it for me? Does it have strange animals and really big insects? Is he an only child too? Were the holes in his jeans there when he bought them, like Dad's, and if not, how did he get them?

But nothing is coming out. Which is lucky, because people don't tend to like it very much when I interrogate them relentlessly while they're trying to sleep.

"Do you often hide under furniture?" I manage eventually. He grins at me and his smile is so wide that it breaks his face into little pieces and my stomach immediately feels like a washing machine on spin-dry mode.

"I don't make a habit of it. You?"

"All of the time," I admit reluctantly. "*All* of the time."

Whenever I panic, actually. Which means, because I panic a lot, that I've been under many types of things. Dining tables, desks, side tables, kitchen counters... Any kind of furniture that allows me to disappear. Which is, actually, how I met Nat.

And I've just remembered what I'm doing here.

14

In case you're wondering, I met Nat under a piano.

It was the second day of school and I'd had enough. Alexa had already taken a shine to me – or whatever the opposite of that is – and I had become the butt of all of her most intricate five-year-old jokes. Who smells the most? Harriet. Who has hair like a carrot? Harriet. Who spilt their milk on their lap, but *actually, it's pee*? Harriet.

So I'd waited until everyone else had gone outside and then I'd crawled under the piano. Where I'd found a heartbroken Nat, crying because her dad had just run off with the check-out girl at Waitrose. We bonded straight away, probably because we both only had half of a parenting team left: a bit like discovering the missing bit of a friendship necklace. I'd offered her a part-time share in my dad, she'd offered me a bit of her mum and – just like that –we'd become Best Friends. And we have been ever since.

At least, from that moment until… *this* one.

"Harriet," a voice says from somewhere outside the table cloth. Two red shoes can be seen underneath it. "I don't know whether you're under some kind of impression that you've become invisible in the last thirteen minutes, but you're not. I can still see you."

My stomach swoops again and this time it has nothing to do with the boy sitting next to me. "Oh."

"Yes, *oh,*" Nat agrees. "So you may as well come out now."

I look back at the Lion Boy, who still has his eyes shut, whisper, "Thanks for sharing the table," and struggle back out of my terrible, terrible hiding place.

Nat looks furious. Even more so than when I accidentally knocked her new bottle of Gucci perfume out of the window as a result of an impromptu dance routine that she didn't want to see in the first place.

"What," she whispers to me, glancing in confusion at Wilbur, "are you *doing,* Harriet?"

"I…" I start, already panicking. "It's not what it—"

"I can't believe this," Nat interrupts. Her cheeks are getting redder and redder and her eyes keep flicking to Wilbur. "I *know* you don't like shopping, Harriet, and I *know* you didn't want to come today, but hiding under *this* table… I mean, of all the tables…" She looks at

Wilbur again in total embarrassment.

I frown. What is she talking about? Then I realise, in a horrible rush. Nat doesn't know I've just been spotted. She didn't see me having my photo taken. She just saw me here and assumed I'd followed her and then crawled under a table because being a total plonker is the only thing I really excel at. And – at exactly the same moment – I glance at Wilbur and a jolt of shock hits my stomach. His expression is totally blank. He's not interested in Nat. *She hasn't been spotted.* Which means – and my stomach suddenly feels like it's been electrocuted – that I haven't just accidentally hitched a ride on the back of Nat's lifelong dream.

I've *stolen* it.

I look at Nat in alarm. "Well?" she says and her voice starts to wobble. "What's going on, Harriet?"

I can save this, I think in a rush, *it's not too late.*

I don't have to break Nat's heart and crush her dream, and I don't have to do it in the most humiliating way possible: in the very place she thought it would come true, in front of the very person who could have given her what she wanted.

"I was looking for unusual table joints," I say as quickly as I can. "For woodwork homework."

A beat and then, "Huh?"

"Woodwork homework," I repeat, trying hard to look into Nat's eyes. "They said local craft can be very interesting and we had to look in other parts of the country. Like... Birmingham."

Nat opens her mouth and then closes it again. *"What?"*

"So," I say, my voice getting fainter, "I thought from a distance that this particular table looked very... solid. In terms of construction. And I thought I'd have a closer look. You know. From... underneath."

"And?"

"And?" I repeat blankly. "And what?"

"What were they?" Nat asks, her eyes narrowing even more. "What kind of table joints? I mean, you were under there quite a long time. You must have been able to tell."

She's testing me. She's checking to see if I'm telling the truth and I can't really blame her. After all, I started the day by covering my face in talcum powder and red lipstick.

"I think that..." I start, but I have absolutely no idea. And there's a really good chance that Nat's about to kneel on the floor and check. "They're..." I say again and the sentence trails to an end.

"They're dovetail," a voice says and Lion Boy climbs

out from under the table.

"Nick!" Wilbur cries, looking delighted. "There you are!" And then he looks at the table in astonishment, as if it's some kind of door to an alternative universe. "How many more of you are there under there?"

Nat stares at Lion Boy and then at me. And then at him again. The creases in her forehead are getting deeper. "*Dovetail?*"

"Yep, dovetail," Nick confirms, flashing her a lopsided smile.

Nat looks at me and blinks three or four times. I can see her trying to process the situation, which is obviously totally unprocessable.

"Mmm," I say in a faint voice. "That's what I thought too."

There's a silence. A long silence. The kind of silence you could take a bite from, should you be interested in eating silences. And then – just as I think I might have got away with it and everything is going to be OK – Nat glances at Wilbur's hand. There, in his grip, are the three damning Polaroids of me. Developed purely to show Nat the truth of my evil lies, like three miniature pictures of Dorian Gray.

The silence breaks. Nat makes a sort of sobbing noise at the base of her throat, and I automatically step forward to try and stop it. "Oh, *no*, Nat, I didn't…"

Nat steps away from me with her face crumpled. She knows, and she found out in the worst way possible. In public, smack bang in the middle of me lying to her.

I should have stayed in bed this morning.

Or at least under the table.

"*No,*" Nat whispers.

And with that final word – the one neither of us can take back – she jumps off the stage and runs away.

15

People Who Hate Harriet Manners
Alexa Roberts
Hat Lady
Owners of stalls 24D 24E 24F 24G 24H
Nat

Back-stabber. Betrayer. Fink. Apostate. Miscreant. Quisling. Snake. It's a good thing I brought my thesaurus with me because Nat refuses to speak to me for the rest of the day so I have an awful lot of time to ponder my wrong doings.

Quisling. I quite like that word. It sounds like a baby quail.

What's even worse is that by the time I've pulled myself together enough to move from the dirty little corner I'm scrunched up in, a *real* security guard has found me and dragged me into an office full of yet more people who look angry with me. Apparently I – or my legal guardians – owe The Clothes Show

69

stallholders £3,000.

This is what happens when you set tables covered in ink pots next to tables covered in dresses next to tables covered in hats next to tables covered in hot wax candles and every single one of them has a **YOU BREAK IT YOU BUY IT** sign and insufficient insurance.

I'm not one to moan unnecessarily. In fact, I like to think of myself as a positive, life-affirming person, albeit one who also has a full grasp of the darkness and tragedy inherent in modern living.

But it has to be said: today is turning out to be just *full* of sugar cookies.

The rest of my Thursday can be summarised thus:

- Nat tells me to bite her.
- I don't.
- I am forced to sit next to Toby for the entire two-and-a-half-hour return coach journey.
- He tells me that water is not blue because it reflects the sky, but actually because the molecular structure of the water itself reflects the colour blue and therefore our art teacher is wrong and the authorities should be alerted.

70

- I pull my jumper over my head.
- I stay under my jumper for the next two hours

By the time we get back to school I'm so high on my own carbon dioxide and deodorant fumes that my powers of apology have been severely stunted. Before I can even focus my eyes properly Nat has raced off the bus and disappeared, and I'm left to walk home on my own.

And no, in case you're wondering. None of this makes sense to me either. I've turned the facts over and over in my head like Chinese marbles for eight hours, but there is still no feasible explanation for anything that has happened today. Unless I have somehow landed in an alternative universe where everything is inside out and all the trees are upside down and people talk backwards and we walk in the sky with the earth as a ceiling and flowers growing downwards. And that seems unlikely.

I've even worked out an equation for the situation.

$$M = (1/W/H \times P + NSM) C + S + X$$

Here, M stands for *Model*, W is *Weight*, H is *Height*, P

is *Prettiness*, NSN is *Nice-shaped Nose*, C is *Confidence*, S is *Style* and X is *Indefinable Coolness*. Each element (apart from Weight and Height, obviously measured by the metric system) is given an objective mark out of ten, and the higher the overall result, the better you would be as a model.

By my calculations, Nat comes out at 92.

I'm 27.2. And I was being quite kind about my nose.

Anyway, I've given up thinking about it. There has clearly been some kind of mistake, and at this precise moment somebody is smacking Wilbur round the head and putting him in a nice jacket that ties his arms behind his back.

And – just so you know – I'm not thinking about Nick either. He hasn't popped into my head once, with his big liony curls and his lime-green smell and his duck-tail tuft at the back. In fact, I can barely remember him. I meet head-smashingly beautiful foreign boys all the time. I can't hide under a table without finding one there. There is no reason whatsoever that this one would stick in my memory or make my stomach twirl at intervals.

And I definitely *didn't* walk past the Infinity Models stall six or seven times during the rest of the day in case he was there. Which he wasn't.

Unfortunately, there isn't a *whole* lot else to think about. My head feels like it's fallen off the top of a great wall and I'm waiting for all the king's soldiers to come and put it back together again. There's only one thing left to occupy myself with. And it isn't that much fun to dwell on. Can you guess what it is yet?

Uh-huh.

Now I have to go home and tell my parents.

16

Debt = £3,000
Pocket money = £5 per week
Total time to pay off debt = 600 weeks = 11.1 years
Age when debts cleared = 26.11

Conversation Starter Option One

Dad? Annabel? I've been spotted by a modelling agency and I owe £3,000. Oh, and can you wash my jeans? They smell of sick.

Conversation Starter Option Two

Dad? Annabel? I owe £3,000 and I've been spotted by a modelling agency. Oh, and can you wash my jeans? They smell of Coco Pops.

Conversation Starter Option Three

Dad? Annabel? I'm moving to Mexico and yes, this is a fake moustache.

74

The problem with making meticulous and well-constructed plans is that people tend to ignore them. Other people. Not me; I stick to them religiously.

As I open the front door, I'm already clearing my throat. I've decided to lead with the modelling because hopefully my parents will be so paralysed with confusion and shock that I can slip the vast quantity of money they now owe various stallholders in there without them noticing: like doing a root canal after local anaesthetic.

"Dad?" I say nervously, shutting the door behind me. "Annabel?"

Hugo immediately barrels into my legs and starts pawing at my stomach. He has obviously just been to the hairdresser's because I can now see where his eyes are instead of just guessing by their proximity to his nose.

"Hey, Hugo," I add, bending down. "You're looking very elegant." He licks my face, which I think means, "Thanks very much," or possibly, "You smell of hotdog." Then I look back up. "Dad? Annabel?"

Silence.

You know what? The welcoming atmosphere in this house needs to be worked on. I've been away all day and it's dark. Why aren't they standing in the hallway, waiting anxiously for me to arrive home safe and in one unharmed piece? What kind of parents *are* they?

"Dad?" I repeat again, getting a bit snarly. "Annab—"

"Harriet?" Annabel interrupts from the living room. "Come in here, please."

I sigh loudly, put my satchel down on the floor and then do as I've been told. Annabel is sitting on the sofa in her office suit, inexplicably eating sardines out of a tin, and Dad is in the armchair opposite her.

You know what I was saying about young children, and how non-uniform doesn't really exist? It's the same for lawyers. Annabel's either in her suit, or her dressing gown, or she puts her dressing gown on top of her suit. When she goes out for dinner, she has to buy an outfit especially.

"What are you *eating*?" I ask immediately, sitting down on a chair and looking at Annabel's tin.

"Sardines," Annabel says – as if I didn't mean *why are you eating that?* – and she pops another one in her mouth. "Now, Harriet," Annabel says as soon as she's swallowed it. "Your dad's in trouble at work."

"Annabel!" Dad exclaims. "For the love of... Don't just throw that at her! Lead up to it, for God's sake!"

"Fine." My stepmother rolls her eyes. "Hello,

76

Harriet. How are you? Your dad's in trouble at work."
Then she looks at Dad. "Better?"

"Not even slightly." Dad scowls. "It's nothing,
Harriet. Just a small difference in opinion."

"You told your most important client to go and
French Connection UK himself, Richard. In the middle
of reception."

Dad picks a bit of fluff off the sofa. "Well, he wasn't
supposed to *hear* it, was he?" he says in his most
defensive voice. "It just came out loudly because of the
acoustics. That place is all stone walls."

"And we're keen that you have a sterling example
of adult behaviour to follow, Harriet."

"*It was the walls*," Dad shouts in exasperation.

I look at Annabel. Under a cosy layer of flippancy
she looks really worried. "How bad is it?"

Annabel puts another sardine in her mouth. "Bad.
They've called him into a disciplinary tomorrow."

"It's just a formality," Dad mutters. "I'm creative:
I'm supposed to be unpredictable. I'm the sort of guy
who wears brown suede shoes when it's raining; they
just don't know what to do with me. I'll probably get a
pay rise for being such a maverick."

Annabel lifts one eyebrow and then rubs her eyes.
"Let's hope so because we really can't afford to just

live on one salary at the moment. Anyway. What about you, Harriet? Did you have a nice day? I hope you had a fragrant day at least because when I went into the bathroom, it was knee-deep in your grandmother's vanilla talcum powder."

"Oh." I look at the floor. "Sorry. I meant to clean that up."

"Of course you did. If only your actual cleaning was as good as your intended cleaning, we would have a very tidy house indeed. Did you manage to get out of whatever it is you were trying to avoid this time?"

"Actually," I say, ignoring this extremely slanderous insinuation, and then I take a deep breath and stand up. "I have something to tell you both."

On second thoughts, maybe I won't tell them about the money *right* now. Honesty is very important within families. But so is timing. Especially when it comes to amounts like £3,000 while your father is in the process of throwing his job out of the window.

"Well?" Annabel prompts after a pause. "Spit it out, sweetheart."

"I, uh," I start. "Well, it's…" I take a deep breath and prepare myself for the…well, whatever reaction you get from parents to news like this. "*I've been spotted*," I finally manage to blurt out. There's a silence. "Today,"

I clarify. "I've been spotted today."

There's another silence and then Annabel frowns. "*What?*" she snaps. "Let me see." She puts the sardine can down and drags me up from the chair and pulls me under the light. She looks carefully at my face, and then she looks at my hand and turns it over. She stares at my wrist and the inside of my upper arm. Then she gets Dad to stand up and look at my wrist and the inside of my upper arm. What the hell are they doing?

"No, Harriet," she finally says firmly. "There're a couple on your forehead, but I think that's just teenage acne."

"Since *when* is spotted a human adjective?" I snap impatiently. "I'm not a leopard or a stingray. *Spotted*. Verb, not adjective. Scouted. Picked up. Discovered. Found." They still look blank, so I continue even more crossly. "By a *model* agent. By Infinity Models, to be more specific."

Annabel looks even more confused. "To do what?"

"To pack potatoes."

"Really?"

"No! *To be a model*," I yell in distress. It's one thing thinking you're not pretty, but it's quite another having that confirmed by the only people in the world who are supposed to think otherwise.

Annabel frowns again. When I look at Dad, however, he appears to be shining with the light of a million smug fairies. "They're my genes, you know," he says, pointing to me. "Standing right there. That's my genetics."

"Yes, dear, they're your genes," Annabel repeats as if she's talking to a child. And then she sits down again and picks up her newspaper.

I look from Annabel to Dad. Is that *it*? I mean, *seriously*?

OK, I didn't expect them to start dancing round the coffee table, waving their Sudoku books in the air like exotic bird feathers, but a *bit* more enthusiasm would be nice. *Fantastic, Harriet,* they could say. *Maybe you're not as totally disgusting to look at as we all thought you were. How wonderful for the whole family.*

Or something that acknowledges that this would be the most exciting thing that had ever happened to anyone, if I was someone else and this was a totally different family.

Annabel looks up to where I'm still standing, mouth open. "What?" she says. "You can't do it, Harriet. You're too young and you've got exams coming up."

"*She can't do it?*" Dad repeats in an incredulous tone. "What do you mean she can't do it?"

Annabel looks at him calmly. "She's fifteen, Richard. It's totally inappropriate."

"It's Infinity Models, Annabel. Even *I've* heard of them."

"Hundreds of beautiful women in one place? I bet you have, darling. But the answer's still no."

"Oh my *God*," Dad yells at the top of his voice. "*This is so unfair.*"

You see the problem? It's really hard being a child in my family when that space seems to already be taken.

"I don't actually want to do it," I interrupt. "I'm just telling you. But you could say well done or something."

"*You don't want to do it?*" Dad yells at me.

Oh, for God's sake.

Annabel looks at me. "It's modelling. Fashion." She pulls a face. "What's there to be excited about? Why is everyone getting so worked up?"

I look from her to Dad and then at Hugo. Hugo gets off the chair, tail wagging, and promptly licks me. I think he knows I need it.

"Right," I say in a slightly deflated voice. "Fine."

The only remotely exciting thing that has ever happened to me and it's over already. It lasted about as long as I thought it would. I feel a little bit like sulking. Dad still looks totally shell-shocked.

"Now," Annabel says, shaking the remote control to get the batteries working and turning the television on. "Who wants to watch a documentary about locusts?"

17

I sulk for about twenty-five minutes and then get bored and spend the rest of Thursday night a) *not* thinking about Nick and b) getting ready to woo Nat into Best Friendship again. Flowers, cards, poetry: I even bake special, personalised, sugar-free muffins with photos of me and her on top (not edible photos – I didn't have time – real photos). And then I put them all in my satchel and prepare to take them to school, where I will ambush Nat and convince her of my guilt and/or innocence.

Whatever it takes to make her anger with me disappear.

It's all a total waste of time and effort and flour. Apparently I don't need to woo Nat at all. On Friday morning, at precisely 8am, the doorbell rings.

"Nat! You're here!" I gurgle in surprise, halfway through a jam sandwich. It comes out a sticky, strawberry-flavoured, "*Nnnnnaaatcchh uuuhhh hhiiii!*"

"For *breakfast*?" she says, looking pointedly at the

other half, which is perched in my left hand.

I stick my nose in the air in my most dignified way. "Jam sandwiches have all the necessary nutrients needed to survive. Sugar, vitamins, carbohydrates. I could live entirely on jam sandwiches and lead a totally normal life."

"No, you couldn't," Nat says, pulling me out of the door. It's lucky I already have my shoes on or I'd be walking to school in my socks. "You'd be The Girl Who Only Eats Strawberry Jam Sandwiches and that's not normal." She looks at me and then coughs. "Can I have the other half, though? I'm totally starving."

I give her the other half in surprise and then look at her while she eats it. Firstly, Nat never eats food with high sugar content. *Ever*. Not since that fateful disco, eight years ago. And secondly, is this *it* then? The big dramatic scene I've been dreading all night? I made muffins without sugar especially and now *nobody* is going to eat them.

"Nat," I start and at exactly the same moment she says "Harriet?" and then she clears her throat.

"I'm sorry. For getting mad at you and stomping off."

"Oh." I blink in shock. "That's OK. I'm sorry too. For… getting spotted and stuff."

"The lying was the main problem, Harriet." Nat twists her mouth up in an awkward half-smile and licks her fingers. "Can we just forget about yesterday?"

"Of course we can," I beam at her.

A huge wave of relief washes over me: it's all OK. I was being neurotic and oversensitive as normal.

And then – just like waves – the relief abruptly disappears. Nat clears her throat and I look at her again, but a little more carefully this time. Suddenly I can see what I didn't notice before: that her neck is tense and her shoulders are all bunched up. Her collarbones have gone red and splotchy. The rims of her eyes are pink. She keeps biting her bottom lip.

"Cool," Nat says after an infinitely long pause, and then an anxious flush climbs up her cheeks and sits there, staring at me. "So…"And she clears her throat. "Did they…"She swallows. "You know… ring you?" She clears her throat for the third time. "Infinity? Did they ring you?"

She hasn't forgotten about yesterday at all. Not even a little bit.

"No." *I didn't give them my number*, I add in my head, but somehow I'm not sure saying that out loud is going to help.

"Oh." Nat's cheeks get darker. "That's a shame. I'm

sorry. So let's just put it behind us, right?"

I frown. *I thought we'd already done that.* "OK."

"And pretend it never happened," Nat adds in a tense voice.

"…OK."

Every time she tells us to put it behind us, it's becoming more and more clear that Nat hasn't done that.

"We'll just carry on as normal," Nat adds.

"…OK."

Then there's a long silence and it's not comfortable. In ten years, it might be the first uncomfortable silence there has ever been between us. Apart from the time she peed herself on the ballet-room floor and it hit my foot. That was a little bit awkward too.

"Anyway," Nat says after a couple of minutes, as she pats her hair and straightens her coat and pulls up her school tights with one hand. "So, Harriet." She looks at the bite of sandwich left in her hand. "Where's the protein in this thing, huh? I'm sorry, but I don't think you've done your research properly."

Finally, the topic has moved back to territory I can handle.

"I *have* done my research properly!" I shout back, pretending to be totally outraged. "The protein's in the…" What can I say to move the conversation as far from modelling as it is possible to move it? "Chicken," I finish and then grin at her. "There's chicken in it too. Did I forget to mention that? Strawberry and high-protein chicken sandwiches. Mmmm. My favourite."

"Strawberry and *chicken*?" Nat laughs and my shoulders relax a little bit.

"You can totally live on strawberry and chicken sandwiches," I clarify, trying not to meet her eyes. Is there any way we can just avoid the subject of yesterday until it goes away completely? Is that how Best Friendship works? Maybe. Maybe not.

But we both spend the rest of the journey to school trying to find out.

18

The really great thing about Toby Pilgrim is that you can always rely on him to treat a delicate situation with sensitivity and consideration.

"Woooooaaah," he says as Nat and I walk into the classroom. We've got to school in one piece – just. I've talked about the Greek origin of the delphinium flower (*delphis*, because it looks like a dolphin), just how many wives Henry VIII *actually* had (between two and four, depending on whether you're Catholic or not) and the fact that the Egyptian pyramids were originally shiny and white with crystals on the top. Nat has stared into the distance, nodded and grown progressively quieter, stiffer and pinker around the collarbone.

But the important thing is we've managed to avoid talking about modelling or dream stealing or the bone-crushing disappointment of thwarted lifelong ambitions. Or the fact that there's palpable tension between us.

Anyway. "Woooooooaaaah," says Toby. "Look at the

palpable tension between you! It's like the Cold War, circa 1962. Harriet, I think you're probably America. You're sort of trying to make lots of noise in the hope it goes away. Nat, you're more like Russia. All kind of cold and frosty and covered in snow." Then he pauses. "Not literally covered in snow," he clarifies. "Although it's terribly wintry today, isn't it? Do you like my new gloves?"

And then he holds out a pair of black knitted gloves with a cotton-white skeleton hand attached to the back. There's an embarrassed silence while Nat and I put a lot of energy into getting our books out of our bags. All our morning's hard work has just been totally undone.

Thank you, Toby.

"You know," Toby continues obliviously, turning his gloves over and over with an affectionate expression, "I had to sew these bones on myself. I was inspired by an old Halloween costume, but it just wasn't warm enough for December." He holds a glove up to my face. "Plus, I thought it would be an excellent way of developing my medical knowledge."

I can now see that on quite a few of the 27 white bones in the hand he's written in grey pen the Latin name for them: *carpals, metacarpals, proximal phalanges, intermediate phalanges, distal phalanges.*

"Very nice, Toby," I say in a distracted voice because Nat's already getting out of her seat.

"I've just got to go hand in my biology homework," she says in an awkward voice. "See you at breaktime, OK?"

For the record, Nat and I don't have any lessons together. Despite trying very hard to get put in the same sets last year (Nat studied more and I did my best to answer things wrong), I'm still in the top sets and Nat is in set two or three for everything.

"OK," I say. She's still not really looking at me. "Meet you in the school canteen?"

"Sure," she says, and then she flicks me a smile and shoots out of the classroom faster than I've ever seen Nat shoot out of anything.

The rest of the day can be summarised thus:

- *Every time I see Nat, she smiles and ducks behind her hair.*
- *At morning breaktime, she has a detention to go to.*
- *At lunchtime, she has another detention to go to.*
- *At afternoon breaktime, she has a third detention to go to.*

· *I spend the entire day on my own.*

By the time the final class comes around and she tells me she's going to be kept behind after school as well, I'm fairly convinced that Nat is specifically getting detentions just to avoid me. I'm torn between being devastated and simultaneously impressed by her extremely cunning strategic bad behaviour.

Toby has been making the most of Nat's absence to follow me around like a small kitten follows a ball of wool; he even pats me now and then to check that I'm still there.

"*Harriet,*" he whispers during sixth period English literature. "Isn't it lovely to spend so much time together?"

I make a noncommittal grunt and doodle another eye on my textbook.

"I really feel that I know you better now," Toby continues enthusiastically. "For instance, I know that at ten o'clock exactly you tend to go straight to the toilet, and when you come back out, your hair is much neater so I can only assume that you redo your ponytail in front of the bathroom mirror."

I continue doodling.

"And," he whispers in excitement, "at five past

twelve you go back to the bathroom and when you come out at twelve fifteen, your eyes are sort of pink and gummy around the edges. Which I can only conclude means that you go in there to cry in private."

I glare at him. "I don't do that every lunchtime, Toby."

"No?" He gets out a little notepad and opens it to a page that appears to have a list on it. He draws a line through the corresponding entry.

I can sense that I'm about to lose my temper. I've hurt Nat, it's been a rubbish day and I suspect that Toby is about to bear the brunt of it.

"And," he continues, "at approximately three pm you go to the bathroom again, but this time you're in there for the entire break so I believe you might be avoiding me. Either that or you're... you know. Engaged in intricate bowel activities."

I can feel my cheeks suddenly flame. He was right the first time, but I'm not happy with that second insinuation. I don't like talking about bowel activities, regardless of intricacy.

"Could you just leave me alone perhaps?" I whisper and I can feel my voice getting louder with every word. "I mean, is there any chance that you could – I don't know – *find someone else to stalk*?"

Toby looks astonished. "Who?" he says, looking around. "There's nobody else worth stalking, Harriet. You're the only one."

I grit my teeth. "Then don't stalk anyone." My voice is getting more abrasive. "How about you just don't stalk anyone, Toby? Otherwise known as LEAVE ME THE HELL ALONE."

And then there's a silence. Toby looks at me in astonishment. A low snigger ripples round the classroom.

When I look up, Mr Bott has paused writing on the board and is staring at me with an expression that a geek like me doesn't see very often. One of anger, frustration and a fervent desire to punish.

It looks like I might be seeing Nat after school today after all.

19

I look at Mr Bott with round eyes.

"Miss Manners," he says icily from the front of the classroom, and I suddenly remember that we're supposed to be reading act four, scene five of *Hamlet*. "Do you have a thought you would like to share with us?"

"No," I say immediately and stare at my desk.

"I find that very hard to believe," Mr Bott says in an even sharper voice. "You always have a thought to share with us. In fact, it's usually difficult to stop you from sharing it with us."

"I've no thoughts," I tell him in a meek voice.

"Good to know. That's what I like to see: a student approaching her exams with nothing at all in her head."

Alexa looks up from where she's been texting somebody under the desk and snorts with laughter.

Oh, yes, Alexa's in the top sets too. Unfortunately, she's both mean and smart. I have at least another three years left of her to look forward to, and then

she'll probably follow me to university. Although, given the amount of time she spends on her phone in our classes, I can only assume she's really, really good at last-minute cramming.

"Alexa?" Mr Bott snaps, whipping round to face her. "Is something funny?"

Alexa looks over to me and raises an eyebrow. "No," she says in a meaningful voice. "Quite the opposite. Mostly sad, I'd say."

Nice. She's managed to insult me in front of the teacher and he hasn't even noticed.

"Well," Mr Bott says, but he doesn't look happy either. In fairness, he rarely looks happy. I don't think he teaches because it fills him with a deep inner light. "How about Little Miss Shouter and Little Miss Giggles both come up to the front here and give us your perspectives on a little question I have."

Alexa's face goes suddenly pale, and as we walk to the front, she's throwing metaphorical daggers in my direction.

"Now," Mr Bott says, "turn and face the whole class, please."

My cheeks are getting hotter and hotter. I turn so that my body is in the right direction, but try to focus on the floor.

"So, Alexa Roberts and Harriet Manners." Mr Bott sits down and gestures gracefully to the board. "As you are both clearly fascinated by this text, would you like to explain the significance of Laertes in *Hamlet*?" He looks at Alexa. "Please go first, Miss Roberts."

"Well..." Alexa says hesitantly. "He's Ophelia's brother, right?"

"I didn't ask for his family tree, Alexa. I want to know his literary significance as a fictional character."

Alexa looks uncomfortable. "Well then, his literary significance is in being Ophelia's brother, isn't it? So she has someone to hang out with."

"How very kind of Shakespeare to give fictional Ophelia a fictional playmate so that she doesn't get fictionally bored. Your analytical skills astound me, Alexa. Perhaps I should send you to Set Seven with Mrs White and you can spend the rest of the lesson studying Thomas the Tank Engine. I believe he has lots of buddies too."

Alexa's face suddenly goes bright red and she looks utterly humiliated. I feel really sorry for her, actually.

Mr Bott then turns to me. "It's your go, Miss Manners. Anything to add?"

I stare at the floor for a few seconds. Answering interesting intellectual questions correctly in public is possibly my single greatest weakness. Every time I do it,

I make myself even less popular. But I can't help myself.

"Well," I say slowly, and even though I know I should say in my most stupid voice, *No idea, sorry*, I say: "Laertes is a literary mirror for Hamlet. The play is *ostensibly* about Hamlet avenging the murder of his father, but actually, it's about Hamlet procrastinating instead. Laertes is a sort of alternative universe Hamlet, because when Hamlet murders *his* father, Laertes takes immediate revenge and pushes the play to its conclusion straight away. So as a *literary construct*, I think he's there to show what would have happened if Hamlet had been somebody else instead. It's sort of Shakespeare's way of saying that our stories are driven by who *we* are and what *we* do, and not by the events that happen to us."

I take a deep breath. Toby starts clapping, but I shoot a look that stops him.

"Very good, Harriet," Mr Bott says, nodding. "Excellent in fact. Possibly even a degree-level answer, although a distinctly second-class one." He looks at Alexa coldly. "Alexa, English literature doesn't have any right answers. But it has a hell of a lot of wrong ones. And your cracker was one of them."

"Sir!" Alexa exclaims indignantly. "This isn't fair! We haven't got to the end of the play yet! Harriet cheated!"

"It's not called cheating," Mr Bott says tiredly, putting his hand over his eyes. "It's called having a vague interest in the storyline." Then he puts his fingers briefly on the bridge of his nose and breathes out.

"But—" Alexa says, cheeks even redder.

"I can see my time here is well spent," Mr Bott interrupts. "And on that encouraging note, I am going to go and collect some more textbooks from the staffroom. At least three members of this class appear to be reading *Romeo and Juliet*, hoping I won't notice the difference." He sweeps a look of total disdain round the classroom. "Entertain yourselves for five minutes. If you can."

And then he leaves. Like a circus master who has just bashed an angry tiger on the nose and then locked it in a cage with his assistant.

I turn slowly to face Alexa, and somewhere in the distance – outside of the terrified buzzing that has just started in my head – I can hear the sound of thirty fifteen-year-olds sucking in their breath at the same time.

"Well," Alexa says eventually, turning to look at me, and I swear she sort of growls. "I guess now it's just you and me, Harriet."

20

You know in romantic films, there's always that moment where the love interest just can't hold back how they feel any more and has a sudden need to declare themselves in public?

It's always totally predictable, and always totally expected, yet the heroine is always shocked and surprised, as if it's out of the blue. I've never understood that. I mean, how dense is she? Couldn't she see it coming a mile off? Couldn't she feel the gradual build-up of tension, like everyone else?

Now it all makes a little bit more sense. You don't see things happening *to you*. Only when they're happening to somebody else. Alexa's passionate, inexplicable hatred for me has nowhere else to go. It has come to a big pulsing head and now it's going to come bursting out.

I look at the door desperately. Should I try to escape? Or keep my head down and try to get through it? We're at school. Just how bad could it be? And you

know the scary bit? There's still a part of me that's about to correct her grammar. "You and I," I'm tempted to reply. "Not you and me. Now it's just you and *I*, Alexa."

"Well," Alexa says again and I can tell the whole class is still holding its breath. "Harriet Manners."

I swallow and take one step towards my seat.

"Oh, no. No, no. You're not going anywhere." She grabs the back of my school jumper and pulls me to the front of the class. It's not a violent tug; it's gentle, almost like a mother trying to stop her child from walking across the road when a car is coming. I stop and stare at the floor, making myself as small as possible.

"Could you have made me look any more stupid?" Alexa asks, almost conversationally. "I mean, *ostensibly*? Did you actually use the word *ostensibly*?"

"It means 'apparently'," I explain in a whisper. "Or 'supposedly'."

Why didn't I use 'supposedly'?

This seems to make her even angrier. "I know what it means!" she shouts. "God, you really do think I'm thick, don't you!"

"No," I whisper.

"Yes, you do. You and your smart little comments and your crap little facts and your geeky little face." She pulls that expression again: the one with the crossed eyes and protruding teeth. Which is really unfair: she knows I had my braces taken off years ago, and my left eye is only lazy when I'm tired. "You really think you're better than everyone else, don't you, Harriet Manners?"

"No," I mumble again. The humiliated burn has spread to my neck and my ears and is creeping up my scalp. I can feel the entire class staring at me the way they stared at the monkey at the zoo with the red bottom. "I don't."

"I can't hear you," Alexa says more loudly. She walks closer – way past my personal space boundaries – and for a brief second I think she's going to slap me. "I'll rephrase. *Do you think you're better than everyone else, Harriet Manners?*"

"No," I say as loudly as I can.

"Yes, you do," she hisses, getting even closer, and even in my shock I can't believe the expression on her face: pure, almost shining, hatred. As if it's burning on the inside of her and lighting her up like one of those little round candles with pictures of penguins on the outside. "You have no idea how much of a loser you really are."

"That's not true," I whisper.

Because I totally do. I know *exactly* who I am. I'm Harriet Manners: A++ student, collector of semi-precious stones, builder of small and perfectly proportioned train sets, writer of lists, alphabetiser and genre-iser of books, user of made-up nouns, guardian of twenty-three woodlice under the rock at the bottom of her garden.

I'm Harriet Manners:

GEEK.

Alexa ignores me. "So I think it's time we put it to the test," she continues and then she looks around the room. I can feel my eyes filling up with water, but I'm totally frozen. Even my tongue feels numb. *"Who in this room,"* Alexa says slowly and loudly, *"hates Harriet Manners?* Put your hand up."

I can't really see anything because the whole room is wobbling.

"Toby," Alexa adds. "Put your hand up or you're going down the toilet every lunchtime for the next week."

I close my eyes and two tears roll down my face. I think it's really important that I don't see this.

"Now open your eyes, geek," Alexa says.

"No," I say as firmly as I can.

"Open your eyes, geek."

"*No.*"

"Open your *eyes*, geek. Or I will make this worse for you today, and tomorrow, and the day after that. And I will keep making it worse for you until you realise what you are and what you are not."

So even though I know precisely what I am – and even though I'm not sure it's even possible to make it worse – I open my eyes.

Every single hand in the classroom is up.

I wish she had just punched me.

And, with that final thought, I burst into tears, grab my satchel with GEEK written all over it and run out of the classroom.

21

People Who Hate Harriet Manners
Alexa Roberts
Hat Lady
Owners of stalls 24D 24E 24F 24G 24H
Nat?
Class 11A English literature

By the time I get home, I'm crying so hard it sounds like somebody sawing wood.

I'm not really a crier, though, and there's a good chance my parents won't understand what I'm doing, so I scoot into the bush outside my house until I can be absolutely certain – without a shadow of a doubt – that I can breathe without either hiccuping or a bubble of snot coming out of my nose. Then I sit in the bush in the hole that Toby's made for himself in four years of stalking and sob quietly into the sleeve of my school jumper.

104

I'm not sure how long I cry for: it's like a never-ending circle of tears because every time I calm down and look up, I catch sight of the red letters on my satchel and it sets me off again. It even feels like they're getting bigger and bigger, although rationally I know they must be staying the same size.

GEEK

GEEK

GEEK

GEEK

GEEK

And I can't pretend it doesn't matter any more because it does. Because they just won't leave me alone.

I'm so tired of it all. I'm tired of not fitting in; of being left out; of being hated. I'm tired of having everything I am ripped up and strewn around the room the way a puppy wrecks an abandoned toilet roll. I'm tired of never doing anything right; of constantly being humiliated; of feeling like I'm just not good enough, no matter what I do.

I'm tired of feeling like this. And most of all, I'm tired of being a polar bear, wandering around the rainforest on my own.

When the letters are two metres high and flashing, I finally lose it completely. I give a little scream of frustration and attack the word with my belt buckle until the material's so ripped you can't read anything. And then – finally calmer – I curl out of a ball, climb out of the bush, wipe the mud off my uniform and try to pretend that I'm behaving in a totally rational way for 4pm on a Friday afternoon.

I sniff my way to the front door.

"Dad?" I say quietly as I open it, wiping my nose on my sleeve. "Annabel?" Then I stop, startled. Because Annabel, Dad and Hugo are all standing in the hallway.

And they all appear to be waiting for me.

22

OK, are you *kidding* me?

Now that I just want to go straight to bed without being hassled my parents have finally started working on the house's welcoming atmosphere?

"What's going on?" I ask, embarrassed and quickly rubbing my eyes with my hand. Hugo jumps up at my trousers and starts experimentally licking at the mud. "Is everything all right? Dad, did you have your meeting?"

Annabel frowns and peers at me. "What's wrong, Harriet? Have you been..." And then she stops, confused. I can see her searching her mind for a word that matches my face. "*Crying?*" she finishes uncertainly.

"I have a cold," I explain firmly, sniffing. "It started this morning." And then I look at Dad, who has his mouth clamped shut. "Dad? Your important meeting? Did it go OK?"

"Huh?" Dad makes a face. "Yeah, no problem. They

said I was a maverick like I predicted they would, but I asked for a pay rise and they said no." Then he looks at Annabel and bounces up and down on his toes a couple of times. "Tell her, Annabel." Dad nudges her with his elbow. "Tell her."

"Tell me what?" I look at Annabel and she stares back in silence. "*What?*"

Annabel sighs. "They rang, Harriet," she finally says in a reluctant voice. "The modelling agency. They rang. While you were at school."

My mouth opens slightly in shock. "They rang? But…" I stop for a few seconds in total confusion. "I didn't give them my number. How could they ring?"

"Well, they found it anyway and they rang!" Dad shouts, exploding and punching the air. Hugo responds by taking a few steps backwards and barking. "*Infinity Models*, Harriet! This is *massive*! This is more massive than massive! This is *massiver*! They rang and they said they love the photos and they want to see us all! Tomorrow, first thing! In the agency! With them! And us! And them again!"

"*Massiver* is not a word, Richard," Annabel sighs. "Anyway, what they want is irrelevant. As we discussed, Harriet's not doing it. She doesn't even want to do it." Then she looks at me. "Right?"

There's a long silence.

"*Right?*" Annabel repeats in confusion.

I look at my parents – Annabel with her hands on her hips and Dad bobbing around like a happy little duck – and suddenly I can't really see them. I can't really see anything at all. It's as if the whole world has just gone strangely dark and quiet and I'm standing in the middle, waiting for everything to start making light and noise again.

And then it hits me, like a metaphorical train or a hammer or a fist or something fast and heavy and absolutely inescapable. And it's so clear I don't know how I didn't see it before, except that maybe I couldn't because I didn't need it like I need it now, at this exact moment.

This is it.

This is what I can do to change things.

This could be my metamorphosis story, like Ovid's or Kafka's, or Hans Christian Andersen's *The Ugly Duckling* or even *Cinderella* (originally called *Rhodopis* and written in Greece in 1BC). I could go from proverbial caterpillar to butterfly; from tadpole to frog. From larva to dragonfly (which is actually only a half metamorphosis, but still – I think – worth mentioning).

MODELLING COULD TRANSFORM ME. And I'd no

longer be Harriet Manners – hated, ignored, humiliated. I'd be… someone else. Someone different. Someone cool. Because if I don't do something now, I'm going to be me forever. I'm going to be a *geek* forever. And people are just going to keep hating me and laughing at me and putting their hands up. Forever. And things will never, ever change.

Unless I do.

"I…I…" I start stammering, and then I stop and swallow because I can hardly believe what I'm about to say.

"Well?" Annabel and Dad say, except with totally different tones.

"I… think maybe I want to see them."

There's a stunned pause. "*What?*" Annabel finally gasps. "*You want to what?*"

"I want to see them," I repeat, but this time my voice is clearer. For a few seconds, Nat's face flicks into the back of my mind. My Best Friend's tense, flushed, miserable, heartbroken face. And then Alexa's flicks up next to it like a double slide show and I switch them both off. "I want to go and see the modelling agency," I confirm.

Dad jumps up in the air. "You *said*, Annabel!" he

crows. "Do you remember? We fought and I won and you said if she wanted to do it, we'd go and see them!"

"I didn't think she'd actually want to," Annabel huffs. "You tricked me, Richard. I can't believe you tricked me."

"Please?" I say, looking at her with my widest eyes. When I look to the side, Dad's doing the same thing. "Just to see? Please, Annabel?"

Annabel opens her mouth and then shuts it again. She's looking at my face as if it's a maths sum and the answer is harder than she was expecting it to be. "You actually want this?" she asks in a totally shocked and slightly disgusted voice, as if I've just said I'd like to pick fleas from stray cats for the rest of my life, and possibly eat them. "*Clothes*, Harriet? Photographs? Fashion? *Modelling?*"

"Yes," I say and I look her straight in the eye. "Maybe," I clarify.

Annabel looks straight back for a few seconds and then sighs and puts her head in her hands. "Has the world gone topsy-turvy?"

"Definitely," I confirm.

"Then…" And Annabel breathes out crossly. "Well, I'm sort of trapped by my own integrity, aren't I?"

"*Yesssss*," Dad shouts as if he's just scored a goal,

and – when Annabel gives him a short, sharp look – he clears his throat. "I meant, good decision, darling. Excellent. Very sensible."

"Don't get carried away, Richard," Annabel snaps. "I said we'd *see* them. That is all. I've made no other promises. I'm not agreeing to anything right now."

"But of course," Dad says in an apparently insulted voice. "That's also very sensible, darling."

But as Dad winks at me and runs off into the kitchen to do a celebration dance, I realise I'm not really listening. Because all I know is – after ten years – I'm finally doing something to make things better.

And – frankly – it's about time.

23

The first thing any good metamorphosis needs is a plan. A nice, well thought out, structured, considered and firm *plan*.

And if that plan happens to be in a bullet-pointed list, typed out and then printed from the computer in Dad's 'office' (the spare room) then so much the better.

It goes like this:

<u>Plan for Today</u>
- Wake up at 7am, and press the snooze button precisely three times.
- Don't think about Nat.
- Find an outfit from my wardrobe suitable for a visit to a modelling agency.
- Go downstairs wearing said outfit. My calm and supportive parents say things like ooh and aah and tell me they didn't realise I had so much inherent style.

113

- Blush prettily and agree because I probably do have inherent style.
- Don't think about Nat.
- Leave the house at 8.34am on the dot, to catch the 9.02am train to London.
- Arrive just in time to eat a pain au chocolat and drink a cappuccino in the local café because this is what models do every morning.
- Get transformed into something amazing.

Admittedly, the last point on the list is a bit vague – because I'm not quite sure what they're going to do, or how they're going to do it – but it's fine. As long as I have control over the rest of my plan, everything should go exactly as it's supposed to.

Unfortunately, nobody else appears to have read it.

"*Richard Manners,*" Annabel is shouting as I come down the stairs. It's already not going well: I pressed snooze fifteen times, and finally got out of bed to the calming, dulcet sounds of my parents trying to scratch each other's eyes out. "I cannot *believe* you ate the last of the strawberry jam!"

"I didn't!" Dad is shouting back. "Look! There's some here!"

"What use is that much strawberry jam to anyone?

Do I look like a fairy to you? With little tiny fairy pieces of toast? I'm five foot ten!"

"How do I answer that without accidentally calling you fat?"

"Be *very careful* what you say next, Richard Manners. Your life depends on the next sentence."

"Well… I… *Harriet*?" and Dad turns to me. I'm not sure how the argument's turned to me when I'm barely in the room, but apparently it has. "What the hell are you wearing?"

I look down indignantly. "It's a black all-in-one," I say with my nose as high as I can get it. "I don't expect you to understand because you're old. It's called fashion. *Fash-ion*."

Now it's Annabel's turn to look confused. "Is that last year's Halloween outfit, Harriet?" she says, scraping some of the jam off Dad's toast and putting it on her own. "Are you dressed as a spider?"

I cough. "No."

"Then why do you have a leg hanging off your shoulder?"

"It's a special kind of bow."

"And why are there seven remaining circles of Velcro down your back?"

"Style statement."

"And the cobweb stuck to your bottom?"

Oh, for God's sake.

"Fine," I snap. It's not that I'm unnecessarily emotional or worked up, but *why won't anyone just stick to the plan*? "It's my Halloween Spider outfit, OK? Happy now?"

"I'm not sure that's the best choice for today," Dad says dubiously as he starts stealing his jam back, and I can tell he's trying not to laugh. "I mean, there are other trendier insects. Bees, I hear, are very big this season."

"Well, tough," I bark again. "*Because it's all I have, OK?*"

"What about a wasp?" Dad offers, voice breaking.

"*Everything else I own has a cartoon on the front.*"

"Or a grasshopper?" Annabel suggests, winking at Dad. "I like grasshoppers."

At which point I lose it completely. They're not being calm or supportive at all. "*Why are you such terrible parents?*" I yell.

"*I don't know,*" Dad yells back. "*Why are you such a naughty little spider?*" And then Annabel bursts out laughing.

"Aaaargh!" I scream in frustration. "I hate you I hate you I hate youihateyouihateyouihateyou."

Then I run out of the room with as much dignity as I can muster.

Which – as my spare leg gets caught in the door frame until Annabel unhooks me in peals of laughter – isn't much.

24

My door doesn't slam nearly as loudly as it used to. I think my parents must have sanded it down. Which is very underhanded of them, and also suppresses my legal freedom to express myself creatively. I shut it three times to make up for it.

Once I'm lying flat on my bed, though, I start to feel ever so slightly ashamed of myself. The thing is I broke the plans myself before I'd even got down the stairs. I've been thinking about Nat all morning. It was the first thing I thought about when I woke up, and that's what I was doing for fifteen snoozes. Picturing Nat's face when I tell her where I've been today. Imagining Nat's expression when she realises I've stolen her dream, for all the wrong reasons. Not because I love fashion, but because it's my short cut out of *this*.

And I can't get it out of my head.

So, yes, I'm pretty irritated with my parents for going on about insects, and I'm also a bit frustrated that the inherent style I was hoping I might have is either not

there or is so inherent that it's never going to come out. Like the last bit of toothpaste.

But mostly I'm just angry at myself.

"Harriet?" Annabel says as I'm huffing and puffing and helping myself to one of the chocolate bars I keep stashed in my bedside table. "Can I come in?"

She never normally asks, so this must mean she's feeling quite sheepish.

"Whatever," I say in a sulky voice.

"Now you know 'whatever' isn't a grammatically correct response to the question, Harriet." Annabel puts her head round the door. "Try again."

"If you must," I correct.

"Thank you. I will." Annabel comes into the room and sits down on the bed next to me. Her arms are full of plastic bags and despite myself I'm curious. Annabel likes shopping about as much as I do. "Sorry we wound you up," she says, brushing a strand of hair out of my eyes. "We didn't realise you'd be so nervous about today."

I make a noise that is intentionally ambiguous.

"Is something wrong?" she sighs. "You're all over the place at the moment. You're normally so sensible."

Maybe that's the problem. "I'm fine."

"And there's nothing you want to talk about?"

For a few seconds all I can see in my head are thirty hands in the air. "…No."

"Then…" and Annabel clears her throat, "I've bought you a present. I thought it might cheer you up."

I look at Annabel in surprise. She rarely buys me presents, and when she does, they absolutely *never* cheer me up.

Annabel unfolds a large bag and hands it to me. "Actually, I bought this for you a while ago. I was waiting for the right moment and I think this might be it. You can wear it today." And she unzips the bag.

I stare at the contents in shock. It's a jacket. It's grey and it's tailored. It has a matching white shirt and a pencil skirt. It has very faint white pinstripe running through the material and a crease down each of the arms. It is, without any question of a doubt, a suit. Annabel's gone and bought me a mini lawyer's outfit. She wants me to turn up looking exactly like her, but twenty years younger.

"I guess you're an adult now," she says in a strange voice. "And this is what adults wear. What do you think?"

I think the modelling agency are going to assume we're trying to sue them.

But as I open my mouth to tell Annabel I'd rather go as a spider *with all eight legs attached*, I look at her face. It's so bright, and so eager, and so happy – this is so clearly some kind of Coming of Age moment for her – I can't do it.

"I love it," I say, crossing my fingers behind my back.

"You do? And you'll wear it today?"

I swallow hard. I don't know much about fashion, but I didn't see many fifteen-year-olds last week in pinstripe suits.

"Yes," I manage as enthusiastically as I can.

"Excellent," Annabel beams at me, shoving some more bags in my direction. "Because I bought you a Filofax and briefcase to match."

25

The entire plan was a total waste of time. And Dad's paper and printer ink.

By the time I'm dressed up like some kind of legal assistant and my parents have stopped fighting about Dad's T-shirt ("It hasn't even been washed, Richard,"; "I won't bow down to the rules of fashion, Annabel,"; "But you'll bow down to the rules of basic hygiene, right?"), we've missed our train and we've also missed the train after that.

When we eventually get to London, there isn't time for a *pain au chocolat* or a cappuccino, and apparently, even if there was, I wouldn't be allowed to have one.

"You're not having coffee, Harriet," Annabel says as I start whining outside the window.

"But *Annabel*…"

"*No.* You are fifteen and permanently anxious enough as it is."

To make matters worse, when we finally locate the

right street in Kensington, we can't find the building: mainly because we're not looking for a blob of cement tucked behind a local supermarket.

"It doesn't look very…" Dad says doubtfully as we stand and stare at it suspiciously.

"I know," Annabel agrees. "Do you think it's…"

"No, it's not dodgy. I saw it in the *Guardian*."

"Maybe it's nicer on the inside?" Annabel suggests.

"Ironic, for a modelling agency," Dad says, then they both laugh and Annabel leans over and gives Dad a kiss, which means they've forgiven each other. Honestly, they're like a pair of married goldfish: squabbling and then forgetting about it three minutes later.

"Well," Annabel says slowly and she squeezes Dad's hand a few times when she thinks I won't notice. She takes a deep breath and looks at me. "I guess this is it then. Are you ready, Harriet?"

"Are you *kidding* me?" Dad says, ruffling my hair. "Fame, fortune, glory? She's a Manners: she was born ready." And – before I can even respond to such a shockingly incorrect statement – he adds, "Last one in is a total loser," and runs to the door, dragging Annabel behind him.

Leaving me – shaking like the proverbial leaf in a

very enthusiastic proverbial breeze – to sit down on the kerb, put my head between my knees and have a very non-proverbial panic attack.

26

After a few minutes of heavy breathing, I'm still not particularly calm.

This might surprise you, but here's a fact: people who plan things thoroughly aren't particularly connected with reality. It seems like they are, but they're not: they're focusing on making things bite-size, instead of having to look at the whole picture. It's procrastination in its purest form because it convinces everyone – including the person who's doing it – that they are very sensible and in touch with reality when they're not. They're obsessed with cutting it up into little pieces so they can pretend that it's not there at all.

The way that Nat nibbles at a burger so that she can pretend she's not eating it, when actually she's eating just as much of it as I would.

Despite my rigorous planning, I can't break this down into any smaller pieces. Walking into a modelling agency and asking strangers to tell me objectively whether I'm pretty or not is one big scary mouthful,

and the truth is I'm terrified.

So, just as I think things can't get any worse, I abruptly start hyperventilating.

Hyperventilation is defined as a breathing state faster than five to eight litres a minute, and the best thing you can do when you're hyperventilating is find a paper bag and breathe into it. This is because the accumulation of carbon dioxide from your exhaled breath will calm your heart rate down, and your breathing will therefore slow.

I haven't got a paper bag, so I try a crisp packet, but the salt and vinegar smell makes me feel sick. I think about trying the plastic bag that came with the crisp packet, but realise that if I inhale too hard, I'm going to end up dragging it into my windpipe, and that would cause problems even for people who weren't struggling to breathe in the first place.So, as a last resort, I close my eyes, cup my hands together and puff in and out of them instead.

I've been puffing into my hands for about thirty-five seconds when I hear a human kind of noise next to me.

"Go away," I say weakly, continuing to blow in and out as hard as I can. I'm not interested in what Dad thinks. He plays games of Snap with himself when he's stressed.

"This isn't Singapore, you know," a voice says. "You can't just fling yourself around on the pavement. You'll get chewing gum all over your suit."

I abruptly stop puffing, but I keep my eyes closed because now I'm too embarrassed to open them again. My suit is grey and the pavement is also grey; perhaps if I stay very still and very quiet, I'll disappear into the background and the owner of the voice will stop being able to see me.

It doesn't work.

"So, Table Girl," the voice continues, and for the second time today somebody I'm talking to is trying not to laugh. "What are you doing *this* time?"

It can't be.

But it is.

I open one eye and peek through my fingers, and there – sitting on the kerb next to me – is Lion Boy.

27

Of all the people in the whole world I didn't want to see me crouched on the floor in a pinstripe suit, hyperventilating into my hands, this one is at the top of the list.

Him and whoever hands out the Nobel Prizes. Just – you know. In case.

"Umm," I say into my palms, thinking as quickly as I can. *Hyperventilating* doesn't sound very good, so I finish with: "Sniffing my hands."

Which, in hindsight, sounds even worse. "Not because I have smelly hands," I add urgently. "Because I don't."

I take a quick peek through my fingers again and see that Lion Boy is lazily flexing his feet up and down and staring at the sky. Somehow – and I don't know how he has done this – he has managed to get even better looking than he was on Thursday.

"And how are they?"

"A bit salty," I answer honestly. Then I nervously

blurt out: "Do you want to smell them?"

I trawl through fifteen years of knowledge, passions and experience and the best I can come up with is: *Do you want to smell my hands?*

"I'm trying to cut back," he says, lifting an eyebrow. "But thanks anyway."

"You're welcome," I reply automatically and then there's a short silence while I wonder if – in an alternative universe somewhere – another Harriet Manners is having a conversation with a ridiculously handsome boy called Nick without making herself sound like a total idiot.

"So," Nick says eventually. "Are you ready to go upstairs yet? Because your parents are waiting in reception, and judging by the look on your mum's face five minutes ago, everybody up there may already be dead."

Oh, sugar cookies. I knew Annabel was going to start channelling *Tomb Raider*: she's been in a scratchy mood all morning. "How do you know they're my parents?" I ask coolly, hoping to pretend that I've never seen them before in my life.

"Your mum is wearing exactly the same thing as you, for starters. And you have the same hair colour as your dad."

"Oh."

"And they keep saying, '*Where the hell is Harriet?*' and looking out of the window."

"Oh," I say and then I stop talking. My hands are shaking and I'm not sure I can handle any more shades of embarrassment. I'm already purple as it is. "You know," I say, after giving it a little thought, "I think I might just stay here."

"Hyperventilating on the kerb?"

I look up and see that Nick is grinning at me. "Yes," I tell him curtly. He has no business laughing at breathing problems. They can be very dangerous. "I am going to stay here and I am going to hyperventilate on the kerb for the rest of the day," I confirm. "I've made an executive decision and that is how I shall entertain myself until nightfall."

Nick laughs again, even though I'm being totally serious. "Don't be daft, Harriet Manners." He stands up and a little flicker of electricity shoots through my stomach because I've just realised he has remembered my name. "And don't be nervous either. Modelling's not scary. It can actually be sort of fun sometimes. As long as you don't take it personally."

"Mmm," I say because frankly I take *everything* personally. And then I watch as he starts wandering lazily back towards the building. Everything Nick does is slow, as if he lives in a little private bubble that's half the speed of everything around it. It's mesmerising. Even if it does make me feel like everything I do and say is too fast and frantic and sort of unravelling like the cotton on my grandma's sewing machine.

"And you want the *really* good news about modelling?" Nick says, abruptly turning round.

I glare at him suspiciously and try and ignore the flip-flop feeling as my stomach turns over and starts gasping for air, like a stranded fish. "What?"

"It's an industry *full* of tables to hide under. If you decide you don't like it, you can literally take your pick."

Then Nick laughs again and disappears through the agency doors.

Forty-eight hours ago, the most exciting thing that had ever happened to me was having my hand accidentally touched by the least spotty boy in the local bookshop, and that was just because he was handing me a book. Now I'm expected to get off the pavement and follow the best-looking boy I have ever seen into an internationally famous modelling agency as if it's the most natural, normal thing in the world.

So let me clarify something, in case you don't know me well enough by now.

It's not.

28

I wait as long as I can because it's important to maintain a high level of personal dignity at all times and also to show that you're not madly in love with someone by chasing them up the stairs. And then I get off the kerb and walk as fast as I can.

It's no use: Nick stays just ahead of me, as if he's the carrot and I'm the eternally optimistic donkey. By the time I reach the reception of Infinity Models (three floors up) he has disappeared completely, and all that's left is a slightly swinging door to convince me I didn't just invent him in the first place.

One quick glance, however, shows me that he was right and Annabel is totally fuming. While Dad bounds around the room, annoying the hell out of the receptionist, Annabel is sitting in total silence, bolt upright, with her back nowhere near the chair. The tendons in her neck are standing out like the bubbles in our living-room wallpaper.

Then I realise why. Somewhere in the direction

133

Annabel keeps looking, I can hear the distant sound of a girl crying.

"Where have you *been*?" she demands as soon as I walk in, but I'm saved by Wilbur, who bursts through the reception door in an explosion of orange silk trousers and a shirt with paint splashes all over it, except they're clearly not a result of anyone painting.

"Gooooood mooooorrrnniiiinnng," he squeals, clasping his hands together. "And if it isn't Mr and Mrs Baby-baby Panda! Just right there in front of me, like two little matching pots of strawberry fromage frais! Ooh, I could just eat you both up. But I won't because that would be terribly antisocial."

Annabel's eyes have gone very round and her mouth has dropped open. Even Dad has stopped bounding and he takes a slightly frightened seat next to her.

"What?" she whispers to him. "*What* did that man just call us?"

"This is fashion," Dad murmurs reassuringly, taking her hand gently as if she's Dorothy and he's the White Witch. "*This is how they speak here.*"

"And it's Mini-panda herself!" Wilbur continues obliviously, waving at me. "In a suit this time, no less! What's the inspiration this time, Monkey-chunk?"

I glance quickly at Annabel and see that she's

mouthing *Monkey-chunk?* at Dad, who shrugs and mouths *Mr Baby-baby Panda?* back. "My stepmother's a lawyer," I explain.

"My Stepmother's a Lawyer," Wilbur repeats slowly, a look of growing amazement on his face. "Genius! I'm Wilbur, that's with a *bur* and not an *iam*," he continues happily, semi-skipping over and grabbing Annabel and Dad's hands, "and I am so thoroughly, *thoroughly* giddy to meet you both."

"It's an – erm," Annabel manages, and Wilbur holds his fingers up to her mouth to stop her speaking.

"Sssssshhh. I know it is, my little Pumpkin-trophy. And I have to tell you I'm totally *incandescent* right now about your beautiful daughter's *visage*. It's special. New. Interesting. And we don't get much of that round here. It's all legs up to *here,*" (he points to his neck) "and eyelashes out *here,*" (he moves his hand a few centimetres in front of his face) "and lips out here," (he keeps his hand in the same place). "Dull, dull, dull." He turns to me, beaming. "You don't have any of those things, do you, my little Box of Peaches?"

I open my mouth to answer, and then realise he's telling me I don't have any of those things. Otherwise known as *beauty*. Fantastic.

In the meantime, Dad is still staring at the hand

Wilbur is holding. "Um," he says, trying to tug it away as politely as he can.

"I know," Wilbur agrees, holding on tighter. "Doesn't it feel like a whirlwind of adventure?"

And before either of them can say anything else he pulls both Annabel and Dad to their feet and starts dragging them across the reception floor.

29

"**N**ow I'd love to stand on ceremony," Wilbur says as he physically pushes my parents into a little office at the back of the room. "But we don't have a minute to lose. I have another engagement in six minutes. So let's get this done speedio and make the magic happen, right?" He holds his hand up to Dad.

"Right!" Dad says and high-fives him.

"For crying out loud," Annabel sighs as Wilbur shows us to little plastic seats. "Will somebody other than me please take this seriously? And you should know that I'm making notes," she adds sternly, getting out her notepad.

"How funalicious!" Wilbur cries. Annabel writes one word down, but I can't see what it is. "Now," he continues, "are we definitely set on the name Harriet?"

We all look at him in shock because… well, it's my *name*. I've been sort of set on it for the last fifteen years.

"My name," I tell Wilbur in the most dignified voice

I can find, "was inspired by Harriet Quimby, the first female American pilot and the first woman ever to cross the Channel in an aeroplane. My mother chose it to represent freedom and bravery and independence, and she gave it to me just before she died."

There's a short pause while Wilbur looks appropriately moved. Then Dad says, "Who told you that?"

"Annabel did."

"Well, it's not true at all. You were named after Harriet the tortoise, the second longest living tortoise in the world."

There's a silence while I stare at Dad, and Annabel puts her head in her hands so abruptly that the pen starts to leak into her collar. "*Richard*," she moans quietly.

"A *tortoise*?" I repeat in dismay. "I'm named after a *tortoise*? What the hell is a tortoise supposed to represent?"

"Longevity?"

I stare at Dad with my mouth open. I don't believe this. Fifteen years of the worst name ever and I can't even blame my dead mother for it?

"We could try Frankie?" Wilbur suggests helpfully. "I don't believe there were any famous reptiles, but I'm sure there must have been a cat or two."

"She stays Harriet," Annabel says in a strained voice.

"You have to admit it was worth a punt," Wilbur whispers to me, but I'm too busy giving my father the evil eye to say anything back.

"Now," Annabel continues. I can see that she has a list in front of her. "Wil*bur.* You're aware that Harriet's still at school?"

"Of course she is, Fluff-pot; the others are decidedly too old."

Annabel glowers at him. "I see I need to rephrase that. *What happens with Harriet's school work?*"

"We work around it. Education is so *very* important, isn't it? Especially when you stop being beautiful and perhaps get a little fat."

Annabel's eyes narrow a bit more. "How much is this going to cost?"

"Gosh, she's to the point, isn't she?" Wilbur says approvingly, winking at Dad. "If it's a testshot, everyone works for free and it costs nothing. If it's a job, Harriet gets paid and the agency gets a cut of that. That's sort of the point, isn't it? I'm not here just for the free dinners." Wilbur pauses thoughtfully. "I'm a little bit here for the free dinners," he corrects. "But not entirely."

"And who looks after her? She's only fifteen."

"You do, poppet. Or Panda Senior over there. At fifteen she has to have a chaperone at all times, and I'm going to suggest that it's one of you two because the total strangers we drag off the streets just don't seem to care as much."

I glance quickly at Dad and note that his excitement levels are getting dangerously high. Annabel scowls at him. "And who was that crying earlier?" she hisses. "*Why* were they crying?"

Wilbur sighs. "We had to turn a girl away, Darling-cherub. If we made everyone who wanted to be a model a model, we'd just be an agency for human beings, wouldn't we? Fashion's exclusive, my little Butternut-squash. That means *excluding* people."

"That was a child," Annabel says in an angry voice.

"Maybe, maybe not," Wilbur shrugs. "It's hard to tell: sometimes they just don't eat very much. Confuses the growth hormones, you know? Either way, we sent them packing." And then he beams at us all. "I won't be sending *you* packing, though, because you're here by special invitation of *moi*." And he throws the Polaroids from The Clothes Show on the table. "Your daughter is adorable. I've never seen such an alien duck in my entire life."

"A *what*?"

"Frankie here looks just like the ginger child of an alien and duck union, and that is so *fresh* right now."

"*Her name is not Frankie,*" Annabel hisses in barely contained frustration. "It's *Harriet.*"

"Could you not at least have smiled, Frankie?" Dad sighs as he studies the photos. "Why do you always sulk?" He looks apologetically at Wilbur. "She ruined eighty per cent of our photos when we were in France last summer."

"*Her name is Harriet!*" Annabel almost shrieks at Dad.

"Oh, no," Wilbur says earnestly. "That works for me. People like their high-fashion models to look as deeply unhappy as physically possible. You can't have beauty *and* contentment: it would just be unfair." He looks at the photos again with a satisfied expression. "Harriet looks thoroughly miserable: she's perfect. Once we've straightened out that lazy eye, obviously."

"*What are you talking about?*" Annabel shouts and her voice is getting higher with every sentence, as if she's singing it. "*Harriet does not have a lazy eye.*"

"Sorry, sorry," Wilbur says, waving his hands around in an attempt to calm her down. "What's a more politically acceptable way of putting it? Directionally challenged?"

Annabel looks like she's about to bite him.

"Are you sure," I finally manage to interrupt before Annabel rips the entire room to shreds, "that I'm what you're looking for? That there isn't some kind of mistake?"

Because with all of the nerves and the tension and the shouting, I haven't been able to get a word – or a thought – in edgeways, but some of the things I've heard have kind of stuck. Words like: *ginger, tortoise, alien, duck, lazy* and *eye.* This isn't quite the magical metamorphosis moment I was looking for. I don't feel very beautiful at all. In fact, I think I feel worse than I did before I came in here.

"My little Tortoise," Wilbur says, reaching out to grab my hand as my squinty, directionally challenged, short-lashed alien eyes start welling up. "Cross-eyed or not, there's no mistake. You're perfect just the way you are. And it's not just me that thinks so."

"No, your daddy does too," Dad says, leaning over and ruffling my hair in an attempt to make peace with me. I growl and bat his hand away crossly.

Wilbur smiles. "*Actually*, I'm rather enigmatically referring to an *enormously* important fashion designer who saw the Polaroids and wants to meet Harriet asap." He pauses and looks at his watch. "Asap is an abbreviation of as soon as possible," he adds.

There's a long silence while Annabel, Dad and I stare at Wilbur with blank expressions. After twenty seconds of nothing, Annabel finally snaps. "What the hell are you talking about, you strange little man? *When?*"

Wilbur's watch starts beeping. "Now," he says, grinning and standing up. "It's the other engagement I was talking about."

"*Now?*"

"Yes." And then Wilbur looks directly at me. "She's sitting next door."

30

Now I know many things.

I know that the word 'mummy' comes from the Egyptian word for 'black gooey stuff'. I know that every year the moon steals some of the Earth's energy and moves 3.8cm further away from us. I know that when you sneeze, all bodily functions stop, including the heart.

And I know nothing about modelling.

However, I'm pretty sure that this is not how the story is supposed to go. The agency are supposed to assess me and then think about it, we're supposed to assess them and think about it, and then we're all supposed to make lots of careful decisions and go through lots of boring waiting time before anything interesting happens. *If* anything interesting happens.

They're not just supposed to lob a fashion designer at me the way Alexa lobs a netball at my head before the game has even started. What's more, I haven't

been transformed at all yet. I'm not ready. *I'm still a caterpillar.*

"*What?*" Annabel finally stammers in total disbelief. "She's *what?*"

In the meantime, Wilbur has manually picked me out of my chair and is pushing me towards the door on wobbly Bambi legs. "She's next door," he repeats. "You know, they sell the most fabulous little ear syringes in chemists that will clear these hearing problems right up for you."

"I don't think so," Annabel hisses, starting to get out of her chair too.

"Oh, they do," Wilbur insists. "It's like *pop*, and suddenly you can hear again."

Annabel clicks her tongue in frustration. "I mean, Harriet's going nowhere."

Wilbur looks at Annabel in confusion. "But it's a *super important designer*, my little Door-frame. I don't think you quite understand. Frankie's a very lucky little girl to even get a chance to meet them."

"I don't give a flying duck if they're Queen of the World," Annabel snaps. "Harriet's not just being thrown into it like that."

Wilbur sighs. "Let's be rational about this, *non*? You haven't signed anything and you haven't decided anything. You can still say no. But isn't it best to know what you're saying no to? That's just basic maths."

"It's not maths," Annabel sighs. And then her head furrows in the middle. I can see the logic has started worming its way in.

"Plus, Annabel," Dad says anxiously. *"What if it's the Queen of the World?"*

"Oh, for the love of *Pete,*" Annabel says after staring at Dad for a few seconds, and then she turns to me. ("Are you Pete?" I hear Wilbur whisper to Dad.) "Do *you* want to meet this person?"

"Uh," I say because everything has suddenly gone very far away and quiet, and my whole body is shaking – even my thumbs.

This cannot be happening. This is not on the plan. This is not on *any of the plans.*

They want me to go in without a plan?

Yes. Apparently that's exactly what they want me to do.

"Perfectomondo!" Wilbur cries and – before I can work out what my next thought is going to be – he pushes me out of the door and closes it behind us.

31

"**N**ow," Wilbur says as we stand alone in the hallway and I start hyperventilating again. I knew I should have bought the crisp packet with me. "There's nothing to worry about, Plum-cake. This woman can't hurt you." He thinks about this statement for a few seconds. "Actually, that's not totally true. She can and she might. But try and forget about that because if she smells fear on you, it'll make her worse. She's like a vicious Rottweiler, except with less muscle mass and much better table manners."

"B-b-but who is it?" I stammer.

"If I tell you, you'll panic," he says, frowning at me.

I'm already panicking. I'm not sure he can say anything that's going to make it worse. "I won't," I lie.

"You will. You'll panic, and then I'll panic, and then you'll panic again, and she'll be able to tell we're weak and she'll eat both of us."

"Wilbur, I *promise* I won't panic. Just tell me who it is."

147

Wilbur takes a deep breath and grabs my arms. "Darling Strawberry-mush," he says in a reverential voice. "It's *Yuka Ito*."

And then he waits for my reaction. Which is obviously extremely disappointing for him because, after a short silence, he shakes me gently and taps my head. "Are you still in there? Has the shock killed you?"

"Who?"

"*Yuka Ito.*" Wilbur waits a little longer for the penny to drop and then sighs because the penny is clearly going nowhere at all. "Legendary designer, personally discovered at least five supermodels? Best friends with eight *Vogue* editors around the world? Has her *own personalised seat* at New York Fashion Week? Current Creative Director of Baylee?" Wilbur pauses and then sighs again. "Bunny-button, this woman doesn't work in fashion, she *is* fashion. She is the beginning of it and she is the end of it. A bit *more* panic might be appropriate."

According to scientists, the slowest that information travels between neurons in the brain is 260mph. I don't believe them because my brain is working nowhere near that fast.

My mouth has gone suddenly dry. I haven't heard of Yuka Ito, but I have heard of Baylee. People at school buy the fake version handbags at the local market. And they're just going to send me in like *this*? In a *suit*? Without any preparation at all? Where the hell is my metamorphosis?

"B-b-but w-w-what do I d-d-do?" I start stuttering because my ears have done what they always do when I'm extremely frightened: they've gone totally numb. "W-w-w-what do I s-s-say?"

Wilbur sighs in relief. "That's better. Total breakdown. A much more respectable reaction." He pats me and pushes me towards the second glass cubicle. "*You* don't do anything, Doughnut-face. Yuka Ito *does*. Trust me, she'll know straight away if you're what she's looking for. And if you're not... Well. She'll probably just bite you."

"B-b-b-but..."

"It's OK, she's totally sterile. This is the moment when the rest of your life takes shape, Harriet," Wilbur says, putting his hand reassuringly on my shoulder. And then he considers this statement. "Or fails completely," he amends. He opens the door. "No pressure," he adds.

And pushes me forward.

32

OK.

Deep breaths. In, out. In, out. But keep them subtle: I don't want Yuka Ito to think I'm going into labour.

Everything is dark, except I don't know whether it's just my brain closing down in shock or my eyes adjusting to the light. The whole room is pitch-black, and there's just a small lamp in the corner. And right in the middle, sitting in a chair, is a very small woman.

She's very still, and very silent, and she's wearing black from head to toe. *Everything* is black: her long hair is black, her minuscule hat is black and the lace hanging over one eye is black. Her dress is black and her shoes are black and her tights are black. The only thing on her that isn't black is her lips, and they're bright purple. Her hands are folded very neatly in her lap, and the only other way I can think of to describe her is that she's everything that Wilbur isn't: quiet, controlled and absolutely rigid. She looks exactly like a fashionable spider.

I *knew* I should have stuck to my first outfit choice.

As if on cue, Wilbur cries, '*Sweetheart!*' and flounces across the room to greet her. 'It's been tooooo long!'

She looks at Wilbur without a flicker of expression on her perfect, pale face. "I saw you eight minutes ago. Which I believe is two minutes longer than we agreed."

"Precisely! Tooooooo long!" Wilbur runs back to me, totally unfazed, and pushes me forward. "I had difficulty retrieving this one," he explains happily, as if he's Hugo and I'm some kind of really nice stick. "But retrieve her I finally did."

He gives me another nudge with his fingertips until I'm standing awkwardly in front of Yuka. There is something so queenly about her that I find myself suddenly dropping into a curtsy, the way I was taught to in ballet class before the teacher asked Annabel not to bring me back because it was "impossible to teach me grace".

Yuka Ito looks at me with a stony face and then – almost without moving – touches a little button on a remote control on her lap. A bright spotlight fades in dramatically, almost directly above me, and I jump a little bit. Seriously. What kind of room *is* this?

"Harriet," she says as I squint upwards. There's no

inflection to her voice, so I'm not sure whether it's a question or a statement or whether she's just practising saying my name.

"Harriet Manners," I correct automatically.

"Harriet Manners." She looks me up and down slowly. "How old are you, Harriet Manners?"

"I'm fifteen years, three months and eight days old."

"Is that your natural hair?"

I pause briefly. Why would anyone dye their hair this colour? "...Yes."

Yuka raises an eyebrow. "And you've never modelled before?"

"No."

"Do you know anything about clothes?"

I look down at my grey pinstripe suit. It must be a trick question. "No."

"And do you know who I am?"

"You're Yuka Ito, Creative Director of Baylee."

"Did you know who I was before Wilbur told you thirty seconds ago?"

I glance at Wilbur. "No."

"But she's *very* bright," Wilbur bursts enthusiastically, clearly no longer able to contain himself. "She picks things up ever so quickly, don't you, my little

Bumblebee? Once I told her who you were she didn't forget straight away at all."

Yuka slowly slides her gaze over to him. "At what point exactly," she says in an icy voice, "did it seem as if I was attempting to engage you in conversation, Wilbur?"

"None at all," Wilbur agrees and takes a few steps back. He starts gesturing at me to get behind him.

"And," she continues, looking at me, "how do you feel about fashion?"

I think really hard for a few seconds. "It's just clothes," I say eventually. Then I close my mouth as tightly as possible and mentally flick myself with my thumb and middle finger. *It's just clothes?* What's wrong with me? Telling the fashion industry's most powerful woman that *It's Just Clothes* is like telling Michelangelo, *It's Just A Drawing.* Or Mozart, *It's Just A Bit Of Music.* Why is there no kind of net between my brain and my mouth to catch sentences like that, like the one we have in the kitchen sink to catch vegetable peel?

"Would you mind explaining why you want to be a model in that case?"

"I guess…" I swallow uncertainly. "I want things to change."

"And by *things* she means," Wilbur interrupts, stepping forward, "famine. Poverty. Global warming."

"Actually, I mean *me* mainly," I clarify uncomfortably. "I'm not sure fashion is going to help with anything else."

Yuka stares at me for what feels like twenty years, but is actually about ten seconds with a totally blank expression on her face. "Turn around," she says eventually in a dry voice.

So I turn around. And then – because I'm not sure what else to do – I keep turning. And turning. Until I start to worry that I'm going to be sick on the floor.

"You can stop turning now," she snaps eventually, and her voice sounds high and strained. She flicks her finger again and the light above me abruptly switches off and plunges me back into the dark. "I've seen enough. Leave now."

I stop, but the room continues spinning, so Wilbur grabs me before I fall over.

I can't believe it. That was my chance and I blew it. That was the escape hatch from my life and I managed to shut it on myself within forty-five seconds. Which means I'm stuck being me forever.

Forever.

Oh, God. Maybe I am actually a moron after all. I

might have to recheck my IQ levels when I get home.

"Go, go, go," Wilbur whispers urgently because I'm still standing in the middle of the room, staring at Yuka, totally paralysed with shock. "Out, out, out."

And then he bows to Yuka, shuffles backwards out of the room with me behind him and shoves me back into the real world.

33

The real world, as it turns out, is even icier than the fashion one.

I stomp back miserably into the little office where my parents are waiting: Annabel, with her head in her hands, and Dad, pointedly ignoring her and staring out of the window in huffy silence.

"Tell your stepmother you don't mind being named after a tortoise," Dad immediately demands, still staring out of the window. "Tell her, Harriet. She won't talk to me."

I sigh. Today is really going downhill. And given the start, I wasn't sure that was possible. "I suppose I should just be grateful you weren't browsing the FBI's Most Wanted lists as well as scanning the *Guinness Book of Records*, Dad."

"Tortoises are incredible creatures," Dad says earnestly. "What they lack in elegance and beauty they more than make up for in the ability to curl up and defend themselves from predators."

 156

"What, like me?"

"That's not what I was saying, Harriet."

"Then what are you saying?"

"No," Annabel snaps suddenly, lifting her head.

Dad remains nonplussed. "They do, Annabel. I saw a documentary about it on telly."

Annabel whips round and her face is suddenly the colour of the paper she's still gripping in her hands. "Why you felt the need to tell her about that bloody *tortoise* I have no idea. What's wrong with you?" Dad looks at me for help, but I'm not going to drag him out of this one. "And," she continues, turning to look at me, "I mean *no*; you're not modelling. Not now, not next year, not ever. Full stop, the end, *finis*, whatever you want to put at the end of the sentence that makes it *finite*."

"Now hang on a second," Dad says. "I get a say in this too."

"No, you don't. Not if it's a stupid say. It's not happening, Richard. Harriet has a brilliant future in front of her and I'm not going to have it ruined by this *nonsense*."

"Who says it's brilliant?" I ask, but they both ignore me.

"Have you been listening to a single word that crazy

man has been saying, Richard?"

"You just want her to be a lawyer, don't you, Annabel!" Dad shouts.

"And what if I did? What's wrong with being a lawyer?"

"Don't get me started on what's wrong with lawyers!"

They're both standing a metre away from each other, ready for battle.

"Do I get a say in this?" I ask, standing up.

"No," they both snap without taking their eyes off each other.

"Right," I say, sitting down again. "Good to know."

Annabel puts her handbag over her shoulder, quivering all over. "I said I would think about it and I have. I've even made notes and I have seen nothing that convinces me that this is right for Harriet. In fact, I've only seen things that convince me of exactly the opposite: that this is a stupid, sick, damaging environment for a young girl, it was a terrible idea and it needs to stop now before it goes any further."

"But—"

"This conversation is over. Do you understand? *Over.* Harriet is going to go to school like a normal fifteen-year-old and she is going to do her exams like a normal fifteen-year-old and have a normal, fifteen-year-old life so that she can have a brilliant, successful, *stable* adult one. Do I make myself clear?"

I could point out that it's irrelevant – seeing as I've just blown any chance I have – but Annabel looks so scary and we can both see so far up her nostrils that Dad and I both duck our heads and mutter, "OK."

"Now, when you're ready, I'll be outside," Annabel continues from between her teeth. "Away from all this *rubbish.*"

And Dad and I continue to stare at the table until we hear the front door close, with Annabel safely on the other side of it.

34

We continue to stare at the table for quite some time: me absorbed in thought and Dad possibly just really interested in the table.

You know, the human brain never stops surprising me. It's always evolving: not just through the centuries, but from day to day, and minute to minute. Always in a constant state of flux. Forty-eight hours ago, I would have laughed if somebody had told me I couldn't be a model or perhaps stared at them as if they were strange alien beings with feet coming out of their heads. I've always wanted to be a palaeontologist, or maybe a physicist. But... I don't want to go back to my life the way it was.

Not now I've imagined an alternative.

I look at Dad and realise he's studying my face. "What do *you* want, Harriet?" he says gently. "Never mind Annabel, I think it must be her time of the month. You know, when she turns into a werewolf. What is it

160

you want to do?"

I think about Nat and how devastated she would be if this went any further. I think about Annabel and her fury, and then I think about Yuka Ito and her open contempt.

"It doesn't matter," I say in a small voice. "It's not going to happen anyway."

At which point Wilbur bursts back into the room and flings himself dramatically into the chair that Annabel just vacated. He doesn't seem to realise that anyone's missing.

"You got the job," he says abruptly, flinging his arms out in a wide motion. "She loves you."

I stare at him in silence. "B-b-but – no, she doesn't, she *hates* me," I finally manage to stammer. "She turned the light off on me and everything."

"*Hates* you?" Wilbur tinkles with laughter. "Golly-knickers. Did you *see* what she did to the other girls? Well, no, obviously not. We'd have all sorts of tribunals on our hands if anyone did. She does not hate you, my little Goldfish. She didn't even turn the light *on* for most of the other candidates."

"What's going on?" Dad is still saying. At least, I think he is. My brain is making that high-pitched TV noise again. "*What job?*"

"The job of the century, my little Crumpet of Loveliness; the position of the millennium. The employment opportunity to end all employment opportunities."

"Which *is*?" Dad snaps crossly. "Drop the jazz, Wilbur, and just tell us."

Wilbur grins. "Gotcha. Yuka Ito wants Harriet to be the new face of Baylee. We're on a deadline, so we start shooting tomorrow. In Moscow. For a twenty-four-hour whirlwind of fashion."

I feel like I'm in an elevator, dropping thirty storeys in three seconds. My stomach doesn't even feel remotely attached to my abdomen.

Dad opens and shuts his mouth a few times.

"For real?" he says eventually, and even in my catatonic state I cringe. I wish Dad would stop trying to be 'street'.

"So real it could have its own TV show," Wilbur confirms seriously. "We've been looking for the right person for ages. The advertising spaces are already booked and the crew is on standby. Now we've found her, it's *lift-off*."

"Gosh," Dad says and he suddenly looks strangely calm. I thought he'd be up and dancing around the room, but he looks very composed and very – you know

– *fatherly*. "Right," he says in a faraway voice. "Wow."
He looks at me again. "So it's actually happening then.
Who'd have thought it?"

The white noise in my head is getting louder and
louder. "Dad?" I manage to squeak. "What do I do?"

Dad clears his throat, leans toward me and puts
his hand on my head. "Harriet," he says gravely, in his
most un-my-dad-like voice. "Think about it carefully.
If you don't want this, we walk now. No questions. If
you do want it, I'm behind you."

"But Annabel…"

Dad sighs. "I'll deal with Annabel. She doesn't
frighten me." He thinks about this. "OK, she frightens
me. But I'll just frighten her back."

I try to swallow, but I can't. The door has just been
thrown wide open when I thought it was locked. This
is the forked road that the poem talks about. I can
take my old life back. I can be Harriet Manners: Best
Friend to Nat, Prey to Alexa, Stepdaughter to Annabel,
Stalkeree to Toby. Stranger and total Hand-sniffing
Weirdo to Nick. *Geek*.

Or I can try to become something else entirely.

Something inside me breaks. "I want to do it," I
hear myself saying. "I want to try and be a model."

"Well, *duh*," Wilbur says happily.

163

"But what happens now?" Dad asks, taking hold of my hand and squeezing it. I squeeze it back. My whole body is trembling.

"Now?" Wilbur says, laughing and leaning back in his chair. "Well. Let's just say that Harriet Manners is about to become very fashionable." And he laughs again. "Very fashionable indeed."

35

So Dad and I have worked out a cunning plan. It's not particularly complicated and it consists of one simple step: *lie*. And that's it.

We debate the telling-the-truth option for about thirty seconds, and then decide that it's probably much better all round if we just... don't. Because we're scared mainly. As Dad says, "Annabel is absolutely *bonkers* at the moment, Harriet. Do you really want to awaken the Kraken?"

So we're going to lie to Annabel. And – I add this silently in my head – Nat. We're obviously not going to lie to them forever. That would be ridiculous. We're just going to keep the truth from them until the timing is right. And it feels like a suitable moment.

And we have absolutely no other alternative. Which makes me feel no better about anything at all, so as soon as we're home from the agency, I make my excuses and go straight to the only place in the world I go when I need to run away.

The local launderette.

It's about 300 metres away from my house, and I've been coming here since I was allowed to leave the house on my own. For some reason it always makes me feel better. I love the soft whirring sounds, I love the soapy smells, I love the bright lights, I love the warmth coming out of the machines. But most of all I love the feeling that nothing could ever be bad or wrong in a place where everything is being cleaned.

I dig fifty pence out of my pocket and put it in one of the tumble dryers. Then – when it's switched on and hot and vibrating – I lean my head on the concave glass window and shut my eyes.

I don't know how long I sit with my head on the dryer, but I must nod off because I suddenly jerk awake to the sound of: "Did you know that the average American family does eight to ten loads of laundry each week, and a single load of laundry takes an average of one hour and twenty-seven minutes to complete from wash to dry? That means that the average American family spends approximately 617 hours a year doing laundry. What do you think it is for England? Less, I think. We just seem to be a bit dirtier."

And there – sitting on top of a washing machine – is Toby.

I stare at him in silence.

"Hey, you're awake!" he observes. "Look!" And then he points to his T-shirt. It has a picture of drums on it. "It's interactive! When I press the drums, they make the sound of drums." *Thud, thud.*

"Toby. What are you doing here?"

"Did you hear that?" He's wearing a yellow bobble hat and it's bobbling in excitement. *Thud, thud, thud.* "They're realistic, aren't they? Do you think if you got one with a guitar on it, we could start a band?"

"No. What are you doing here?"

"Obviously I'm doing laundry, Harriet."

I raise my eyebrow. He looks completely at ease with this terrible excuse, which – considering the fact that he has no laundry with him – is a little worrying. "Did you just follow me here?"

"Yes."

"Why?"

"You looked sad. And also because it's dark and it could be dangerous if you wander around on your own."

I scowl. "Yes, Toby. I might be at risk from *stalkers*."

Toby looks around us. "I think it's just me, Harriet.

I've not run into any others while on the job. Are you excited about the modelling assignment?"

I stare at him for a few seconds. *"How the hell do you know about that?"*

How am I supposed to keep it a secret from Nat and Annabel if I can't even keep it secret from Toby?

"Well, I wouldn't be a very good stalker if I didn't, would I?" Toby laughs. "I'd have to hang up my stalker gear in shame." He thinks about it. "Which would be unfortunate because all I've really got is this flask and I'm quite attached to it." He pulls out a red flask and shows it to me. "Soup," he explains. "In case I get hungry."

"Toby, nobody is *supposed to know.*"

"So that makes this a secret between the two of us, right?" I glare at him. "Which makes us kindred spirits? And – correct me if I'm wrong – *soulmates*?"

"We're not soulmates, Toby. You can't just go round stealing secrets and then forcing people into being your soulmate."

"OK." He seems unabashed by the rejection. "But you're glad I gave that model man your number."

For a few seconds all I can do is stutter without any noises coming out. *"You* gave the modelling agency my number?"

"You ran off at The Clothes Show so quickly I think you forgot. Good, huh?" Toby grins at me and the yellow bobble bounces up and down cheerfully. "Now the whole world is going to see you the way I already see you. I've always been a little bit ahead of the trends."

I point to the scraped-up word on my satchel. "And what if they see me the way everyone at school sees me, Toby?"

Toby considers this for a few moments. "Then I think you're going to need a bigger bag." And he hits the drum on his T-shirt. *Thud, thud.*

Suddenly I'm not so sure the launderette was a good idea after all. "I'm going home."

"OK. Would you like me to follow a few metres behind?" I frown at him, but he doesn't seem to notice. "By the way," he adds, "did Nat tell you what she did yesterday? She was amazing, Harriet. Like Boadicea, except without the chariot. Or the horses, or the swords, but still: it was *awesome.*"

I stop near the door. "Nat?" I say, totally confused. "What are you talking about?"

"She heard what happened to you in Mr Bott's English class and she went *crazy.* She stormed into the changing rooms while Alexa was getting ready for hockey and did a whole world of yelling." Toby pauses. "I didn't see this because they wouldn't let me in. Apparently that room is only for girls and I am not one of those, Harriet. I assure you. Whatever Alexa might say. I am all man."

My blood is running cold, and not just because Toby just said the phrase *all man*.

"And you want to know the best bit?" Toby adds, apparently totally unaware that every single muscle in my face is now twitching with guilt and horror. "You want to know what else she did?"

"What?"

"Honestly, you won't believe it when I tell you."

I almost snarl at him, I'm so tense. "*Tell me*," I pretty much shout across the launderette. "*Tell me what she did.*"

"She chopped Alexa's ponytail off. Right off. At the base. With some scissors. And then she said, '*Now let's see how you like everyone laughing at you,*' and stormed off." Toby laughs. "Apparently Alexa looks a bit like she's all man too now."

Oh my God. I groan and put my hand over my eyes. This is the school equivalent of the assassination of Archduke Franz Ferdinand in Sarajevo in June 1914, which led to Austria-Hungary declaring war on

Serbia, which led to Russian mobilisation, which led to Germany declaring war on Russia. *Which led to World War One.*

Nat just started a war for me. In defence of me. Because of me.

And I am not worth it.

This is about as horrible as it's possible to feel. I've reached new heights of self-shame (or lows, depending on which way up the scale is). "I...I..." I say faintly, holding on to the door handle. "I really have to go home, Toby."

And I run out of the door as fast as my legs will carry me.

36

I run all the way home.

OK, that's not true. I don't run *all* the way. I just wanted you to think I could if I needed to. Because I probably could. I run most of the way and then I Brownie Walk for the rest of it (walk twenty paces, run twenty paces). But I can't run fast enough to get me away from what it is I'm running from. Which is me, mainly.

What am I doing? I'm about to screw over my Best Friend while she defends me, my stepmother while she protects me and possibly – depending on exactly how bad I am at this modelling thing – Wilbur and the entire fashion industry.

My head feels like it's starting to rattle with words bouncing around inside it like balls. Every time *Moscow, Nick, Baylee* or *Metamorphosis* hit the side, my entire body jolts with excitement. Every time *Nat* and *Annabel* make contact, I feel like I'm about to implode with guilt and anxiety. And every time the *Alexa* ball

bounces, I feel like vomiting.

But it's too late. I've made my choice. So I spend the rest of the evening making an imaginary box in my head. And into this box I put all of the balls. I close the lid. And then I lock it up and temporarily misplace the key.

I'm going to Russia, I'm going to be transformed and there is nothing anybody can do to stop me.

First thing on Monday morning, the lies begin.

Lie No.1
Nat, I have a bad cold. Really do this time. Not coming to school today or tomorrow probably. Hope you're OK. See you Wednesday XX

Lies No.s 2 and 3
Annabel: "Why are you wearing your Winnie the Pooh jumper, Harriet?"

Me: "…It's non-uniform day."

Annabel (*long silence*): "And why haven't you gone to work already, Richard?"

Dad: "It's non-uniform… Hang on. No. Late start today. Going in later. Look: I bought some strawberry jam."

Annabel: "Why? I *hate* strawberry jam."

Lie No.4

Me: "Annabel, do you know where my passport is?"

Annabel: "Why on earth would you want your passport at 8am on a Monday morning?"

Me: "…International school project?"

Annabel: "Why does that sound like a question? Are you asking me or telling me?"

Lie No.5

Toby, have gone to Amsterdam for a shoot. H

By the time Annabel's frowned at both of us, checked me for a temperature and gone to work, Dad and I are running late for the airport so packing consists of throwing everything I own into a little suitcase, bouncing on top of it to get it to shut and contemplating just trimming round the edges as if it's some kind of pie.

I've decided if I'm doing this, I have to do it properly, so I've made a bubble chart plan on the computer and given a copy to Dad. My lies are pink bubbles, Dad's lies are blue bubbles and the lies we have to share are – obviously – purple.

In synopsis: Nat thinks I'm at home, sick, Annabel thinks I'm at Nat's tonight for a sleepover, followed by school, and Annabel also thinks that Dad's flown to Edinburgh for a late emergency client meeting that will run over until tomorrow evening.

"I can't believe you made a *bubble chart,*" Dad keeps saying in disbelief as we finally climb into our plane seats.

"It's the most suitable kind of chart for this kind of plan," I tell him indignantly. "I made a flow chart and a pie chart, but they didn't work nearly as well. This one is a lot more sensible."

Dad looks at me in silence. "That's not what I meant," he says eventually.

"I made a timeline graph too," I tell him as we buckle our seatbelts. "The lies are spread across it on an hourly basis. But if I show it to you, you might get confused. I think it's best if I simply alert you when you're supposed to be saying something that isn't true."

Dad stares at the bubble chart again. "Harriet, are you sure you're my kid? I mean, you're sure that Annabel didn't bring you with her and swap you in?"

I scowl at him and then wince in pain because the universe has apparently decided to wreak vengeance upon me by making my metaphorical devil horns literal. By the time the air hostesses start pointing to the exits, my entire forehead is hot and throbbing; by the time they bring round the free peanuts, I can't really frown without it hurting, and by the time we start the descent into Moscow, Dad's calling my brand-new and massive zit "Bob" and talking to it like a separate entity.

"Would Bob like a drink of orange juice?" he asks every time a flight attendant walks past. "Perhaps a piece of cracker?"

It takes every single bit of patience I have not to ask the pilot if we can just turn round and drop my father back in England because he is *not behaving*. None of this, however, is enough to crush my excitement.

I'm going to Russia.

Land of revolutions and preserved leaders with lightbulbs stuck in the back of their heads. Land of the Kremlin and the Catherine Palace and the lost Amber Room, which was covered in gold and somehow 'went missing' during World War Two. Land of big fur hats and little dolls that fit inside each other.

And if I have to model while I'm there, so be it.

"This is it," Dad says as the plane comes down. He nudges me with his elbow and grins. "Do you know how many teenagers would kill for this, sweetheart?"

I look out of the window. There's a flurry of soft white snow and everything is covered in white powder, like a postcard. Russia looks exactly as I imagined it would. And trust me, I've imagined it a lot. It's on my Top Ten List of Countries to Visit. Number Three, actually. After Japan and Myanmar.

I swallow hard. Things are starting to change already. From this point on, everything is going to be different.

"You're living the dream," Dad smiles at me, looking back out of the window.

"Yes," I say, smiling back at him. "I think I just might be."

37

The really great thing about Moscow airport is that it's so *Russian*.

The signs are in Russian. The books are in Russian. The brochures are in Russian. The shops are in Russian. All the things in the shops are Russian. All the people are Russian. OK, maybe all the people aren't *Russian* – most of them are getting off planes from the UK and America, and if I'm totally honest, everything is also in English – but everyone looks sort of… different. Exotic. Historical. Revolutionary.

Even Dad looks more sophisticated, and he's still wearing that nasty T-shirt with the robot on the front of it. None of which seems to have made any impression on Wilbur.

"Oh, my Billy Ray Cyrus," he sighs when we finally find him. He's sitting on top of a pink suitcase, wearing a silk shirt covered in little pictures of ponies, and the second he gets close to me he puts his hands over his eyes as if I'm about to poke them out with my

zit. "Where did *that* come from? What have you been *eating*?"

"Chocolate-chip cereal bars," Dad informs him helpfully. "She had three for breakfast."

"You look like a baby unicorn, Twinkletoes. Could you not have held off for another twenty-four hours before you started sprouting horns?"

I scowl in humiliation, wince, and try to push the spot back in again. "It's only one," I mumble in embarrassment. "Horn, *singular.*"

"Stop trying to *climb* the mountain with your fingers, Cookie-crumble," Wilbur sighs, gently smacking my hand away. "Unless you're planning on sticking a flag on top for posterity."

Dad laughs so I thump his arm. Adults really need to learn to be more sensitive about teenage skin problems. They can be devastating to mental health, and to confidence, and also – I'd imagine – to modelling careers. "It'll cover up with make-up, though, right?" I ask nervously.

"Treacle-nose, putting make-up on *that* is like sprinkling sugar on the top of Mount Fuji. Thank God for computers, that's all I'm saying." Then Wilbur takes a step back and surveys my outfit. "*Luckily*," he exclaims, "we've saved the day with another moment of sheer fashion brilliance. Turn around, my little Rhino."

I squint at him and then look down. "My Winnie the Pooh jumper?" I say in disbelief. "And my school skirt?"

It was all I had that still fitted and wasn't a) in the wash, covered in sick, b) a football kit c) a suit or d) designed with an insect as a template.

"Winnie the Pooh Jumper and School Skirt," Wilbur says, looking at the sky in wonder and slapping himself on the forehead. "You are truly an original, my little Jellyfish. *Anyhoo*, while I could stand here all day and talk about dermatological disasters and your sense of style, sadly I'm being paid to make sure I don't."

And he starts wobbling across the airport with his suitcase in one hand and the other held inexplicably high in the air.

"But where are we going first?" I say as Dad and I trot along behind him. I'm so excited now that little insects feel like they're rocketing around my stomach, the way they rocketed around the jam-jar trap we made at primary school. "The Gulag History Museum? The Tretyakov Gallery? The Novodevichy Convent? The Worker and Kolkhoz Woman is in Moscow, you know. It moved from Paris."

Not that I've spent the entire journey reading a guidebook about Moscow or anything. Or – you know – three. And studying a map.

"Oh, good Lord. They sell lots of vodka here, right?" Dad asks. "I think I might need one."

"My little Ginger-cakes," Wilbur says, turning to look at us with his hand on his hip. "We're not sightseeing *or* drinking vodka. This isn't a romantic weekend for three, although – " and he looks at Dad – "Mr Panda Senior over here is definitely a cutey."

Dad looks momentarily stunned, and then grins and winks at me. "I keep telling Annabel I am, but she never believes me."

"So where are we going?" I repeat impatiently. I'm going to throttle Dad before this trip is over.

"We're going straight to set, Sponge-finger," Wilbur says in a businesslike voice, "and we don't even have time to drop your bags off at the hotel first. However, we *do* have to find the other model before we go anywhere."

I stare at Wilbur in shock. He's started walking towards the taxi rank and is waving his hands around as if his feet are on fire. "Wooohooo?" he adds at the top of his voice. "*Avez-vous* a spare taxi, anyone? Silver plate?"

I continue looking at his back, slightly distracted by

the fact that he seems to think we're in France. "Other model? What other model?"

Another model is *not* on the bubble chart.

"It's a paired shoot, Puppy-toe," Wilbur explains, looking at his watch. "I'm certain I explained it all to you, although that could have been a dream. And not one of my most interesting ones either." He looks at his watch again and sighs. "But he's predictably late, *as usual.*"

My stomach falls into my knees. "*He?*" I finally stammer.

"That's the personal pronoun we use when the subject is male, Petal. And, if I remember correctly, you've met this one before. You were talking about doves, or was it pigeons? Some sort of bird anyway."

My stomach drops all the way to the floor. And then my heart and my lungs and my kidneys and my liver all follow it until they're lying in a smashed-up pile at my feet.

There is *no way* this is happening.

"*Finally*," Wilbur says, turning round and waving. Because there – leaning against a lamp-post in the snow, wearing a big army jacket and looking impossibly beautiful – is Nick.

Again.

38

What were the chances?

I'll tell you what the chances were. Approximately 673 to one. And that's if Yuka Ito was only casting male models who were based in London. If you count the rest of the globe – which is equally full of beautiful people – then the statistics get even more improbable. Thousands to one. Thousands and thousands to one little tiny one.

And how have I worked this out so quickly? That's not important. But if, say, I *happened* to stumble upon all the main modelling agency websites while I was bored last night, and I *happened* to count up all the male models, and I *happened* to calculate the chances of seeing Nick again soon, then that would be my prognosis. If I *had*.

As I said, it's not important.

Approximately 673 to 1 and yet here he is, climbing into a taxi next to me. And my dad. Which is mind-boggling because I sort of assumed that if my planet and Nick's planet weren't supposed to collide then his planet and my *dad's* planet were probably on different orbits, in different solar systems, in totally different universes.

Dad takes one look at Nick, sitting on the backseat next to me with his hair covered in snowflakes, and coughs. "I think I'm starting to understand why you were so keen to be a model, Harriet," he says in the most unsubtle voice I've ever heard. I kick him on the ankle.

"What?!" Dad pretends to look innocent and offended. "I'm just saying, from a fifteen-year-old girl's perspective, things are making a lot more sense all of a sudden." And then he grins at me.

It's not possible to be this embarrassed. If I open the taxi door while it's moving and physically *push* my dad out, will I get arrested for murder? It might be worth it.

"*Dad*," I whimper and stare out of the window as hard as I can. Moscow is zooming past — all snow and big buildings — but I can barely focus on it. Not only is Nick here when he's not supposed to be, he's even *more* handsome than last time I saw him. He gets better looking every day, as if he's taking some kind of magic beautifying potion made from the tongue of a unicorn and the hair of a dragon or something.

Perhaps I should ask if he has any spare.

"You met under the table at The Clothes Show, do you remember?" Wilbur says innocently, waving his hand between us.

Dad's all-knowing expression has deepened. "Is that *so*?"

Nick half smiles at me and puts his feet up on the seat in front of us. "Harriet Manners," he says in his slow, lazy voice. "Dedicated to law enforcement."

"She gets that from her stepmother," Dad explains and I quickly try to calculate how much injury I'll cause if I wait until there's a red light and then just casually kick Dad's car door open.

"I didn't know you'd be here," I say as nonchalantly as I can.

Nick shrugs. "I got the Baylee gig a while ago," he says as if he's just landed a Saturday job at the local supermarket. "They were just waiting to find the right girl."

Oh my God. *I'm* the Right Girl? I'm usually the Girl That Will Have To Do I Suppose Because That Other One Got Chicken Pox (Year Five play *Cinderella*).

Wilbur leans forward. "Plum-pudding," he says in an awe-filled voice. "He's done it all. Gucci, Hilfiger,

Klein, Armani. Barely sixteen years old and one of the most successful young male models in London. You're very lucky to work with him, my little Pot of Bean Paste. He can hold your hand. Walk you through it."

I look briefly at Nick's hand. *I wish*, I think wistfully. And then my cheeks go pink.

"It's nothing to be worried about, honestly," Nick says in a calm voice, staring out of the window. "We rock up, we do our job, we get snowed on, we go home again. It's no biggy."

I nod quickly, my whole head now zinging with nerves. *No biggy.* The closer we get, the more real it's starting to feel, and the more I can feel the panic rising. The last few days have been less like a funfair rollercoaster and more like one of those round balls they strap astronauts into in preparation for space. I'm never quite sure which way is up any more.

But it's fine: this is *no biggy.* It's just me, Dad and Wilbur, hanging out in Moscow for twenty-four hours, taking photos. Casual, breezy photos, with a really expensive camera. And one of London's top male models and a famous photographer. And maybe fashion legend Yuka Ito drinking coffee 100 metres away and switching lights on and off with a disgusted look on her face. Just six people and one of them is Lion Boy.

No biggy. Sure.

My heart is starting to hammer like one of the little toy soldiers in a Christmas cartoon, and my mouth has gone suddenly fuzzy. I lick my lips and try to focus. This is what I wanted. This was my choice. This is what I'm lying for. And what's the point if I'm so scared I can't enjoy my own transformation?

I look out of the window while I try to calm my breathing down. It *is* really beautiful. The buildings are massive and majestic, everyone is wrapped up in furry hats and scarves and there are Christmas lights twinkling between the snowflakes. And every so often, if you look really hard, it's possible to see a man in uniform, standing on a corner with a massive gun in his hands.

Which distracts a little bit from the Christmas *ambience*, but still.

And then there's the river: huge and shining with the lights stretching out in reflections across the water. Exactly like the books I have at home and much, *much* better than *La Seine* in Paris.

Which is not being racist towards rivers. I'm just saying.

"We're nearly here, my little Chocolate-drops,"

Wilbur says as the taxi turns a corner. "Baby-baby Unicorn, how are you feeling? Calm? Cool? Deeply and irretrievably fashionable?"

I give the least convincing nod of my life. "I feel fine," I lie as the taxi stops. My hands suddenly feel like live fish in my lap: all slippery and incapable of staying still. "I feel great," I continue, looking out of the window. "I feel—"

Then I stop. Because in front of us is a huge square, filled with snow. On one side is an elaborate red wall and on the other side is a large white palace, delicately carved. I know that if I was to turn round, there would be a red castle behind us, but directly in front of us is the most beautiful building I have ever seen. Red, and blue, and green, and yellow, and striped and starred and carved like the most expensive cake you could possibly imagine.

And in front of that are about thirty-five people, sixty lights, trailers, chairs, hangers full of clothes, clusters of passers-by and – inexplicably – a small white kitten on a pillow, wearing a lead.

And it looks like every single one of them is waiting for us.

39

Lion Boy lied.

There's no other way of putting it: he totally and utterly lied. This *is* a biggy, in every possible sense of the word. As soon as we get out of the taxi in Red Square – which is where I've already worked out we are – we're surrounded. It's like being in some kind of zombie movie, except that instead of the undead wearing ripped clothes and trying to eat us, it's fashionable people wearing black and fur and trying to talk to us about our journey.

"At last!" somebody shouts at the back. "They're finally here!"

"Sweetums," Wilbur announces as he gets majestically out of the car. The snow has slowed down, but Wilbur still opens a huge umbrella in case his hair gets "damp". "I'd like to say it was the traffic, but it really wasn't. It's just so much easier making an *entrance* when everybody's waiting already, isn't it?"

I'm glaring at Nick so hard that my eyebrows are starting to hurt. "No biggy?" I hiss as we're helped out into the snow. "*No biggy?*"

Nick grins at me and shrugs. "Oh, come on," he says in a low voice. "If I'd told you the truth, you'd have just tried to climb out of the taxi window."

He's right. "I would *not*," I snap back because climbing out of windows isn't a very elegant image for him to have of me, and then – to regain a little bit of dignity – I toss my head as angrily as I can. Although it's pretty hard staying mad when you're standing in the middle of a fairytale in front of a castle with somebody who looks just like a prince.

Not that I think of Nick like that. We're just colleagues.

Dad, in the meantime, is sucking the attention up as fast as physically possible. "*My* daughter," he's saying to anyone who will listen. "The strawberry-blonde one. Can you see?" He keeps pointing to his own hair. "Genetically mine. It's actually a recessive gene so she was very lucky because her mother was a brunette."

"*Dad*," I whisper again and roughly four more ways to kill him race through my head. "*Please.*"

"Harriet, this is all *so... so...*" Dad sighs happily while he looks for the right word, dusting off his nineties vocab. "*Rad*," he finishes and I have to put my hand over my face to hide my embarrassment.

It's not enough to ruin this moment, though. I'm in *Red Square*. To my left is the Kremlin, which houses Lenin's Mausoleum, and in front of me is St Basil's Cathedral, one of the most amazing and famous pieces of architecture in the entire world. There's the GUM department store, and the State Historical Museum, and the Kazan Cathedral. There's even a bronze statue of Kuzma Minin and Dmitry Pozharsky, although it's so covered in snow I can't see who is who.

It's stunning, which shouldn't really be a surprise. It's not called Red Square because it's red. It's because the Russian word for red – *красная*– also means *beautiful*. This is their *beautiful square*.

There are so many people making so much noise – so many objects I don't really recognise – that it takes me quite a few moments to realise that Nick has disappeared completely again and the crowd is starting to part in the middle, like the Red Sea except Black.

It slowly gets quieter and the parting widens until there's a distinct snowy pathway up the middle. Even Wilbur stops talking and the only sound left is the kitten, who now and then makes a small squeaking sound like a door shutting.

"Here she comes," somebody whispers in what sounds a lot like terror, and all heads turn in one direction.

Stalking up the pathway on the highest black heels I've ever seen is Yuka Ito. And she's staring directly at me.

40

Now I could be wrong, but Yuka Ito appears to be wearing exactly the same outfit, except with bright orange lipstick instead of purple. For somebody so high up in the fashion industry, she seems to have even fewer wardrobe options than I do.

Yuka stops two metres away from where we're all standing, totally mesmerised. She doesn't look happy. Although obviously I'm not sure what happiness looks like for Yuka Ito. Let's just say the snow on her shoulders doesn't appear to be melting in the slightest.

"Wilbur," she says in a voice so appropriately icy it's like it's coming from the sky. "What, precisely, do you think your job is?"

"Other than being generally fabulous?"

"Debatable," Yuka snaps. "Would you say that your job entails getting my models to me at the time I've asked you to get them to me?"

Wilbur thinks about this for a few seconds. "I would say it's definitely on the list, yes."

"Then could you explain why they're both forty-five minutes late?"

"Darling," Wilbur sighs, rolling his eyes. "Turning up on time is so *keen*. Not *cool*. Plus –" and he makes a little gesture and lowers his voice, as if telling us a secret –"it's *snowing*."

"Yes, I was vaguely aware of that. Although everybody else managed to get here on time because in Russia snow is not, shall we say, *unexpected*." Yuka's lips press together in a straight line and then she looks at me. "Could you also explain why the female face of my new collection is sporting some kind of head accessory?"

Head accessory? What is she... *Oh*. My whole being goes bright red. She's talking about the spot. If there was a light above my head, I suspect it would be turned off about now.

"If you cast a *teenager*," Wilbur says patiently, "that's a risk that comes with the territory. They're skinny, yes, but just *full* of hormones and pus. It's like employing a tiger and then complaining because it has whiskers."

Yuka looks at me impassively. I've definitely felt prettier. She makes a clicking noise with her tongue. "Fine," she says in a snipped voice. "We'll digitally enhance her beyond recognition anyway. Take her to the hotel to get ready while we set up and do Nick's solo shots. You've got an hour and a half." And then she clicks her fingers at a handful of people standing directly to her right. "There's a list. Follow it *exactly*. Let me make this clear: this is *not* your time to shine creatively." She scowls at the crowd in general. "*Now*," she adds. "Why are you all still standing there? I'm finished."

And then she walks back through the black sea, which closes neatly around her.

I look at Wilbur in bewilderment.

"List?" I say finally. "What list?"

"I believe, Munchkin-face, that'll be the list of what we're going to do about *this*." And then he waves his hand in my direction.

Apparently by *this* he means *me*.

"But," I finally manage to blurt, "I thought you said I was perfect just the way I was?" At which point Wilbur throws his head back and roars with laughter.

And that, apparently, is my answer.

41

So I have a confession to make: I haven't come here totally unprepared. I mean, I can't expect them to do everything, can I? If I want to be cool, I have to put a little effort in. Participate in my own metamorphosis.

So I spent a few hours last night doing some research on the internet. I know a whole lot more about the fashion industry than I did before. And I'm kind of excited because now I get a chance to prove it and, maybe, start making a little progress in the right direction.

"Sit down, sweetheart," one of the women wearing black says. I've been taken out of the snow and put into a little hotel room just behind Red Square. I've never seen so many beauty products, make-up items and hairbrushes. There's even one of those headlamps set up, like the one my grandma uses when she gets a perm.

I sit down. Another woman gets a piece of paper out and looks at it. "Are you kidding me?" she says

196

in disbelief. *"No cat eyes?* Doesn't Yuka know it's all about cat eyes this season?"

The other woman shrugs. "Prada have just done it so it's officially over already."

I blink. This isn't quite the conversation I was gearing up for, but I shall do my best to keep up.

"You know," I say, clearing my throat and trying to look as casual as possible, "cats' eyes have a mirror-like membrane on the back to maximise light exposure. That's why they shine in the dark."

The two ladies look at me. "That's... nice."

"And on the subject of fashion," I add quickly, mentally trawling through the research I did last night, "did you know that in the eighteenth century it was very hip to stick on eyebrows made out of mice skin?"

They gaze at me in silence.

"Also," I add, determined to keep going until they're impressed, "did you know that there are buttons on coat sleeves because Napoleon ordered them to stop his soldiers wiping their noses on their jackets?"

"That's gross," one of them points out.

"But weirdly interesting," the other one adds.

See? I told you my research would pay off. I've already won over a little bit of the fashion industry with my hip knowledge.

"Now," she continues, looking at the list again, "we've got just enough time to do your make-up after. And get you into the clothes."

I stare at her and then I stare at Dad who's wandering around the room picking things up and putting them down again. ("Look, Harriet! A Russian Bible! It's all in Russian!") Dad shrugs nonchalantly as I raise my eyebrows at him. "No idea what anyone's talking about, sweetheart. Don't look at me."

"After what?" I ask tentatively, looking at Wilbur.

We've got an hour and a half. How much time does it take to put on a bit of lipstick and a dress? How much time does it take to make me into a model? How ugly do they think I am?

Wilbur claps his hands together. "Ah, my little Pineapple-chunk, this is the best bit," he explains. "I've been excited about it ever since I saw The List."

I look around the room and already I can feel a sense of impending doom. "What's going on?"

"Oh, come on," Wilbur shouts in excitement, starting to jump up and down. "What happens to the Ugly Duckling to turn her into a swan?"

The blood drains from my face. "You're making me go swimming?"

"Yes!" Wilbur shouts excitedly. "We're making you

go—" and then he stops. "What? No, honey. We're *giving you a haircut.*" At which point the door opens.

"And *that*," Wilbur adds, pointing to the incredibly short man who has just walked in, "is the wizard who is going to transform you."

Right, I'm not sure what fairytales Wilbur has been reading, but at no stage in any of Hans Christian Andersen's stories does the Ugly Duckling get a haircut.

The Ugly Duckling gradually becomes the beautiful bird on the outside that he always was on the inside. It's a story about inner beauty and embracing who you truly are and fulfilling your destiny (and also ignoring mean ducks who have a go at you in the process).

He doesn't just *get a haircut*. I've tried explaining this to Wilbur, but he's having none of it. "What are you talking about, Treacle-bottom?" he says distractedly, still dancing round my chair like some kind of excited leprechaun. "So how does he go from all ratty and grey to beautiful and smooth and white then? Are you telling me a hairdresser wasn't involved?"

I'm not quite sure what to say to that, so instead I shut up and stare at the hairdresser – a French man called Julien – who is walking solemnly round in the opposite direction.

199

"Now," Julien says, "*ma petite puce*. Wot iz your name again?"

"Harriet Manners," I say, sticking my hand out awkwardly. Did he just call me a *flea*?

Julien stares at my hand in shock. "*Mon Dieu*," he says, appalled. "I am *French*. We do not *touch 'ands*. It is un'igienic."

"Sorry," I say, pulling it back as quickly as possible and wiping it on my trousers.

"*Non*, instead we do a little kissin'. Like zis." And he leans forward and kisses Wilbur three times on the cheeks and then once lingeringly on the lips.

Wilbur giggles. "Best bit of my trip," he whispers to me behind his hand. "I do *love* Frenchmen."

"Ze lip bit was just for Wilbur," Julien explains. "We don't do zat in France. *Alors.*" He grabs my face and stands behind me, looking into the mirror. Then Wilbur's face pokes up to the right, and Dad's face pokes up to the left until all three are staring at me like a bad eighties album cover.

"Zis 'air," Julien continues. "It iz big."

"Yes," I agree.

"It iz *too* big. It iz… 'ow you say… *flooding you*."

"Drowning?" Dad offers helpfully.

"*Mais oui*. You are nuthin' but a little wave in an

200

ocean of 'air. We cannot see your features. It iz all lost." Julien looks at Wilbur and then looks back at me. "Yuka iz right," he says finally, and Wilbur gives a little squeal as if somebody just trod on his toe and he's happy about it. I'm not feeling as comfortable with this conversation as I should be.

"Your 'air," Julien explains in a nonchalant voice, "iz too big for your 'ead."

"It's *supposed* to be," I explain. "More room to hide."

"*Non*." Julien pushes me back down again. "A little 'ead needs little 'air."

"And a little ego needs *lots*," I argue, but it's too late. Julien has put a thick lock of my hair between his scissors and he's moving them closer and closer to my head. "Dad!" I yell. "Do something!"

"Touch a hair on my daughter's head," Dad says firmly, standing up, "and my wife will sue you all."

"OK," Julien shrugs.

And then he lops the whole lot off.

42

My dad is having a breakdown.

He keeps looking at my head and then murmuring, *Oh God, Oh God, Oh God*, and putting his hands over his eyes. "I think Annabel is going to notice this one," he says eventually.

I touch the hair clutched between my fingers. An hour ago it was waist-length and now it's bobbed to just below my ears. I also have a short spiky fringe which is going to be standing vertically for the rest of my teens.

Julien is calling this look *"La Jeanne d'Arc* for the New Decade". I think it means that I'm going to be sent to the wrong toilet in restaurants until it grows back again.

"Darling," the stylist says, patting me on the shoulder, "I know you must be gutted: the loss of your femininity and so on. But we don't really have time for this. We need to get you ready."

I nod, and then pull myself together and get off

the bed. I can't complain just because my idea of a *transformation* apparently isn't the same as anyone else's, i.e. to make me look better.

"OK," I say bravely, getting into the make-up chair. I'm going to just let them do whatever it is these people want to do.

Which is, apparently, bore me to death.

Being transformed is incredibly dull. It's like watching somebody you don't know paint by numbers. They inexplicably paint my face with something the same colour as my face, then put pink stuff where I was blushing before they covered it up, and then give me lots of black mascara that goes into my eyes, and then bright pink lips.

Then they put shimmery stuff on my shoulders, and shimmery stuff in my hair, and then they hand me my 'outfit'. I've used quotation marks, for the record, because it's not an outfit. It's a short fake fur coat and a pair of the highest red heels I have ever seen. And that's it.

No, sorry. I've also got a pair of big black knickers you *just* can't see under the coat and a sheer pair of tights that are totally transparent and do nothing apart from make my legs look weird and shiny, like the legs of a Barbie.

I stare at it all for a few seconds in disbelief and then take it into the bathroom to maintain my modesty, which for some unknown reason everybody seems to think is really funny. Then I sit on the seat of the toilet to put 'the outfit' on.

Ten minutes later, I'm still sitting there.

"Harriet?" a concerned voice eventually says, accompanied by a knocking on the door. "It's Dad. Are you all right, sweetheart?"

"She's probably so mesmerised by her own beauty she can't move away from the mirror," I hear Wilbur stage-whisper. "It's why I'm always late." Then he knocks on the door as well. "*Look away from the reflection, baby*," he shouts through the wood. "*Just look away and the spell will be broken.*"

"Dad? Can you come in here? I'm on the toilet."

There's a pause. "Darling, I love you very much. You're my only child and the apple of my eye and whatnot. But I'm not coming in there if you're on the toilet."

I sigh in frustration. "With the seat *down*, Dad. I'm sitting on the toilet. As a chair."

"Oh. OK." Dad pokes his head round the door. "What are you doing?"

"I can't stand up."

"You're *paralysed*? How did that happen?"

"No, I literally can't stand up. The heels are too big, Dad. I can't walk in them." I try to stand up and my ankles buckle and I collapse back on to the toilet.

"Oh." Dad frowns. "Why hasn't Annabel been teaching you how to walk in heels? I thought we had an agreement: I teach you how to be cool and she trains you how to be a girl."

I stare at him in silence. This explains so much. "I've never worn heels before. So what am I going to do?"

Dad thinks about it and then starts singing 'Lean on Me' by Al Green. He bends down and I take one wobbly step and hang on to his shoulder like a tipsy baby koala hanging on to a eucalyptus tree. Then Dad spins me round so I'm facing away from the door.

"What are you doing?" I snap crossly. I'm currently failing to be a *girl*, let alone a model. "The exit's that way."

"Before we go anywhere, I want you to see this," Dad says and he points in the mirror.

Next to a reflection that looks exactly like my dad is a girl. She's got white skin and sharp cheekbones and a pointed chin and green eyes. She has thin long legs and a long neck and she's sort of graceful yet clumsy-looking, like a baby deer. It's only when I lean forward

205

a bit and see that her nose turns up at the end just like mine does that I fully register that it's me.

That's *me*? Wow. The beauty industry actually works. I look… I look… I look kind of *OK*.

"You can say what you like," Dad says after a moment. "But I think me and your mum must have done something right."

I make an embarrassed but pleased peeping sound.

"Don't get me wrong, I'm taking full credit for the hair. But she had all the beauty. She'd be so stoked right now." Then Dad spins me round again so that my toes are on top of his feet and starts half-carrying, half-dancing me out of the bathroom. "Roar for me?" he demands.

"*Rooooaaaar.*"

"That's the one. Now let's go get 'em, Tiger."

"I think this is leopard, actually," I point out, looking at the coat. "Tigers have stripes."

Dad gives me his widest grin. "Then let's go get 'em, Leopard."

It takes another four minutes to get out of the bathroom, and by the time I'm back in the hotel room, Dad has corrected the leopard analogy to "baby giraffe learning how to ice-skate".

Which is extremely unkind. I'd like to see *him* try and walk with eight-inch spikes attached to his feet. Plus, giraffes never lie down and there are at least three points where I'm sort of horizontal.

"Well, *this* isn't going to work, is it?" Wilbur points out eventually. "At this rate you'll be *way* too old to model by the time we get down to the shoot, Angelmoo. You'll probably be in your early twenties and what good is that to anyone?"

"I could put my trainers back on?" I suggest, getting them out of my bag.

Wilbur visibly flinches. "A next season, perfectly cut, limited edition Baylee coat worn with... are they supermarket own-brand trainers?" He swallows. "I think I just sicked up in my mouth. Fashion sacrilege. I can't allow it. Not while there's a breath left in this beautiful body of mine." He frowns and looks around the room. "Luckily I'm brilliant as well as stunning," he adds happily. "And I have an idea."

Ten minutes later, I enter Red Square with my entourage behind me. It's not *exactly* the entrance I was hoping for. In fact, I believe I've got my head in my hands for all of it.

Nick takes one look at the wheelchair, accurately

guesses why I'm in it and gives a very uncool shout of laughter so loud that pigeons fly off the top of a nearby statue. Yuka isn't quite as impressed.

"Would somebody like to tell me," she hisses as she stalks towards where I'm sitting, glaring at the seven people standing behind me, *"who broke my model?"*

43

Elegant. Dignified. Graceful.

Three words that don't describe me in the slightest. Five people have to pick me out of the wheelchair and carry me to where Nick is waiting in the snow, in front of St Basil's Cathedral, and when they plop me down, it takes another few minutes to get me balanced enough to remain vertical on my own. Which I can just about manage. As long as I focus really hard, don't move a muscle and scrunch my toes up into claws inside the shoes for leverage. And keep my hands out at the sides like a tightrope walker. None of which is aided by Dad's continuous laughing.

Or – for that matter – Nick's.

I'm briefly introduced to the photographer, Paul, who is a thin blond man without – as far as I can see – one single flamboyant tendency. He looks totally focused on the job, which is actually even more worrying. At least with Wilbur, it's possible to forget

209

that there's a great deal riding on me.

It's not a little metamorphosis experiment any more. It's a job. It's very expensive. It's very important. And it matters to a lot of people.

"Look at me doing wheelies in the snow!" Wilbur screams in the background, spinning around in the wheelchair.

The photographer takes one look at him, grinds his teeth and looks back at Nick and me. "I just need to set up lighting," he says in a tense voice, looking up at the sky. It's starting to snow harder and the sky is a little darker than it was before. "Can somebody get my light reflector?"

A young boy races off and then runs back with a big gold circle.

"Just make yourself comfortable for a few minutes," he says, fiddling with a little black box as the boy starts flicking the gold circle around. "I'll take a few test shots when everything's perfect." He fiddles with the box again and then looks up. "Somebody might as well get Gary."

Gary? *Gary?* Who the hell is *Gary*?

I look at Nick, who I've managed to avoid making eye contact with since I came back from the hotel. I feel extremely self-conscious now that my hair's all gone.

Like the Wizard of Oz after the curtain's come down. Nick has his hands in the pockets of a large army-style coat and his hair gelled into a Mohican. He scrunches up his nose at me and my internal organs turn inside out again.

Shouldn't I be immune to him by now? Or is he like the human version of the common cold?

"You want to watch out," he says in his slow drawl. "Gary's vicious."

I look around in alarm. "Is Gary another model?" I whisper in terror. "A stylist? A hairdresser? Yuka's assistant?"

"Nope," Nick says and the corner of his mouth is twitching. "Worse. He's a monster. Raises hell wherever he goes." And then he looks past me and nods. "Here he comes. Watch yourself." And out of the crowd comes a woman holding the teeny-tiny white kitten.

OK, first impressions are deceiving. As soon as the lady hands him over to me, Gary nips my finger and starts clawing his way up my shoulder, hissing like an angry kettle. It's just not natural for something so cute and fluffy to be so nasty.

I look at Nick in distress. "Why is he spitting at me?"

"Maybe he thinks he's a llama."

I grab the kitten, who has changed his mind and is now scrabbling back down and trying to use my arm as a springboard. I don't think that's a good idea. He's small and white: if he lands in the snow, there's a really good chance we'll never find him again.

"OK, guys," Paul finally says. "We're ready to do some test shots." He pauses and looks at me. "Harriet. What are you doing to that animal?"

I look down to where I'm sort of hanging on to Gary by his back legs while he scrabbles away with his front ones. "Bonding?" I offer weakly.

"Could you bond in a way that looks a bit less like animal cruelty?" Paul clears his throat. "Right, I'm going to take a dozen or so frames. It's not *too* important what you do now, but this might be a good time to practise."

I nod nervously, grimly hold on to the cat and try to pretend that there isn't a large group of people in a semicircle, all watching every single thing we do.

Right, this is it. I'd expected a little more training – perhaps a little step-by-step instruction sheet on modelling – but... this is fine. I'll just go with it. Let the inner model out. Wilbur and Yuka obviously saw something deep within me, which has just been waiting to burst forth and impress everyone. Like a...

dragon. Or a really big dog.

I stare at the camera with my most modelly face. There's a pause and then Paul looks up. "What are you doing, Harriet? What's that face?"

I gulp. "It's my modelling face."

"Your…" Paul says in confusion and then he rolls his eyes. "You *have* a modelling face, Harriet. You don't need to strain it as if you've got a bad case of constipation. *Relax.*" There's another silence. "*Now* what are you doing?"

"Smiling?"

Paul sighs. "Have you ever seen a fashion magazine in your life? Take a look at Nick, Harriet. What is he doing?"

I look at Nick. "He's, erm… Just standing there."

"Precisely. He's being natural, in the best-looking way possible. Just pretend the camera's not here, sweetheart, and focus on being as beautiful as you can be."

The cat's clearly not convinced that I'm capable of this either; he makes a mewling sound and scratches in terror at my other shoulder. Which makes me wobble dangerously on the heels, so I have to reach out and grab Nick's shoulder.

"Sorry," I mumble in embarrassment and stare

hard at the snow.

Why didn't anyone explain that there was actually some kind of *skill* involved in being a model? Why didn't somebody tell me I'd have to actually *do* something? Why didn't they know I'd be rubbish?

I can feel my eyes starting to well up, and somewhere in the background I hear the make-up artist starting to panic loudly about my mascara. I look at Nick in open desperation and he gives me a crooked smile.

"Right," he says under his breath. "Give me the cat," and he takes it off me. Gary immediately makes a small meowing sound, curls up happily in Nick's arm and goes to sleep. Even *Gary* is in love with him.

"Now blow a raspberry."

I look at him for a few seconds in silence. "You want me to blow a raspberry?"

"Yup. Loud as you can. Make it a nice wet one."

I can feel my cheeks getting pink under the foundation. "I'm not blowing a raspberry," I tell him in a dignified voice. "I'm nearly an adult."

"Blow a raspberry."

"No."

"Blow it."

"No."

"Blow."

"*Fine*," I snap in exasperation and I blow a half-hearted raspberry.

Nick frowns at me. "That wasn't even a strawberry."

"Oh, for the love of…" I sigh and then I blow a much louder raspberry. I'm not even going to look at Yuka. I don't think this is why she employed me. "Happy now?"

"Much better. Now wiggle your shoulders. And your neck."

I wiggle my shoulders and my neck.

"Knock your knees together."

I knock my knees.

"And do the funky chicken."

I giggle and obediently do the funky chicken.

"Can you handle cold feet? Because if you can, I reckon you should take those stupid shoes off and hold them."

I glance at Paul, who is concentrating on adjusting one of the lamps to his right. And then I glance to the left where Yuka Ito is sitting in a black chair, glaring at us both with the face Annabel pulls when she eats oysters.

"OK," I say, shrugging, and take my shoes off. I'm so nervous I can't feel my feet anyway. Plus, I'm not sure I can get much worse at this. The only way is up.

Apparently Nick's thinking the same thing. Literally. "Now," he says, grinning. "I'm going to hold your hand. And when I say jump, *jump*, as high as you can. Look straight at the camera, keep your face calm and *jump*. OK?"

I nod, with my head now numb.

"Relax?"

I nod.

"Funky chicken?"

I nod and waggle my arms a bit.

"*OK, jump*," Nick whispers.

And I jump.

44

I'm holding Nick's hand.

I'm actually holding Nick's hand. And nobody made him do it. He did it for free.

Or, you know. For a modelling fee. *But he didn't have to.*

It was his idea.

Not that this is the only thing going through my head for the rest of the shoot, obviously. I'm a professional. I think about lots of… modelling related things. Like clothes, and make-up, and hair, and sticky eyebrows made out of mice.

And… and… no.

That's all I think about. The fact that Nick is holding my hand and I've never had my hand held by a boy before in my entire life unless you count when I was eight and forced into being Prince Charming's mother in the school play, and I don't.

And this time it's Lion Boy.

This time it's Nick.

*

It turns out that when Nick said *jump*, his idea was that he *also* jumped, and so we both leapt into the air at the same time as high as we could. Nick held on to the kitten, I held on to the red shoes and we both jumped together.

And *everyone* loved it. Paul loved it. Wilbur loved it. Dad loved it. The crowd loved it. Even Yuka stopped threatening to sack everyone in a ten-mile radius. Gary wasn't quite as keen, but you can't please everyone.

When we've finished jumping in the air from a standing position, we throw caution to the wind and try running along from left to right, jumping. And then from right to left, jumping. Eventually I'm so relaxed and having so much fun they actually manage to get me to *not* jump for a few shots, just for variety. They even get close to my face and I don't flinch or start twitching because I'm too busy thinking about… erm. Make-up. And clothes. And hair. And mice. And so on and so forth.

Before I know it, we're done.

I'm a *model.*

"My little Pea-pod!" Wilbur squeals as soon as Paul shuts down the camera. Nick immediately lets go of my hand, and by the time I turn around he's gone again. *Poof.* Like the proverbial genie. "Look at you, just bouncing around like a little kangaroo in the snow!"

Dad pushes past him. "All right, kiddo?" he says, and it looks like his face is going to snap in half, he's smiling so hard. "Chip off the old block, that was. I used to do high jump for the under-sixteens. Won trophies and everything."

"Dad, you won a bronze medallion on Sports Day once when you were thirteen. It's still on top of the fireplace."

"Trophy, medallion, who's counting? Anyway, I'm very proud." He gives me a hug. "I thought for a horrible minute there we were going to have to pay for our own flight home. Now did someone say free vodka?" And he scampers off happily in the direction of the hotel.

I look at my empty hand again. I can't believe Nick's gone already. I've never seen anyone capable of becoming invisible quite so quickly or unexpectedly. And I can't help wishing he wouldn't.

"London, Poppet," Wilbur says kindly, patting my shoulder.

"Hmm?" I'm still gazing in the direction I think Nick went.

"He's gone back to London. He has another shoot for a different designer in the morning."

I swallow in embarrassment and quickly look away. "Who? I don't know what you're talking about."

"Oh, please, Petal-pants. You're all lit up like Lenin, and you don't have the excuse of a lightbulb in the back of your head."

I clear my throat crossly. "Nick and I are just colleagues," I say with as much indifference as I can muster and an improvised shrug. "We work together."

"Not any more you don't," Wilbur says matter-of-factly, patting me on the head. "His bit's over. Yuka's not as bothered about the male fashion end of the spectrum. Not bad money for a four-hour gig, hey?"

A swoop of disappointment hits my stomach and I bite my bottom lip in case it reaches my face. I should have realised. I'll probably never see Nick again, unless it's on the pages of a magazine in a doctor's surgery and half his face will probably be missing from where somebody's ripped out a coupon from the other side.

I can feel my cheeks tingling. And he didn't even say goodbye.

"So," I say as calmly as I can, "is my bit over too then?"

I've done a shoot, I've got a new haircut, I'm wearing make-up and I've held a boy's hand, but…

I still feel like me. Something's not working the way it's supposed to.

Wilbur starts pealing with laughter. "*Is my bit over? Is my bit…* Oh, my little Bookworm," he sighs eventually, bending over and putting his hand in the crease of his waist. "You *do* crack me right down the middle."

Honestly, I wish people would just answer questions properly when I ask them.

"It's not over then?" I reiterate.

"Nope." Wilbur wipes the tears of laughter out of his eyes. "Now is the *really* fun bit. We're going to another part of Moscow."

For some reason, I'm not feeling as excited as I should be. Nick's gone and I'm on my own this time.

"For dinner?"

Wilbur starts squealing again. "*Dinner?* You're a model, Sugar-plum: you no longer *do* dinner. Or lunch. Or breakfast, actually, unless you plan on regurgitating like a little snake. No, we have a Baylee fashion show to attend."

"A fashion show? And I'm going too?"

"Well, I hope so, my little Chicken-wing," Wilbur says, straightening out my fringe affectionately. "Because you're starring in it."

45

OK, how the hell am I supposed to concentrate on turning into a butterfly when I don't have a clue what's going on from one minute to the next?

Although – to be fair – I'm not sure what I'd have done if they'd told me. I am not a big fan of fashion shows. That's not a gloomy, defeatist attitude either. It's hard-won knowledge that comes from plenty of experience. I spent a large portion of my ninth summer walking up and down a 'catwalk' (the patio at the bottom of Nat's garden), holding on to a skipping rope pulled in a straight line down the middle.

It was part of a deal Nat and I made: I practised 'The Walk' with her, she rehearsed lines from *The Song of Hiawatha* with me and we both pretended to enjoy it. But no matter how hard I tried, or how carefully Nat shaped our 'couture' plastic bin-bag dresses or arranged daisies on our heads as accessories, something always went wrong. A stumble. A rip.

A trip over a piece of pavement that resulted in a

trip to A&E and seven stitches.

Until Nat decided it was probably less dangerous if I handled half-time refreshments and 'directed' the show from the safety of a deckchair on the lawn. And she got on with the modelling.

Nat.

Ugh. The metaphorical box in my head feels like it's going to open and the contents are about to burst all over the floor, so I mentally stick an extra nail in each corner.

"Fashion shows are fantabulous," Wilbur reassures me as he forces me into yet another taxi. "Obviously we're going to need to work on your walking skills, Chuckle-bean, because I don't think the wheelchair is going to fit on the catwalk, but we've got at least twenty minutes to train you up."

I feel a bit like vomiting.

I get the Bubble Chart of Lies out of my bag and switch my phone on. "Dad," I say, turning to him, "You need to send something to Annabel to make her believe you're in a really boring business meeting that's running over."

"Like *what*?" Dad asks in confusion.

"I don't know," I snap back irritably. "I can't do *everything*. Just send whatever you'd normally send."

Dad frowns. "First of all, if I'm in a meeting, I don't normally text people under the desk. It's not school. Second of all, Annabel and I have been married for eight years: we don't send texts updating each other on our emotions about everything. And third of all, I'm a man. I *never* send texts updating people on my emotions about everything. *Anything* in fact."

"Oh, for God's sake," I grouch because my head feels like it's about to explode. "Send a text message, Dad. Just *follow the Bubble Chart*, OK? I don't have the energy for your maverickness today."

Dad looks at me, shrugs and gets his phone out. "All right. Don't blame me if she gets suspicious. This is your adventure: I'm just the sidekick."

"You're not the sidekick, Dad."

"I am. I'm like Robin. Or maybe Dr Watson."

I scowl at him. "Try Chewbacca," I mutter under my breath. My phone has been going crazy on my lap. I'm trying to pretend I haven't heard it because I'm not sure I'm ready to deal with the rocket of guilt and shame I'm about to have launched at me.

"Is this a teenage thing?" Wilbur eventually asks in excitement when it beeps yet again. "It's been a couple of years since I was a teenager, so maybe I'm out of the loop. Do you have a special ringtone you can't hear or something?"

Dad coughs. "A couple?" he says, gazing out of the window. "A couple of years?"

Wilbur sticks his nose in the air. "I just have a very carved face," he says haughtily. "Like Wolverine. It's always been carved."

Dad and I both look at him for a few seconds. If Wilbur's under forty, I'll eat that gold light reflector.

"No," I sigh eventually, picking up my phone. "I can hear it. Unfortunately." And then – extremely reluctantly – I click on the text messages.

H, how are you? Wish you were here. Shall I bring round soup after school? I can pick up some of that green Thai chicken stuff you like Nat x

H, no green stuff. Is red OK? Nat x

Dear Harriet, Toby Pilgrim here. Things are erupting at school. To wit: Alexa's torturing Nat. Shall I come to Amsterdam and bring you home to avenge her like a flaming angel? Yours truly, Toby Pilgrim

Harriet, don't forget to floss Annabel

H, is red too spicy? There's a picture of three chillis. Is that bad? Nat

Nausea rises up my trachea and I stare at my phone, totally frozen.

I'm the devil. I'm actually the devil. Any minute now the horn that matches Bob is going to sprout and my hair is going to catch fire. I've been prancing around in the snow like a shoeless idiot, while Nat runs around fighting for me and buying me soup, and Annabel worries about my dental hygiene. And all I can think about is holding a boy's hand.

I touch the painful spot on my forehead and tap my feet on the floor of the car. They're starting to sound a little bit like – oh, I don't know – *cloven hooves.*

I quickly type out a reply.

Nat, no soup thanks – am going straight to sleep. Am also contagious so don't come round. See you soon. H x

I stare at it for a few seconds then press send.

That's another lie. Two in fact. The balls inside the box in my head are going crazy, so I mentally sit on the lid so they don't all come bursting out at the same time.

When I glance to the side, Dad looks pretty uncomfortable too. "Hell's a pretty cosy place, right?" he says, closing his phone. "I mean, it's probably not as bad as they say, I reckon."

"Let's hope not," I sigh as we draw up outside an astonishing, white, beautiful, huge carved building with a red carpet spread out in front of it.

Because I have quite a strong feeling we're about to find out.

46

The Baylee fashion show is being held in a proper red-velvet-seated Russian theatre. A runway has been built down the middle of the room, in the bit where I'd imagine they normally sell ice cream, and there are chandeliers hanging low over the centre of it. Russian architecture isn't exactly known for minimalism: true to form, the entire room is gold and gilt and carved and embroidered and mirrored.

"Oh, my heavenly mango juice," Wilbur says when we walk in, putting his hand over his eyes and making a loud retching sound. "It's like the Sugar Plum Fairy exploded in here."

"If you don't like it, William," Yuka says, stalking past in her heels, "I can send you somewhere a lot less fancy." She walks up to the front of the stage.

Wilbur looks at me in shock. "Where did *she* come from?" he whispers, placing a hand over his heart. "Am I right in thinking that was a physical threat?" He looks resentfully at Yuka, who's now checking the

229

runway. "And it's *bur* not *iam*," he points out loudly.

"I can't begin to tell you how little I care," Yuka snaps and beckons me over to where she's standing. "Harriet Manners," she continues seamlessly. "Everyone's getting ready backstage. Please go and join them. Important people are going to start arriving imminently and I can't have the face of my new campaign standing here in a hamster and horse jumper."

I look down, momentarily stunned. "He's not a *hamster*. He's Winnie the Pooh. A *bear.*" And then I turn round and point to my back. "Eeyore's a *donkey.*"

Yuka studies me for a few seconds. "I don't like donkeys," she decides eventually. "Or bears. Please go away and get into the outfit I've chosen for you, which features neither. Your name is on the tag."

I nod meekly. I'm not sure what to say to a woman who doesn't recognise Winnie the Pooh.

"And Harriet?"

I turn round on the stage, where I'm trying to find my way behind the curtains. My foot is caught in one of them. "Yes?" I say, trying to extricate it as subtly as possible.

Yuka's eyes slide down until she's staring at it. "If somebody offers to shave your legs," she snaps, "let them."

*

Well, I've found all of the Russian people.

All of the really good-looking female ones anyway. They're tucked into a little room behind the stage, crammed together like beautiful, thin, blonde sardines. I've never been so uncomfortable. There is skin *everywhere*. It's not flashes of puppy fat and training bras either. Really tall, toned girls are wandering around, laughing and almost naked, as if it's the most natural state in the world.

And I don't care what documentaries on television say: it's *not*.

I've climbed down the backstage stairs, beyond a screen, and now I'm standing by the doorway. Nobody has noticed I'm here; they're just walking past me as if I'm on work experience. At school, Alexa is the Cool girl, Nat is the Beautiful girl and a girl called Jessica is the girl who insists upon stripping down to her underwear at any possible opportunity. I'm the hairy-legged geek in the corner with the white ankle socks. I think the scale has just shifted and I should be in a hole under the floor somewhere.

I start backing out of the door I just came through.

"My daughter *needs me*," a voice yells from behind me. When I look round, Dad's standing on his tiptoes by the door, trying to see over the screen. "She *needs me*, I tell you."

"I don't need you," I call back.

"You see?" Dad says again, doing little jumps so that the top of his head bobs up and down. "I demand you let me into the room full of tall Russian models *this minute*."

Oh, for the love of sugar cookies.

"Dad," I hiss through the screen, "if you embarrass me any more, I'm sending you home. I mean it."

There's a pause and then Dad sighs dramatically. "*Fine*," he snaps in a sulky voice. "I'll just go and eat pickled cabbage at the back of the hall, shall I?"

"Yes, please."

"Being a sidekick *sucks*," he mutters and strops back into the theatre.

I look at the room again, which is getting more overwhelming by the minute. There's commotion and chaos everywhere: mountains of clothes, dozens of people, the shine of bright lights, the smell of hairspray, the roar of hairdryers and girls. People taking off clothes and putting them back on again. Confidence oozing out of every pore in the room. I am totally and utterly out of my depth.

I reckon if I just tucked myself into a ball in one

232

of the prop cupboards, nobody would notice I was missing. I mean, how important can I be?

"There she is!" somebody shouts, running forward and dragging me into the room by my arm. "The most important model of all!"

Oh.

I guess that's my answer.

47

This is a new start, I keep reminding myself as I'm pulled through the crowd of girls. What's the saying? *You've got to fake it to make it.* It's time I start pretending to belong and then maybe I will.

This isn't school after all. I can be someone else here. Someone cool. Someone different. I don't have to be a geek any more. I look down at my satchel. The red words are still vaguely visible and I hastily put my hand over it. I have *got* to get a new bag.

"Hello," I say confidently to the models who have all stopped what they're doing and are now watching me with their eyes narrowed. "I'm Harriet Manners. It's nice to meet you."

It's totally working. They've all stopped talking, and I can tell from the expressions on their faces that any minute now they're going to stand up, envelop me in a warm group hug and start arguing over who will get to be my Russian penpal. I grin in relief and hold out my hand to an astonishingly beautiful brunette.

234

"Bite me," she says in a strong accent, and then she turns round and continues putting on black stockings.

"Black with no sugar. Don't forget the lemon," another giggles and she high-fives her friend, who starts muttering darkly in Russian.

"I lost the Baylee campaign to *her*? Seriously? Has Yuka gone totally insane?"

"She looks like a little boy," another one says in a perfectly audible whisper.

"Maybe she is. Let's see what happens when she takes off her skirt."

"I reckon she doesn't have *anything* going on down there. Like Action Man."

"Have you ever seen freckles *like* it?"

"Yeah. Definitely. On a, like, *egg*."

"Or, like, a *Dalmatian*."

I can literally feel my face collapsing. This is exactly like school. Except that they've all got a fewer clothes on, which somehow makes it even worse.

I've said nine words so far. How can it have gone so badly wrong already? *How do they know all the same insults?*

"Actually," I say in the most reprimanding voice I can find, "there are no animals that have no reproductive organs at all. Even hermaphrodites have both sets, for instance the great majority of pulmonate snails, opisthobranch snails and slugs. So that is a physical impossibility."

There's a surprised silence and then the room erupts into nasty giggles. It's probably not going to go down in history as one of my most incisive comebacks.

"And," I add, looking at the girl with the stockings, "I'd rather not bite you. I don't know where you've been."

The giggling stops.

That's better, Harriet. That's the sort of thing Nat would have said.

The girl blinks at me a few times in shocked silence. "*What* did she just say to me?" she eventually snaps to the girl next to her and her forehead starts to get all scrunched up in the middle. "I'm the face of *Gucci*. I'm *Shola*. People don't talk to me like that. I *won't be talked to like that.*"

"Don't get worked up, honey," a blonde with huge blue eyes whispers back. "It'll just make you ugly and we're about to go on. *Vogue*'s out there. Stay pretty for *Vogue*."

Shola swallows and concentrates. "Thanks, Rose. I am *so* not getting wrinkles for *her.*" She looks back at me and narrows her eyes. "You're *how* old?"

"Fifteen and three-twelfths."

"My God, you still measure your age in fractions. I'm not getting worked up over a *child*. I'm just *not*. I am a *woman*. I am the face of *Gucci Woman*. It's right there in the title."

"It is," Rose agrees, patting her on the shoulder. "It's right there on the advert under your face, Shola. *Woman*."

"Harriet?" a friendly lady in red says, tapping me on the shoulder just in the nick of time. Models are clearly bonkers. "This is your outfit." And she unzips a clothes bag.

A general hiss goes round the room as I stare at the contents. It's a long, silky gold dress with thousands of tiny little gold feathers layered around the bottom. It has thin straps made of sort of gold fish scales and it shimmers when you touch it, like a magic cloak. It's really, really beautiful: even I can see that. Although it *is* going to make me look a bit like the toffee finger in a box of Quality Street.

"That's mine? For me?"

"It is, darling. You're the Closer."

Another slightly louder hiss goes round the room. "I'm the what?"

"The Closer. You're the last girl on the catwalk. All

eyes are going to be on you, honey."

I quickly look into the mirror, and behind me I can feel every single eye in the room glaring at my back.

"You're the new face of the line," she continues. "Yuka wants you to be as prominent as possible."

I can see Shola's face getting paler under her make-up. She glances quickly at Rose and a look passes between them, but I've no idea what it means.

"OK," I say, trying to ignore the new clenching sensation in my stomach. "But…"And then I take a deep breath. "The… Ummm." I stop. How can I put this subtly? "The… er." And then I take in as much oxygen as I can. "What shoes am I wearing?" I finally blurt out.

The lady smiles at me kindly. "These," she says. And then she holds out a pair of little gold-scaled shoes with one-inch kitten heels. I almost collapse with relief.

"Yuka says she would prefer it if you could stay upright," she says with a wink. "Now, Miss Manners, let's get your hair and make-up sorted so we can have a little practice, shall we?"

48

People Who Hate Harriet Manners
Alexa Roberts
Hat Lady
Owners of stalls 24D 24E 24F 24G 24H
Nat?
Class 11A English literature
Models in general, but particularly Shola and Rose

I can do it.

I can actually do it. I can walk up and down a room with a pretty dress and heels on and not rip anything, ruin anything, break anything or fall over.

It seemed like an impossibility an hour ago. But… I've practised and practised backstage for about an hour until I'm pretty sure I can get through this evening without a disaster. I mean, it's *one walk*. A toddler could do it, with a bit of encouragement and maybe one of those push-along toys. How hard can it be?

"Thank you *so* much," I say to Betty, the stylist who

239

has been helping me. She's even managed to find time to quickly de-fluff both my legs without causing any damage.

Betty winks at me. "My pleasure, chicken. Quick revision: what are you walking in time to?"

"The music," I say eagerly. She gave me her iPod to practise with. I have no idea what the music is, but it's actually quite nice. At least I know when to put each foot forward.

"And what do you do when you get to the bottom of the runway?"

I'm back in my comfort zone: studying and revision. "I pause with one hand on my hip, and then I face towards the left, and then the right, and then I pause again, and then I turn round slowly and walk back."

"Facial expression?"

"Totally blank and slightly bored."

"Excellent. And what side are you walking on?"

"Centre, and when you see a girl coming, keep to the left."

"I think you're set." She smiles at me and points at the door. I was taken out of the area where everyone was getting ready so that I could concentrate, and also so that I could fall over without anyone laughing at me. "Knock 'em dead," Betty adds.

Which – given the probability of that happening – is not the *best* thing she could have said to me.

And she gently nudges me back into the world of fashion.

It is now manic.

The earlier commotion was obviously just the buzz before the mania: the whole room has exploded into a mess of lights and noise and panic. I can hear the music pumping from the stage and I don't think the girls have time to be nasty any more: they're whizzing in and out of clothes and being shouted at by people wearing headsets as if they're working in call centres.

"Next!" an angry man shouts. "Come on! We don't have time for a lipgloss touch-up! Get on the stage!"

There's a small queue of models forming this side of the curtains and I'm totally mesmerised. They're all twice my height, and willowy, and curvy in the right places, with the most amazing faces. Every single one of them looks like a different example of beauty, from a different imagination. And now they look like a collection of amazing birds, or butterflies, covered in greens and blues and reds and sparkles and feathers. It's less fashion, I think, and more… plumage.

It's like that butterfly farm I go to every summer with

Annabel: the room is covered in colours. I feel a sudden pang of envy. I'm the little brown moth, going round and round the light bulb. Then I look at the mirror next to the stage. My eyes have been painted dark black, and my hair's been fluffed up and pinned at the back. My cheeks are pink and flushed and the light is reflecting off the top of my head, and off my shoes, and off the straps over my back. The gold dress sort of shoots straight down because there's nothing to stop it – but... it still looks pretty. Sparkly.

I'm not a moth, I realise with a lurch. I'm not one of them exactly, but maybe I'm still a butterfly. One of those little white ones that doesn't live very long, but is happy just to get the chance to be there for a little while.

"Harriet?" the man with the headset on shouts. "Where's Harriet?"

"I'm here," I say as clearly as I can and realise my hands are damp. Dad's somewhere out in the audience: Yuka reluctantly gave him a seat near the back. I have to make him proud. I *have* to. I have to make Annabel proud too, even though she isn't here and doesn't know about it.

"Get ready," the man says. "You're nearly up."

I stand against the curtains and notice that there

are three girls in front of me. Rose, Shola and a girl I haven't spoken to – or been shouted at – before with a set of earphones in. A very, very beautiful girl with pale brown hair in curls.

"I'm Harriet Manners," I say automatically, holding out my hand and trying to stop it shaking.

She takes her headphones out. "Hmm?" she says. "Sorry. I listen to music to help calm my nerves before a show."

"I'm Harriet Manners," I say again. "Nice to meet you."

"I know who you are," she says, nodding and giving me a wry smile. "I'm Fleur. I'm not the face of anything." And she gives me an almost imperceptible wink.

"This is the Closer," Shola says, nodding at me. Fleur shrugs and puts her headphones back in again, and Shola smiles sweetly. "So they told you about the change of plans, right?"

"What change of plans?"

"*They didn't tell you?* Oh, that's just so *like* them. They told us while you were out the back, doing your little walking practice." She looks at Rose. "*So cute,*" she adds, smirking.

"What's changed?" I can feel myself starting to

tense up again. I've learnt everything by heart; I'm not sure I can just alter details at this late stage. This *never* happens in exams at school. It's why we have revision guides.

"Well, this is *Moscow*," she explains as if I'm not aware of this already. "And we drive on the *right* here. So although Yuka's not Russian, she's decided last minute that models have to go *right* on the runway. Not left as they normally would. To make things more... *realistic.*"

"Huh?" I frown.

"I can't believe they didn't tell you. That was a close call." Shola makes a face of massive relief. "Could have screwed *everything* up."

I take a deep, confused breath. Honestly, I don't know whether to believe her or not. Is she telling me that so I make a mistake, or is she genuinely telling me so that I *don't* make a mistake?

Shola looks at me with massive, heavily made-up almond eyes. "We're on the same side," she says innocently. "Us models. We have to stick together. The better you look, the better I look, right?"

I look at her for a few quiet seconds, my mind twirling like a ballerina in a music box. "OK," I finally whisper. "Thank you." Rose has gone on stage now and it's nearly my time. My legs are starting to wobble and I can feel my feet shaking.

"My pleasure." And then Shola frowns. "What are you doing?"

"Blowing a raspberry," I explain, doing a funky chicken so subtle I'm not sure she can see it. "Sorry. I'm just trying to relax."

"Oh. Whatever," Shola says, turning her back on me and rolling her eyes when she thinks I can't see, and then she walks up the stage steps.

This is it.

I'm so terrified that when I try to lick my lips, my tongue doesn't come out. Somewhere on the other side of the curtains is a huge audience, and in that audience is Dad, waiting for me to be amazing. It's time to prove to him that I can be.

And maybe prove it to myself while I'm at it.

"You're up," the man with the headset says. "Good luck, Harriet."

And I climb up the stairs into the bright lights.

49

For a few seconds, I can't move.

The theatre looks nothing like it did when I walked in. The lights are so bright I can hardly see anything, but there's just enough visibility to ascertain that every single chair in the building is filled. Even the carved golden boxes near the ceiling have people in them, and if there were still tsars in Russia, I'd imagine that's where they'd be sitting.

I glance in terror to the right, where I can vaguely see Yuka sitting in the centre of the front row, her face like a mask. And, somewhere at the back, I think I can see Dad holding both thumbs up in the air.

I stand there, paralysed, for a few seconds. Then I take a deep breath and I start walking.

Apparently I've been walking since I was nine months old and hanging on to the bottom of Dad's jumper, but it has never felt like this before. It's never felt so difficult, or so surreal. It feels less like *I'm* moving forward and

more like it's the floor moving backward and I'm just trying to keep up. Like… ice skating. Or walking down the aisle of a moving coach.

And as we know, I'm not so good at that.

I keep my face totally blank and try to focus on the music. All I have to think about is just one foot in front of the other. Looking as bored as I possibly can.

Somewhere near the bottom of the stage, I see Fleur, pausing and looking to the right and the left, just as I've been told to. Now that she's at a distance I can appreciate what she's wearing: emerald green, covered in little bits of floaty green material like a mermaid. And the biggest silver heels I've ever seen in my life. Bigger even than the red ones I had to wear in Red Square. She hasn't even been given a wheelchair.

Now *that's* what I call a model.

Fleur gives a little dignified toss of her head and starts walking back up the centre of the stage towards me, at which point something in my chest abruptly lurches in a panic.

If I believe Shola, I go right. If I don't believe Shola, I go left. So right or left?

Left or right?

I can trust Shola. I *have* to believe that human beings are essentially good. That girls don't destroy each other just because they can. I start veering towards the right. Then Alexa's face pops into my head. Alexa would send me in the wrong direction. She would want a collision. What if Shola is another Alexa?

So I start moving towards the left. But if I start to believe that everyone is like Alexa, doesn't it mean she's won? If I start to lose faith in humanity, isn't that worse than a million hands in the air? I can't let that happen.

I start veering towards the right again.

We're getting closer and closer and I can see a look of sheer panic starting to appear on Fleur's face.

I don't know what I'm doing.

Oh, God. Left or right? Right or left?

I'm changing my mind by the millisecond, and as I walk, I'm making almost unnoticeable movements towards each direction. They're so small, I don't think the audience can tell. But Fleur can, and the look of panic on her face is getting more and more pronounced. It's like we're in a game of chess, trying to second-guess the other's movements.

We're almost in the middle now and I still don't know which way to go. I can feel myself starting to wobble. I'm going to lose my balance and topple, even on these low heels. And then it hits me: that's what Shola wants. She doesn't want a *collision*. She wants me to fall over.

Which means I *have* to keep going. At which point everything starts happening in slow motion. Fleur starts to wobble too. She sways from side to side like a tree, except that her heels are much, much bigger than mine. And they can't take it.

Time almost stops.

One of her ankles buckles completely.

And – with the smallest of gasps – Fleur plummets like a stone on to the runway.

50

I'm paralysed with horror. The whole audience has taken one loud, audible breath.

I have just ruined an entire fashion show.

And it's *all my fault*.

I stare numbly at Fleur, who is now desperately trying to stand up. Her heels keep slipping, and I can see her eyes filling with tears and her cheeks starting to flame, even under the thick make-up. And with a sick lurch of my stomach, I recognise the humiliation and shame, the disbelief and horror. It's like looking in a mirror. I've just done to Fleur what I promised I would never, ever do to anyone.

I've turned her into me.

The entire audience is staring, but the only thing I know now is I have to do something to help her. *Anything*. Just so Fleur knows she isn't on her own. So I take a deep breath and sit down on the stage next to her.

There's a stunned silence. And then, from somewhere

at the back, comes the sound of one person clapping as hard as they possibly can.

"Woooooooooo!" Dad shouts at the top of his voice. "That's my girl! Woooooo!"

The whole audience turns to look at him and Fleur grabs my hand. Slowly, we stand up.

And together we walk off the runway, back behind the curtains.

51

As soon as I'm backstage, I find the nearest table I can and crawl straight under it.

I don't know much about fashion shows, but I don't think that's how they're supposed to go. And I have a suspicion I'm about to get into really, *really* big trouble.

"Harriet?" a voice says after about forty minutes, and a pair of black trainers appears under the tablecloth.

"Monkey-moo?" another voice says and a pair of shiny orange shoes with blue toes appears next to them. There's a bit of whispering and then I hear Wilbur say: "Is it, like, some kind of fetish? Is it just tables, or all types of furniture?"

"She's frightened," Dad explains. "She's done it ever since she was a baby." And before I know it he's crawling under the table next to me. "Harriet, sweetheart," he says gently. "What you did was very noble. Nobody's going to shout at you."

Wilbur sticks his head under the tablecloth. "That's not *necessarily* true," he amends. "Yuka's on her way

252

backstage now and I've never seen her lips so thin. The bottom part of her face looks like an envelope."

"I'm sorry," I say, with my knees pulled right up to my chest. "I didn't know what else to do."

"*Sorry?*" Wilbur gasps and he puts his hand over his chest. "Baby-baby Panda, Baylee couldn't have *bought* that much publicity if they'd hung Yuka Ito upside down from the chandelier with her trousers down around her ankles."

"Which they're not going to do," a cold voice says from somewhere beyond the tablecloth. Another pair of shoes appears: black and shiny and spiky. "I'm a fashion goddess. Goddesses don't wear trousers."

"Yuka, darling!" Wilbur says, retracting his head. "I didn't see you there! Mainly because I don't have eyes in my bottom."

"Fascinating, William," Yuka snaps. "Harriet? I am going to speak to you immediately. I would therefore prefer it if this conversation was not held with a piece of laminate wood."

I look at Dad, take the biggest breath I can find and crawl out from under the table. "I'm sorry, Yuka."

"I don't recall asking you to do anything other than wear a dress and walk in a straight line. It really shouldn't have been that difficult."

"I know," I mumble. "Am I fired?"

Yuka looks at Wilbur. "William? How did the front row react?"

"It's *bur* not *iam*," Wilbur points out, sighing. "The editor of *Elle* said Harriet was fresh. *Harper's* said she was delicious. *Vogue* thought she had unexpected warmth."

"My daughter's not a loaf of bread," Dad points out in surprise.

Yuka raises an eyebrow at him and then looks at me. "In that case, Harriet, you're not fired and neither is Fleur. But in future, if I want you to sit down, I shall ask you to sit down. I shall give you a step-by-step plan, an X on the requisite spot and a detailed description of how I want you to do it."

"OK," I say, feeling my spirits starting to lift. The more I get to know Yuka, the more I like her. She reminds me of Annabel.

Yuka looks at her watch. "There is an after-party being held in the penthouse suite of our hotel. The other models have gone there, and every important editor and celebrity in Europe is currently drinking my profits."

My stomach twists uneasily and Dad's face starts to beam.

"Yuka," I start anxiously, "I'm not sure that—"

"Obviously," Yuka continues as if I haven't opened my mouth, "you will be going straight to bed and you will go nowhere near it. If I so much as catch you out of your room for the rest of the evening, there will be a world of pain."

I sort of want to hug her. I'm so tired. This has probably been the longest day of my entire life.

"Oh, *what*?" Dad moans under his breath. "This is so unfair."

"The same applies to you," Yuka says to him sternly, narrowing her eyes. "A world of pain. Understood?"

"Understood," Dad says in a shamed voice, staring at the floor. Which makes me feel even more at home.

Because that's exactly what Annabel would have said as well.

52

Somehow, I manage to get a full ten hours of sleep. Despite Dad doing everything he possibly can to sabotage this. I've been given the queen-size bed and he has the sofa on the other side of the room "as befits a sidekick".

"You know," he says as I'm brushing my teeth, "if I were to wake up in the middle of the night, say, and find you putting your make-up back on, I would assume it was a mirage and go back to sleep."

I nod sleepily.

Ten minutes later, as I'm crawling under the duvet in my penguin pyjamas and yawning, Dad coughs. "And if I were to wake up in the middle of the night and see that your bed was empty, I would presume I was dreaming and put it down to an overactive imagination."

"OK, Dad." I close my eyes and snuggle into the pillows.

"And if you were to come back in, smelling of – say

– *celebrity party*, I would say nothing of it the next day. To *anyone*."

"OK," I murmur, starting to drift off. Suddenly the bedroom lights snap on.

"Are you seriously telling me you're not going to this celebrity party?" Dad says in loud disbelief. "You're not going to sneak out for even a little bit?"

"You can go if you want," I mumble with my eyes shut. "I'm going to be asleep."

"Oh, *great*, just guilt trip away, why don't you, Harriet? No, it's fine. I don't need to meet Liz Hurley. I'll just sit here on the sofa and eat pickled cabbage."

I yawn again. What is this obsession with pickled cabbage? "OK, Dad. You do that."

"I will," Dad says, turning off the light again. "Who needs a celebrity fashion party? I mean, who needs to meet Liz Hurley and drink Martinis and eat little olives and bits of cheese on sticks when you can just sit, wide awake, on a spare… sofa… and… eat… pickled… "And the word *cabbage* is replaced by the sound of Dad snoring so loudly it sounds like somebody is drilling through the wall next to my head.

I open my eyes and look at the ceiling. Somewhere, floors and floors above us, a party is going on. A party full of beautiful people and important people and famous people: laughing, drinking, kissing the air, sparkling, having their photos taken. Wearing beautiful clothes and eating beautiful food – or pretending to. And I really couldn't care less.

I listen to Dad snoring his head off for a few minutes and then I close my eyes and join him.

We have the entire following morning to look around Moscow. Yuka has told us that we're "free to do whatever it is ordinary people do during daylight hours".

So we go to the Kremlin and look around the Cathedral of the Archangel where the Romanov tsars are buried, and the Ivan the Great Bell Tower which is covered in beautiful gold leaf and is thought to be the very centre point of Moscow. Then we go to the Peter the Great Monument and the Bolshoi, and a huge park where the lake is covered in ice and peeved-looking ducks. The amazing morning is only ruined by the fact that I keep having to lie to Nat by text and Annabel keeps ringing Dad up and crying.

Which is disconcerting because Annabel never cries. *Ever*. This is the woman who watches gazelles get mauled by tigers on television and gives them marks out of ten for tidiness.

"Sweetheart," Dad says into the handset as we pay

for some authentic Russian merchandise (I've got some hand-painted Russian dolls and a teddy bear that says **I RUSHED THROUGH RUSSIA**, and Dad has a T-shirt that says **RUSSIA HOUR**). "You're wrong. I *do* understand."

There's some squeaking on the other end of the phone. From a distance it sounds a bit like Dad is talking to a mouse.

"But darling, it's just milk. You can clean it up." There's more squeaking. "And we can buy you some more cornflakes." More squeaking. "And a new bowl." *Squeak, squeak.* "Yes, exactly the same shade of white, sweetheart. Now stop crying."

The Russian merchandise seller loudly asks Dad in broken English if he wants his **ONLY FOOLS RUSSIA IN** baseball cap gift-wrapped. There are a few more squeaks on the phone. "Hmm? Wrapped?" Dad says anxiously. "No, Annabel. That's just the… coffee lady. She wants to know if I want my coffee… flapped." *Squeak, squeak.* "It's street talk for… cooled down."

Eventually, Dad puts the phone down, wipes his hand over his face and looks at me.

"Phew. That was close," he says after a long, strained pause. "Luckily I'm an excellent liar. Annabel's gone all Sylvia Plath on us. What are we going to do?"

I swallow guiltily and tug at my shorn hair. "Not show her this?" I suggest.

Dad nods. "We need to wait out werewolf season." And then he thinks about it. "But Harriet... What if she's just... *crazy*?"

We both look at Dad's phone, which has started ringing again. And then Dad looks at the stall in front of us, covered in huge furry Russian hats. "Let's get you one of these," he sighs eventually. "I'll turn off the central heating and we'll tell Annabel you have a cold head."

"Do you think she'll buy that?"

"No." Dad looks at his phone again. "Take a good long look at my face, Harriet, because by tomorrow it'll be chewed right off." He opens his phone. "Darling?" *Squeak, squeak.* "Then throw the burnt bits away, sweetheart. And get some more bread." *Squeak.* "I know it's not the same." And then he looks at me, puts his finger up to his forehead and twirls it. *Bonkers,* he mouths to me.

And I swallow nervously and buy as many Russian hats as I can fit into my bag.

By the time we get back to England, though, everything

is starting to feel a lot more promising. My hair is covered with a nice big Russian hat – it's very cosy and goes well with my orange snowflake jumper – and the world is looking brighter already.

In fact, as we get off the train from London and start walking home – and I say goodbye to Dad and veer off to the shops to buy myself a Welcome Home Harriet chocolate bar – it feels like things are starting to go the right way finally.

I've been to Moscow, I've had an adventure and I appear to have got away with it. OK, I haven't really changed at all, except I'm now considerably less hairy and the owner of a Russian teddy bear. But it *feels* like life might be getting ready to improve. I mean, even caterpillars spend between four and nine days inside a cocoon before anything happens. And I *do* know some things I didn't know a few days ago. Like, for instance, if you put primer on your eyelids, it helps eyeshadow last longer. And pink lipstick has a tendency to get on *everything*.

Maybe it's just a matter of thinking positively. Believing that we can all change, if we try hard enough. Which is when it hits me. Because just as I'm reaching a point where the world is starting to make sense and happy thoughts are making me feel all sort of glowy on the inside, a yellow banana sweet comes flying through the air.

And whacks me straight on the head.

53

It takes a few moments to work out where the bananas are coming from. Within seconds, I've got sweets in my hat, in the collar of my jumper and a half-chewed one stuck to the sleeve of my coat.

Inexplicably, I look upwards.

"Hey, *geek*," a voice yells. It's only as I turn round that I realise the sky isn't raining sweets after all. Alexa is standing on the other side of the road just outside the local shops with her hand in a paper bag. "*GEEK*," she shouts again and then she laughs.

I freeze. Alexa has the single ugliest haircut I've ever seen on a girl in my life. Somehow I don't think this is going to be a friendly encounter. A confused buzzing has started in the back of my head. *Aren't things supposed to be different now?*

"Leave me alone," I say more firmly than I feel and start walking away as fast as I can.

She follows me. "As if that's going to happen." Another banana smacks me hard on the back of

the head. "I saw a documentary about monkeys last night and I think you look just like one, Harriet. And you move like one too. A little ginger orang-utan. All orange and hairy." She looks at the bananas in the bag she's holding. "You know," she adds, "it's lucky these taste like perfume or I'd probably just eat them."

"Umm," I say. Does she want me to thank her?

Alexa looks back at me and her lips pull back so I can see her teeth, except it's definitely not a smile. "What do you think, Harriet? Do you like my hair?" And she points to her head.

Don't engage in conversation. It's going to make it worse. "It's, umm," I say because yet again the connection between brain and mouth has snapped. "Very... snazzy."

"Yeah?" Alexa says. "Personally I'm not so keen." She runs her hands through it. "In fact, I'm pretty hacked off about it."

I burst out laughing at the pun and then bite my lip in horror.

"You think this is *funny*?" Alexa yells, suddenly losing her cool. Her face changes colour. "You think I'm *laughing*?"

"No." I put my suddenly sweaty hands around my satchel straps so that when I have to run, it doesn't slow me down.

"The hairdresser can't fit me in until tomorrow. I've had to go to school like this for *two entire days*. Two days, geek. Do you *know* how many boys have stopped fancying me now?"

"Two?"

"It was a rhetorical question!" Alexa looks furious. "Nat said she did it for you. So *I'm going to make you pay for it.*"

I take a few jittery steps backwards because she's going to hit me. Finally – after years of vaguely promising it – she's going to get down to bullying basics and smack me right in the face.

I quickly run through the options.

- Run.
- Wait until she hits me then run.
- Wait until she hits me, hit her back and then run.
- Hit first then run.

I'm so surprised that I nearly forget about the fifth choice:

- Stand still and stare at her like a total idiot.

"Are you going to punch me?" I ask, feeling numb and strangely relieved. I wish she had done this years ago. Maybe then she'll be finished with me.

Alexa frowns and then laughs. "Punch you? Why would I *punch* you? What on earth would I get out of that, apart from a load of trouble?" Then she pulls something out of her bag. It looks a lot like a newspaper. "You forget, Harriet, that I've known you for ten years. I don't *need* to punch you."

I'm so confused my whole head feels like it has been stuffed with cotton wool. And yet somehow I know that whatever it is Alexa's about to do, I'm going to wish she'd just used her fist.

I look at the paper. "W-w-what's that?"

"This?" Alexa looks at it. "It's an article, Harriet. About some fifteen-year-old schoolgirl apparently. Took the fashion world by storm yesterday in… where was it? Moscow."

My entire body goes cold and I feel like I'm going to throw up.

"That's in Russia," she adds. "In case you were wondering if I knew."

No. *No.* There's no way this could have happened. It would have to have gone to print… Last night.

Sugar cookies.

Alexa smirks and moves close enough for me to see. There – in full glory – is a large photo of me yesterday. Sitting on the catwalk, with Fleur next to me. The headline says English Schoolgirl Knocks Fashion World Off Its Feet.

"I…" I start mumbling, but my insides are ice and my ears are completely numb. "I… I…"

"I, I, I," Alexa echoes and then she looks at it again. "I know. It's beyond me why anybody would want a photo of *you.*"

At the back of my brain, I finally feel the horror of comprehension. "You haven't… *shown* anyone, have you?" I whisper and my voice sounds like I'm being strangled. "You haven't shown anyone else this article?"

Alexa looks shocked. "Like who? Like our headmistress? Who'll be interested to know why you haven't been at school for two days? I went all the way back to school to hand her a copy especially. Punishment for taking time off school without permission is normally suspension, right? Or possibly," and she looks at the paper again, "expulsion."

My head is starting to spin. I'm going to get suspended? I don't get suspended. And I definitely don't get *expelled.* I shake my head. There's something more important. "Have you shown it to... anyone else?"

Alexa crows. "What, Nat? The girl who has made every single class speech about wanting to model since we were seven? The girl who wouldn't talk to anyone after The Clothes Show and has been crying in the loos ever since? The girl who told everyone you were sick with a cold for the last two days *and seemed to believe it*?" Alexa raises her eyebrows. "Why?" she says in a faux-innocent voice. "Was I not supposed to?"

Oh, no. Oh, no, no, no.

Nonononononono.

"Did you tell Nat?" I shout at the top of my voice. *"Did you tell her?"*

"No," Alexa says. "I just dropped an extra copy of this page through her letterbox." And she turns round and touches her hair. "It's known as *retribution*, Harriet. Or *requital. Vengeance. Comeuppance.* Pick any noun you like."

And – just as quickly as it started fitting back together – my whole world falls apart again.

54

I run as fast as I can, but it's no good. As soon as I turn my phone on, I know my life is in meltdown. I have fifteen voicemails from Wilbur and nobody else is picking up their phone.

"Hello. This is Richard Manners. I'm probably with Liz Hurley right now, but leave a message and I'll ring you back when she's gone home. BEEP."

"Dad," I gasp into his answering machine, still running. "We've been caught. Don't let Annabel buy—" and I screech to an abrupt halt on the pavement. I have no idea what paper this article is in. "Don't let her buy *anything*. Just stop her leaving the house. She can't find out this way."

Then I recommence running. I need to get to Nat. Before the newspaper does.

Apparently I'm the only person in the entire world with any sense of urgency. By the time Nat's mum finally opens the front door, I'm screaming *Fire* through the

269

letterbox and scratching at the paintwork.

"Harriet?" she says and even in my panic I stop, confused for a few seconds.

Nat's mum is blue. Not a bit blue: totally blue. Like Annabel, she only really ever wears a dressing gown; unlike Annabel, she doesn't just have one and it doesn't have baked beans down the front. This one is a pale blue silk kimono. She also has a white towel wrapped round her hair and her face is painted in a pale blue face mask. When Nat's mum doesn't look like a giant Smurf, she looks a lot like Nat. Except twenty years older and modified by huge amounts of plastic surgery.

"What's going on? Are we all dying?"

"Yes. I mean no. Not immediately. Is Nat here, please?"

"No idea. Four Botox injections and I can't move a muscle. Look at this!" She makes a pained expression with her eyes.

"I need to see her."

"Is everything all right?"

"Not really." I start removing my shoes so I don't track mud into her white carpet. "Has anything been delivered to your house today?"

Nat's mum strains around the eyes again. "Not as far as I know."

I pause in the middle of a shoelace. The wave of relief is so powerful that for a second I think I'm going to fall over. Maybe Alexa got the wrong address. "Really?"

"I don't think so."

I take a deep breath and feel the panic starting to seep back out. I'm still going to tell Nat, but now I can do it gently, sensitively, apologetically, delicatel—

"Unless you mean the envelope that came through the door half an hour ago."

My breath stops.

"I took it up to her a few minutes ago. I'm not sure I'd call it a *delivery* exactly, but it seemed important. Handwritten and everything."

Oh, no, no, *no*.

And before Nat's mum can say anything else, I rip my shoes off and race upstairs.

55

I'm too late.

That's the only thing I know for certain when I open Nat's bedroom door. She's sitting on her bed in her pyjamas with the newspaper next to her. And on her face is the most hurt expression I've ever seen on anyone. Ever.

"Nat—" I start and then grind to a halt. "Nat, it's not what it looks like." Then I pause because actually, it's *exactly* what it looks like.

"What's this?" she asks in a bewildered voice. She holds the newspaper up. "Harriet? What's going on?"

I'm not sure I've ever heard her sound so young. It's like we're five years old again. "It's... It's..." I say and then I swallow and look at the floor. "It's exactly what it looks like."

"You haven't been sick?"

"No."

"You were in Russia?"

"Yes."

272

"You're a model?"

"Yes."

"I defended you…"

"I know."

"And you left me to Alexa and didn't even tell me why?"

Oh God. "Yes."

"You've been lying about…" Nat pauses for a few seconds. "About *everything*?"

"I was going to tell you, but I was looking for the right way to do it."

"Via national newspaper?"

I stare at her in confusion and then the penny drops. I look at the envelope. On the front is printed in familiar red capital letters: **NAT, IT WAS THE EASIEST WAY TO TELL YOU.**

Alexa really is a piece of work.

"*No*," I gasp. "You weren't supposed to know for *months*." Then I flinch. I'm not sure that's the best thing I could have said.

Nat's eyes widen. "You were going to keep lying for *months*?"

"Well, *no*… you know… just… a few more days," but I'm not even sure what the truth is any more. Was I ever going to be honest, unless I was caught? Have I been lying to myself as well as everyone else?

Nat's cheeks are getting pinker and pinker. "*Why?*"

"Because… Because…" It all made so much sense at the time, but it suddenly doesn't any more. "You were so angry at The Clothes Show…"

"*Because you lied*, not because you were *spotted*. I told you that."

"It would have hurt you."

"More than this?"

I lick my lips. "I thought you would ruin it for me."

"*You thought I would ruin it for you?*" she repeats, amazed. "I'm your *best friend*, Harriet. *Why would I ruin anything for you?*"

"You wouldn't understand and… and… you wouldn't want to be my friend any more."

The excuses are coming thick and fast. But the truth that I can't even admit to my best friend is that I lied because it was easier.

Because I'm a coward.

Because I clearly don't think very much of the people I love.

Because all I was thinking about was me.

Nat stands up and the hurt five-year-old suddenly disappears. "No," she says abruptly. "Now I don't want to be your friend any more. *Get out of my bedroom.*"

"But…" I start. I open my mouth and promptly shut it again. All I've done is think about myself and lie compulsively. I don't have a leg to stand on.

"*Now*," she yells, totally furious, and she starts rummaging in a plastic bag at the foot of her bed.

"Nat, I'm sorry."

"*Out*," she screams and I've never seen her so angry. "What are you waiting for, Manners? *Soup?* You still want *soup*?" And she pulls something out of her bag and throws it. A carton of green Thai soup hits the wall behind me and explodes. "*There's your bloody soup.*" She rummages in her bag again, and before I know it for the second time this afternoon food is hitting my head. "*And there's the bread. I hope you feel better soon. NOW GET THE HELL OUT!*"

And – just as I think things can't get any worse – Nat puts her hand in the air and looks at it. My chin starts to wobble: of all the hands in the air this week, I think this might finally be the hand I actually deserve.

Then, because I'm frozen to the spot, Nat pushes me across the room and into the hallway.

And slams the door behind me.

56

All I want to do is crawl into bed and cry, but I can't. The minute I open the front door I know things are about to get even worse.

Hugo's lying in his basket with his chin on the edge. His eyebrows twitch unhappily and he immediately looks at the wall as if he's blanking me. According to scientists, dogs can make approximately 100 facial expressions and it's quite clear which one Hugo is using right now.

"Annabel?" I whisper. "Dad?"

There's a long silence, so I put my bag down and tiptoe into the living room. Then I tiptoe into the kitchen, and the bathroom, and the garage, and the laundry room, and Annabel and Dad's bedroom. It's only when there's nowhere else to tiptoe that I go into

my own bedroom and find Dad sitting on the floor with his back against my chest of drawers.

He looks at me desolately. "You know," he says, "for somebody so organised, you're incredibly untidy."

There are clothes everywhere: books strewn all over the floor, sweet wrappers across the bottom of the bed, teddybears stuck halfway behind the wardrobe, clothes scattered. He has a point. I'm just not sure it's the most important one right now.

"Dad, where's Annabel?"

"She's gone."

"What do you mean gone?"

"She's gone, is what I mean. She'd gone by the time I got your message and managed to get back to the house. She took her bags with her and the cat."

"But why?"

Dad shrugs. "It was her cat."

"No, why did she leave?"

Dad reaches into his pocket. "She wrote this." And he hands me a yellow Post-it.

SICK OF BEING LIED TO. HAVE GONE.
A

Then he pulls out the article from the newspaper. "This was next to it."

I stare at it, my heart making little sputtering sounds. "This is all my fault."

"Not really."

"Of course it is, Dad. What else would she be talking about?"

"A couple of things maybe." He reaches in his pocket and pulls out another piece of paper. "This was on the kitchen table too."

It's a letter from The Clothes Show lawyers, addressed to my parents.

"Dad, I..." And my voice breaks. "I'm sorry."

The amount I'm saying that at the moment, maybe I should just get a little MP3 track with it on loop so that I can simply press a button and offer out earphones.

Dad shakes his head. "That's not everything." Then he looks at the carpet and rummages around in his pocket again. What he pulls out appears to be a tax form. More specifically a P45. "This was also on the table."

I look at it in confusion.

"I've been lying too, Harriet. I didn't get permission from work to come with you to Moscow."

"But..." And when I look at him, I realise he's been wearing the same clothes now for five days, he smells of vodka and he looks exhausted. In fact, he's looked exhausted all week. I've just been too wrapped up in myself to notice.

"I don't understand, Dad. Why not?"

"Because I didn't need to, sweetheart. The agency lost their biggest client because of me and they fired me on Friday. On the spot."

"But you said…"

"I know. I lied. I thought Annabel would be angry."

"Oh."

"It turns out she's much, *much* angrier now."

It feels like the whole world has tilted up on itself and everything is falling off the top of it. "Oh," I say again.

"Yeah. *Oh* pretty much sums it up for me too," Dad agrees and then he lies down on the carpet. "We're not very good at this, are we, Harriet?" he says.

And he closes his eyes.

It's only once I've helped him up and put him in front of the TV that I turn the yellow Post-it over.

PS HARRIET, YOUR FATHER NEVER TURNS NOTES OVER. DON'T TELL HIM I'M PREGNANT.

57

People Who Hate Harriet Manners
Alexa Roberts
Hat Lady
Owners of stalls 24D 24E 24F 24G 24H
Nat
Class 11A English literature
Models in general, but particularly Shola and Rose
Mrs Miller, our headmistress
Annabel
Harriet Manners

My name is Harriet Manners and I am an idiot.

I know I'm an idiot because I'm lying in my bed, looking up other words to call myself. Ninny. Dunce. Blockhead. Twit. Ignoramus. *Fool*. Which is the origin of the word 'geek' so I think we've just come full circle.

I've made a mess of everything.

Alexa has won. Nat's not talking to me. Annabel has gone. Dad's unemployed. I owe £3,000. The entire

280

population of England is laughing at me. My hair looks like a ball of orange fuzz.

I don't know if I've been suspended or not, but only because I'm refusing to go to school to find out. For the first time in my life, I've decided I don't care about my education. It hasn't made me any smarter at all. I've actually managed to transform in the *opposite* direction. I'm like a caterpillar that's gone back to being an egg, or an unemployed Cinderella without even a hearth to scrub.

One simple metamorphosis story and I couldn't even get *that* right.

Dad and I spend the entire night trying to fix things. I haven't told him about the back of the note, though. I *think* about telling him, but Annabel asked me not to. I've betrayed her quite enough already without adding that to the list as well.

"We've got to do something *dramatic*," Dad tells me sternly after staring at the wall for half an hour. "We have to *prove* to Nat and Annabel how sorry we are."

So we make 'sorry' cakes, we make cards, we film ourselves singing an apologetic song. I take Nat a mix CD, a little silver necklace that splits in half and a box of chocolates. Then a barely used bottle of perfume, then flowers with a cunningly amended poem on the card. She trashes everything apart from the chocolates, which she eats without offering me any.

Dad goes to Annabel's law firm and stands outside with a bunch of flowers and a sandwich board that says *I AM SO VERY SORRY, ANNABEL* (and on the back says *SERIOUSLY. VERY, VERY SORRY*). He stands there until the security guard comes down with a note saying:

GO AWAY, RICHARD, OR I'LL BACK CHARGE YOU FOR WASTING MY TIME.

MY RATES ARE £300 AN HOUR AND YOU OWE ME TEN YEARS.

ANNABEL

Dad says he's not good at maths, but that's not a number he wants to calculate.

Finally, totally defeated and unsuccessful, we give up and sit on the sofa for the rest of the evening. Then we get up the next morning and sit on the sofa for the rest of the next day. I have no idea what we watch on television because I'm not really watching it.

All I'm thinking, over and over and over again, is: *How? How do I make everything go back to exactly the way it was?* Because I'll go through everything again – the bullying, the ugliness, the unpopularity – just to have my old life back. I've traded the only things that mattered to me for a whole load of stuff that doesn't matter to me in the slightest. And I did it on purpose. Out of choice.

My IQ is clearly nowhere *near* as high as I thought it was.

"My little Tadpole," Wilbur gasps when I eventually pick up my phone. "Where have you been?"

"On the sofa."

"Jelly-bean, we have things to do. Everyone wants a piece of you, my little Ginger-cake. Journalists, television shows, designers, big brands. My phone hasn't stopped, Sugar-plum, apart from when I turned it off so I could drink a coffee. The genius that is Yuka Ito has turned your little sit-down-athon into a PR coup. She's telling everyone you've inspired her. You're her new muse."

"Uh-huh," I say without really listening.

"You know what that *means*, my little Frog?"

I continue staring impassively at the television. "No."

"It means you're *hot*, darling. You're at *boiling point.* Your saucepan simmereth over."

There's a silence. Modelling is how I got into this mess in the first place. OK, technically *lying* is how I got into it. But I wouldn't have had to lie if the modelling had never happened. Nothing's going to get better if I keep going down this path.

"I don't care," I say. "Sorry, Wilbur."

Wilbur laughs. "That almost sounded like *I don't care*," he says, giggling. "But obviously I misheard you. This is… this is… the stuff of dreams."

"Not of mine."

And I put down the phone.

I'm not sure what my next plan should be. But it's going to start with Annabel.

58

The best way to make amends for lying is probably not by lying, but I can't really see an alternative. Not after the way Annabel responded to Dad.

Luckily the receptionist is new, which makes the process significantly easier. As long as there isn't a little warning photo of me taped behind the desk: you know, like the photos they have of terrorists and people who steal penny sweets from newsagents.

"May I speak to Annabel Manners, please?" I ask sweetly, taking the fur hat off and making myself look as small and vulnerable as physically possible.

The receptionist reluctantly puts down her magazine. "Do you have an appointment?"

"Yes." I widen my eyes to make my face a vision of innocence. "Gosh, that's a nice ponytail you have. Did you do it yourself?" And when she turns round to try and look at it, I lean over the desk and quickly scan the schedule. "My name is Roberta Adams," I say as she turns back.

285

She frowns at the list. "Bit young to have your own lawyer, aren't you?"

"I'm suing my parents," I say calmly.

Her expression immediately clears. "Oooh, I thought about doing that too. Let me know how much money you get. Go straight up."

And she buzzes me through before I get a chance to change my mind.

This building has always scared me. When I was young, I refused to come in alone when Annabel was working late because I thought it was haunted.

"It's not haunted," Dad said when I told him. "Haunted buildings are full of souls with no bodies, Harriet. A lawyer's office is full of bodies with no souls. There's a big difference."

And then he'd laughed until Annabel put salt in his wine glass.

Even the lift feels like some sort of creepy horror-movie glass coffin. When I finally get to Annabel's office, I can see through the window that she has her head down and is writing some kind of report.

"Ahem," I say softly.

"Roberta," she says without looking up. "Take a seat. I've been going through the file and I think getting custody of the guinea pig isn't going to be a problem."

I take a seat despite not being Roberta and squirm. I've just realised that Roberta is a real person and not just a name on a sheet, and she might actually turn up too. Annabel writes a few more things down and then glances up. She fixes me with a long stare, while I try desperately to activate the dimples in my cheeks.

"Well, Roberta," she says eventually. "Can I just say that you have grown a lot younger in the three weeks since I saw you last. Being away from your husband is clearly doing wonders for your complexion."

"Annabel—"

"And," she says, looking at my head, "that's a great improvement on your last hairstyle. Although as your last hairstyle was a purple rinse, that's not necessarily saying much."

"Annabel, I—"

She looks at the hat in my hand. "I thought for a moment perhaps you had brought the guinea pig with you, but I'm relieved to see that's not the case. I *would* suggest, however, making sure that whatever that *is*, is definitely dead. It looks like it might bite."

"Annabel—"

Annabel leans forward and presses a button on her phone. "Audrey? When the *other* Roberta Adams turns up, please keep her in reception until I alert you otherwise. And for future reference, none of my clients are schoolgirls. Thank you."

And then she leans back in her chair and looks at me in silence.

59

After what feels like forever, I finally manage to say, "Hello, Annabel."

"Hello, Harriet."

"How are you?" This seems like a good conversation opener. Actually, I think this is the only conversation opener. I don't know how she is at all.

"Sleeping on the floor of my office, which is never ideal, but apart from that I'm just dandy, thank you."

I stare at her stomach. It doesn't look any different, but I can't stop staring. It's amazing really. A few days ago it was a stomach containing strawberry jam and now it contains a person. I'm actually really excited, even though it does mean that every minute I've spent in the last five years researching *famous only children* on the internet was a total waste of my time. "So it's true?" I ask. "What you wrote?"

"That I am gravid, parous, fecund, *enceinte*, teeming with child?"

"Umm." I think Annabel's thesaurus is bigger than

mine. "Yes?"

"Absolutely. I'm gestating like nobody's business."

"Wow." I'm so overwhelmed with this information. I don't know anything about babies: it's a massive hole in my general knowledge base. I'm going to have to go home and do some research.

"Does your father know?"

"No, you told me not to tell him."

"Quite right. The man should learn to turn a Post-it over now and then."

It feels like something tight in my chest is finally starting to unravel; as if everything from the last week is starting to melt. Why didn't I just come to Annabel in the beginning? Why did I tell her I was OK when I wasn't?

"Annabel," I say, folding my arms round my knees. "Can I ask you a question?"

"As long as it's not about bodily functions. I'm not going to start discussing disgusting things just because I'm pregnant."

"It's not about bodily functions." Then I close my eyes and say in a rush: "Do you hate me?"

Annabel raises an eyebrow. "No," she says after the longest pause that has ever existed in the history of the world. "I don't hate you, Harriet."

I take a deep breath, and without warning everything in my chest comes pouring out. "I didn't want to lie to you, Annabel, I really didn't. I mean, I *did* want to lie to you because that's why I lied to you, but I didn't do it to hurt you or because I don't respect you or I don't think that you're usually right all the time, because you are. It's just... haven't you ever wanted to be somebody else?"

Annabel looks at me as if I'm mad. "Not really," she says finally. "Who in particular?"

"*Anybody*. Just to see what it's like? Just to see if it's better? To see if things can be different?"

Annabel thinks about it. "No," she admits. "Never."

"Well, that's what I wanted. I was so tired of being me. And I thought maybe if I became a model instead of a geek, I would be somebody else and my life would change, or maybe everyone else would change, or maybe the way they saw me would change."

Annabel crosses her ankles under the desk. "Hmm," she says.

"But nothing's changed and all I've done in the last week is make a big mess of everything, and I don't know what to do to take any of it back."

Annabel folds her hands together. "Huh," she says.

"And my list keeps getting longer," I continue in

a slightly smaller voice. "Longer and longer. I'm in trouble with just about everyone I've ever met and I don't know what to do now, Annabel. I'm out of my depth and I don't know how to fix it. Just… Just… *Please.* Tell me what to do. Tell me how to make it all better again."

I'm not going to cry. I'm *not*. But now I can feel a lump in my throat I can't quite swallow. Like when I'm taking those huge vitamins Dad makes me eat in the winter.

Annabel nods calmly. "And what list is this?"

Oh. I forgot she didn't know about my list. I reach in my pocket, get it out and hand it over the desk. You thought that was just a mental list, for your benefit? No, it's a real one. I carry it around in my pocket and update it regularly.

"Well, it's very neat and well spaced," Annabel says approvingly. "Underlined with a ruler?"

"Of course." I feel a little burst of pride. "Two lines, actually, if you look carefully."

"Nice," Annabel agrees. "Now give me the pen and the ruler. May I mark the list?"

I nod because it's a bit rude to tell her I don't really like other people editing my lists.

"Right. So first of all, we're taking this one off."

And she draws a neat line through her own name. "And I'd appreciate it if you'd stop putting people who love you very much on to lists like this." She looks at the list again with the pen lid in her mouth and crosses another one off. "And you can take off Mrs Miller too."

I shake my head. "She's going to suspend me for missing school."

"No, she's not." Annabel looks straight at me. "Harriet, when are you going to realise that you are just as bad at lying as your father is? I saw your faces when you came out of the agency and therefore kept in daily – sometimes minutely – touch with Wilbur. I gave my permission for you to have your hair cut and I also rang Mrs Miller and explained that you would be taking three days off school and I would supervise the catch-up: two for the trip to Russia and one to recover."

There's a stunned silence while my mouth makes an O shape. "But—"

"However clever you think I am, Harriet, I'm much, *much* cleverer." Annabel looks at the list. "And you can take Hat Lady and the stall owners off too: I paid them. Or, I should say, I recalculated the damages and paid them what they were actually worth, and then I threatened to sue them for extortion."

I stare at her with my mouth still open.

"You can pay me back if you want to, but trust me: the amount you earned this week – and Wilbur promised me he wouldn't tell you how much that is – you won't even notice." Annabel looks at the piece of paper again. "As for the models, we can obviously put that down to the fact that they're models and also women."

She crosses them off as if that explains itself.

"But everyone at school... everyone in my class, they—"

"Put their hand up? Nat rang and told me. Has world history taught you nothing, Harriet? Countries will always side with those who have the biggest weapons. Your classmates were scared of Alexa and not scared of you. You should take that as a good thing, unless you have dictator ambitions."

And she crosses them off the list as well.

I blink a few times. I suppose I hadn't thought of it that way, but countries with lots of nuclear weapons tend to have an awful lot of allies.

"And as for Alexa..." Annabel pauses. "I don't know what's wrong with the girl. The point is: who cares?"

"I care."

"I know you do," Annabel says and her voice is gentler now. "That's the problem. You need to stop caring what people who don't matter think of you. Be who you are and let everybody else be who they are. Differences are a good thing. It would be a terribly boring world if we were all the same."

"But, Annabel, I'm a… I'm a…" I can't get the word out, so instead I lift my satchel and point at what's left of the red word.

"A…" Annabel squints slightly. "CE-H? What's a Ceh?"

"A geek. It says GEEK. Or, at least, it used to."

"Oh." Annabel shrugs. "So? Some of the best people are. And – for the record – I didn't want you to model precisely because I didn't *want* you to become someone else." She picks up the newspaper and points at the article of me. "But I was wrong. You've stayed you and I'm so proud. What you did was kind. It was courageous. It was strangely inspired. It was everything I love best about you. It came from a good place."

"Russia?"

Annabel gives me a long look. "No, Harriet. Not Russia. *You*." She lifts an eyebrow and then looks back at the paper. "Take yourself off the list and you'll find that the rest start to disappear as well."

And she draws the final line.

I can feel my head starting to go swirly again.

Annabel looks at me in silence and then she hands me the paper.

People Who Hate Harriet Manners
~~Alexa Roberts~~
~~Hat Lady~~
~~Owners of stalls 24D 24E 24F 24G 24H~~
Nat
~~Class 11A English literature~~
~~Models in general, but particularly Shola and Rose~~
~~Mrs Miller, our headmistress~~
~~Annabel~~
~~Harriet Manners~~

"There's still one on there," I point out sadly.

"What did I tell you about putting people who love you very much on this list, Harriet?"

"Nat doesn't—"

"Don't be daft – she's just hurt and angry. Nobody likes being lied to by somebody they trust. When you've worked out what it is Nat needs from you, you'll be able to cross her off too."

"Is it…"

"No, it's not personalised flapjacks, Harriet."

I nod and tuck the list in my back pocket. I don't

know why I didn't come here first of all: Annabel always knows how to organise the world for me so it makes sense again. Just as she does when she tidies my room. "Are you coming home, Annabel? Ever?"

Annabel sighs and looks back at her report. "I don't know. Your dad has his own list to think about. And unlike you, he's old enough to do it on his own."

Her phone beeps.

"Annabel? Roberta Adams says if she doesn't get back soon, Fred is going to start getting anxious."

"God forbid I should make a guinea pig feel unloved. Send her up, Audrey." Annabel looks at me. "Now go home and study that list," she adds in her normal sharp voice. "You know where I am if you need me. My bed is in the cupboard."

And as I turn round and walk back out of the office with the paper in my hand, I realise how happy I am that Annabel knew about everything the whole time. It reminds me of that famous fridge magnet: the one about footprints in the sand.

I wasn't as on my own as I thought I was.

60

So I no longer have a plan.

The universe has shown me, repeatedly, that it has no respect at all for bullet points or pointers or lists or charts. Plans don't work and even when they *might* work and *should* work, people ignore them. So I'm going to try a brand-new strategy: not having a plan.

For the first time in my life, I'm just going to attempt to bumble through from one moment to the next and see where I end up. Just like a normal human being.

Or, you know. A bee.

"Are you *kidding* me?" I say as I open the front door. Dad's still in his dressing gown from yesterday, and the only difference is that he now has a family-size packet of gummy sweets nestled in the crook of his arm. I read somewhere that in an average lifetime we each use 272 cans of deodorant, 276 tubes of toothpaste and 656 bars of soap, and it is quite clear that since

Annabel left, Dad hasn't touched one of them.

"Look how depressed I am," he says as soon as I walk into the room. He holds up a sweet, looks at it sadly and then puts it in his mouth. "I'm even eating the green ones. I have nothing to get up for any more. *Nothing.* I think I'm just going to stay here until I grow into the sofa and they have to winch me out of the window every time I need the toilet."

"Dad," I say, sitting next to him. The situation is clearly critical. Dad is starting to sound like he thinks he's in some kind of made-for-TV film. I have to do something. "Dad, does Annabel like strawberry jam?"

Dad frowns and puts another sweet in his mouth even though he hasn't swallowed the one he's chewing yet. "What are you talking about?"

"Does she like strawberry jam?"

"No. She's always hated it."

"So *why is she eating strawberry jam*, Dad?" Then I look at him with the most obvious meaningful expression I can get on my face. I promised Annabel I wouldn't tell him, but I never told her he wouldn't work it out for himself.

Although frankly, at the rate my dad's brain works, there's a really good chance the baby will be in school by the time that happens.

"Do werewolves eat jam?" Dad asks in surprise.

I roll my eyes. "No. They eat people."

"So does Annabel. Do you think maybe she's trying to scramble my brain up and trick me into divorcing her by accident?"

"No." God, this is like pulling teeth. "Is Annabel any plumper than normal?"

Dad nods knowingly. "It's all the strawberry jam. Or people."

I look at him so hard it feels like my eyes are going to pop out. "Yes," I say meaningfully. "*Or people.*"

Dad stares at me blankly.

"So," I continue slowly, "she's *getting fat*. She's *eating things she hates*. She keeps *changing her mind* about things. She's *crying* about inconsequential things and *shouting a lot* and *peeing all the time*."

I'm ticking the points off on my fingers and holding them pretty much under his nose. There is no way he won't get this now. No *way.*

Dad nods slowly, a look of realisation starting to dawn on his face (he has a red and yellow stain on the corner of his mouth and I'm trying really hard not to look at it). "My God," he says in a stunned voice. "She's… she's…"

"Yes?"

"She's… *having an affair with a strawberry jam manufacturer*?"

"Oh, for the love of *sugar cookies*," I shout, standing up. How have I managed to grow into such a balanced, reasonable person with him as a role model? "She's *pregnant. Annabel is pregnant.*" Then there's a long silence while Dad's entire face goes white.

Oops. I didn't mean to just throw it at him like that. He's quite old. Over forty. He'd better not have a heart attack.

"Sh-she *can't* be," Dad finally stammers. "It's utterly impossible."

"Is this the part where I have to tell you about the birds and the bees and the fact that it has nothing to do with either?"

"No, I mean the doctors have always said she can't have children. Almost totally impossible. We've been trying for years."

OK: ugh. That's disgusting.

"Too much information," I interrupt. "Well, she is. The proverbial bun is cooking in the proverbial oven."

"She's *pregnant*?" Dad says again. He looks like he'd fall over if he wasn't already sitting down.

"I just saw her. Trust me, she's pregnant."

Dad inexplicably looks even more astonished. "You

301

just *saw her*?"

"She's not the Loch Ness monster, Dad. She's in her office, doing paperwork."

"She's pregnant. With a baby?" For some reason Dad looks at me questioningly.

"Yes, with a *baby*. What else is she going to be pregnant with?"

"A mini werewolf perhaps," he mumbles. Then there's a long silence while he puts his head in his hands. "I'm an idiot, aren't I?" he mumbles through his fingers. "A total idiot."

There's no beating around the bush here. "Yes. I think it must be in our gene pool."

"I need her. I need to tell her I need her *immediately*."

"No, you don't." I shake my head crossly. "You need to show her that you're there for her when she needs you."

And then I shut my mouth in surprise. Oh. *Oh.*

Is that why Nat is so angry with me?

Dad looks at me in shock. "When did you get so smart, missy?"

I put my nose in the air, totally offended. "I've always been smart, actually."

"Not that kind of smart, you haven't." Dad thinks about it and then stands up and dramatically takes off his dressing gown like some kind of superhero transforming. Underneath, he's wearing jeans, a T-shirt and a cardigan.

"Hey!" I say crossly. "That's my trick!"

"Like I said, I'm a maverick. And you're a chip off the old block." Dad stretches the muscles in his neck. "Now grab your coat, Harriet. We're going to get your not-so-evil stepmother back."

61

I have absolutely no idea where we're going.

"Annabel's office isn't in this direction," I point out as Dad pounds down the street in the steadily increasing drizzle, with me jogging along behind him. I've never seen him looking so purposeful (apart from when he's on the Easter egg hunt, and that has chocolate at the other end of it).

"She's not in her office."

"But she *is*, Dad. I was just there."

Dad looks at his watch. "The cleaners come in at seven and Annabel hates the sound of a vacuum cleaner. She'll have gone. I know my wife. Werewife or not."

He takes another turning and I can feel myself getting steadily more anxious (which is not helped by the fact that my phone keeps vibrating in my pocket). "We're going shopping?" I say as Dad takes an abrupt right turn into a clothes shop.

"Trust me, Harriet." Dad picks up a shopping

basket and throws a green floral dress into it. "This is part of the master plan." I look with concern at the yellow ruffled shirt he's chucking on top of it, followed by a pink catsuit and a sequined boobtube.

"Have you ever met Annabel before?" I ask in concern as he shovels more hideous clothes into the basket. "They're not suits or dressing gowns."

"They're not for Annabel."

I look with alarm at the purple hotpants he's just picked up. "Tell me they're not for you, Dad."

Dad laughs.

"Or *me*," I say sternly. I'm still looking at the hotpants.

"They're not for you, Harriet." Dad marches abruptly into the baby section.

"They're not going to fit the baby either."

Dad picks up a pair of baby socks and strides over to the cashier. If he screws this up, I'm going to have to move into Annabel's office with her. And – frankly – I'm a little concerned about just how many beds she can get in her cupboard.

"Right," Dad says when it's all paid for. "Let's go to the park."

"Annabel's in the park?" I huff as we charge to the bit of grass about fifty metres away. It's not really a park because there are no flowers or trees, but now is probably not the best time to split that particular hair.

"Have you met Annabel before?" Dad says as he hands me the hotpants, puts the baby socks in his pocket, throws the rest of the brand-new clothes in the mud and starts jumping up and down on them. After a couple of minutes, he looks up. "That doesn't look very much like helping me, Harriet," he says.

"But—"

"Pipe down and stamp on the shorts, kid. As hard as you can."

So even though I am quite distinctly not a baby goat, I pipe down, throw the recently purchased hotpants on the floor and start jumping up and down on them like Rumpelstiltskin when he finds out that he's been tricked out of the Princess. Three minutes later, we're both exhausted, dripping wet and covered in mud. We stop and look at each other. "That should do it," Dad says, nodding, and then he grabs the clothes and puts them back in the bag.

"But where are we—"

"All will become abundantly clear imminently," Dad explains in a mysterious voice. "Learn some patience, sweetheart."

Which – frankly – is a bit rich coming from him.

And then he starts charging back towards our house again, trailing mud behind him.

It's only when Dad takes an unexpected turn that I finally realise where we're going. I stop, very still, on the pavement and stare at him.

"We're going to the *launderette*?" I finally manage to say. This makes no sense at all. This is where I come. This is my hiding place.

"It's where Annabel always comes when she's upset, Harriet. She used to take you with her when you were tiny."

Suddenly a memory comes bursting forward. Annabel and I, sitting in the launderette, listening to the washing machines. Me curled on her lap, sleepy and sniffing the soap bubbles and feeling totally content. And then it hits me. I don't come here by chance, or by magic, or by coincidence. I come here when I'm sad or scared or anxious because – without even knowing it – it reminds me of Annabel and makes me feel safe again.

"There she is," Dad says. And my heart figuratively skips a beat, and possibly literally skips a beat too,

I'm so surprised. Because Annabel is asleep in the same chair I fell asleep in a few days ago. Her head on the same tumble dryer.

62

Dad looks at the sleeping Annabel with a silly expression on his face and then opens the door as quietly as he can.

"Annabel—" I begin, inexplicably wanting to climb back into her lap, but Dad motions for quiet. She hasn't opened her eyes yet and I'm guessing from this gesture that he doesn't want her to.

Dad opens the bag of wet, muddy clothes and dumps the contents on the table. Then he opens a washing machine and starts putting each item in, very slowly. My pocket has started vibrating again, but I studiously ignore it.

"The thing is, Harriet," Dad says loudly, "I've made a real mess of things." I look at Annabel; her eyes are still shut. "You see this shirt, Harriet? I really mucked it up. It was lovely, and now it's not, and it's my fault."

I glance at Annabel again. She hasn't moved, but one eye has opened a little bit.

"And do you see this jumper?" Dad continues,

holding up a green one. A big dollop of mud falls off the sleeve on to the floor. "It was beautiful and now it's ruined."

"Mmm," I say and peek at Annabel again.

"I can't help it," Dad continues, picking up a skirt and putting it in the washing machine. "I'm an idiot and sometimes I don't even know I'm mucking things up until they look like this." He holds up a pair of dripping brown trousers. "And I'm so angry with myself because they were such an awesome *pair*." He pauses for a few seconds and then adds, "Of trousers."

Annabel has both eyes open now and is quietly watching Dad fill the washing machine. Dad is pretending he can't see her. "And it's so sad," he says, picking up some gloves, "because they made such an amazing *couple*." He pauses again. "Of gloves. What do you think, Harriet?"

I clear my throat. "I think I messed things up too," I say, pulling out the hotpants and holding them up. "And I'm so sorry because I really love them."

I don't, just to make that clear. I don't love the hotpants. But I love Annabel and that's what the hotpants stand for. At least, I think that's what the hotpants stand for.

"Exactly." Dad continues to fill the washing

machine. "And you should always look after what you love properly and keep it safe." He pauses. "And not jump up and down on it in the mud." Then he makes a large sweeping gesture with his hand and moves into the centre of the room.

"You've gone too far," I whisper to him under my breath. "Rein it in, Dad."

"Sorry," he whispers back. "But maybe," he says more loudly, holding his hands together, "it's not too late. Maybe we can make everything lovely again."

"Maybe," I say, glancing at Annabel again and moving into the middle of the room to support him.

"I hope so. I'll do anything it takes because I really don't want to screw these up too." Dad promptly pulls the clean baby socks out of his pocket and dangles them in the air.

And then – I'm going to assume this is the final scene of the final act – he closes the lid of the washing machine and stands there like a wally, holding the baby socks and staring at Annabel with the expression Hugo makes when he pees on the carpet.

There's a long, long silence, broken only by the comforting sound of a tumble dryer going round and round.

Finally Annabel sits up and rubs her eyes. "You

know what gets things clean?" she says, yawning.

"What?" Dad says eagerly. He takes a few excited, dripping steps towards her.

"Turning the washing machine on." Annabel looks at it pointedly.

"Oh."

"And you know what else gets things clean?"

"Saying sorry again?"

"Washing powder."

Dad and I both stare at the washing machine. We've piled all the clothes into it and then just left them there. Presumably to clean themselves.

"Now just wait a minute," Dad says in a horrified voice. "I actually have to wash the clothes? I mean, *actually* wash them?"

Annabel glances at the ceiling. "Yes, Richard. You have to actually wash them. They're covered in mud and dripping wet."

"But they're a *metaphor*," Dad explains. "They're supposed to symbolise our relationship, Annabel. Are you telling me I have to wash the metaphor?"

"Yes, you have to wash the metaphor. You can't just leave them in the washing machine like that. It's a public washing machine."

"Can I take them out and throw them away?"

"No. We'll wash them and take them to a charity shop."

Dad looks shell-shocked and then visibly rallies himself. "Am I forgiven, though? Will you take me back, with all of my adorable foibles and charming idiosyncrasies?" He thinks about it. "And handsome quirks?" he adds with round eyes.

Annabel's mouth twitches, but I don't think Dad sees it. He looks really anxious, although this might be partly because he really doesn't like doing laundry. "We'll discuss it while you're doing the washing. And the drying. That should take a good couple of hours at least."

Dad sighs and looks at the washing machine. "I guess this is fitting punishment," he says in a humble voice.

"Oh, no," Annabel says, winking at me so that Dad can't see it. "This isn't the punishment, Richard. This is the metaphor for the punishment."

Dad looks terrified, and then sighs and takes her hands. "No matter what you do to me," he says, slipping effortlessly back into B-movie mode, "no matter how hard you try, I'll always be glad I knew where to find you."

"Me too," Annabel says and then she flicks his nose

hard with her thumb and middle finger. There's a pause while they both look at each other and something unspoken passes between them, something I don't really understand. Which is good because I don't think I'm supposed to.

"High five for Medical Miracle Baby?" Dad finally says, holding up his hand and grinning at her. Annabel bites her bottom lip, and then laughs and hits it twice.

"High ten," she corrects. "Although we're going to have to work on a better name than that."

Which must mean Annabel's coming home again.

63

Now I don't want to be smug or anything, but not having a plan seems to be working miraculously well. In fact, you could say that the plan of not having a plan – because that's how I'm now thinking of it – is working a treat. I've fixed Dad and Annabel pretty much single-handedly and left them in the launderette. And next on my not-plan plan is Nat.

My phone rings again.

"*Pamplemousse*?" Wilbur says as soon as I pick it up. It's been vibrating in my pocket at three-minute intervals for the last four hours and I can't ignore it any more. There's a really fine line between playing it cool and just being rude, and I think any more than four hours is pushing it. "Is that you, my little *Pamplemousse*?"

"It's still me, Wilbur."

"Oh, thank holy chicken monkeys. Where have you been?"

"The launderette."

"I can't help but feel your priorities are a little out of whack, my Chestnut-bean. But if clean clothes are what you need to be a star, who am I to argue?"

I sigh. I couldn't feel less like a star now if I tried. I'm covered in splashes of mud and I smell vaguely of washing powder and socks. "Did you want something, Wilbur?"

"Banana-muffin, I need to talk to you about an opportunity that's come up, but they need to see you tomorrow mor—"

"I can't do it." I look at my watch and immediately pick up speed: I need to get where I'm going faster. I frown, and then bend down in a moment of pure inspiration and click the little button on the side of my trainers so that the little inbuilt secret wheels pop out. And *no*, I am not of an age group too old to be wearing these. No matter what Nat says. Just in case you were wondering. They wouldn't make them in this size if I was.

Anyway.

"You *can* do it," Wilbur protests.

"No," I say again as I start wheeling down the pavement. "Whatever it is, I can't do it, Wilbur."

"But you don't underst—"

316

"I'm sure it's great, I'm sure it's amazing, I'm sure that every girl in the world wishes she had the same opportunity." I wheel-hop over a double drain. "But I don't, OK? This isn't me, Wilbur. None of this is me. I'm not the swan. I'm the duckling. No, I'm the *duck*. I just want things to go back to how they were before I met you."

Wilbur laughs. "You really *do* make me giggle, my little Darling-pudding," he titters. "As if that makes any difference!"

I'm so busy calculating if I'll get where I'm going faster if I start running rather than wheeling, but have to stop again in a few minutes – average speed versus immediate speed – that I'm hardly listening to him.

"Difference?" I say distractedly, skipping over a crack in the pavement.

"Kitten-ears, you're under contract."

I slam the stopper on the toes down and abruptly stop in the middle of the road, with the sound of the wheels still whizzing behind me. "I'm under *what*?"

"Contract, Sweet-bean. You know the pieces of paper you signed? That's what they call them in the legal industry apparently. Visa-vee: Yuka owns you.

Plumptious, she wants you to do this so you *have* to do it. Or she'll just go right ahead and sue you."

My stomach abruptly folds in half. *Why do people keep trying to sue me?*

"A contract?" I finally repeat in disbelief. Was I so blinded by the excitement of my own metamorphosis that I signed a contract without actually reading it first? Without making notes? Without looking at every single word of the small writing and then looking it up in a legal dictionary? I mean, of course *Dad* did. Dad would sell his soul for a pink marshmallow. But me*?*

Who have I *been* this week?

"I know! Isn't a 'contract' just the least fun name for anything in the world ever? Annabel was *furious* that you did it, but it still stands: just one parental signature needed, my little Squeaky-kettle. So I'll ring you with details about tomorrow later, OK? Toodle-pip, *bella*."

I make a few confused mumbling sounds, say goodbye and hang up. I can't believe I'm in trouble with the law again. For the second time this week. Doesn't nine years living with a lawyer rub off at all?

I can't think about this now. I'll think about it

later. There's somewhere I need to be and it's far more important.

And I abruptly click the button on my shoes so that the wheels disappear and start running.

64

I was only here a couple of days ago, yet everything feels so different.

It even looks different. Everything is lit by a bright green light and there's a little red flask on the ground. Somewhere in the background, I can hear the faint, tinny sound of *Swan Lake* by Tchaikovsky coming out of a wind-up, hand-held radio. Which was actually performed first at the Bolshoi Theatre in Russia, so everything seems to be fitting into place like a magical puzzle.

Or, you know. A normal one packed simply full of coincidences.

"Toby?" I say, crawling back into the bush outside my house.

He's sitting inside it, just as I suspected he would be, reading a battered copy of *Don Juan*. He looks up, sniffs and then lifts the green torch he's holding so that it shines directly in my face like a sort of Halloween-

320

themed Gestapo. "Harriet!" he says in astonishment. "What an unexpected surprise! I didn't expect you for – " and he clicks the red light on his watch – "another twenty-eight minutes. Did you not get any laundry done? Or did I miscalculate the dryer times?"

OK, Toby is much, *much* better at this stalking malarkey than I thought he was.

"Aren't you cold?" I ask, clambering in next to him.

"Not at all. This flask prevents the energy loss of the vibrating molecules of my soup and thus is still nice and toasty." Toby sniffs again. "Sadly, I think I may need a flask for my nose, as it is suspiciously icy and may be about to fall off, if that is a physical possibility."

I laugh. "Not at this temperature."

"Well, that's a relief." Toby looks around the inside of the bush with an embarrassed expression. "If I'd known you were coming, I'd have tidied up. Honestly, it's not always like this."

"It's OK. Isn't it my bush anyway?"

"Which makes me your tenant, I suppose." Toby fiddles with the volume button on the radio, which is now playing Vivaldi. "I shall try and keep it down so as not to disturb the neighbours."

"*I'm* your neighbour, Toby." I laugh again and make myself a little bit more comfortable on the blanket.

The entire time I was running/wheeling here, I knew I had to ask him something – something important – but I didn't know quite what it was.

Suddenly I do.

I look at Toby's skeleton gloves, and the hat with the little bear ears built into it, and the trainers with the laces that look like piano keys, and the battered copy of a book he'll never *have* to read, not even for university. I look at his flask and his blanket and his face, with the slightly shiny, drippy, wet-looking nose. I look at his simple, transparent happiness that I'm here. And then I take a deep breath.

"Toby," I say, "can I ask you a question?"

"Sure." Toby thinks about it. "Was that it? Did I just answer it?"

"No."

"Then sure, go right ahead."

"OK." I close my eyes, swirl the question around my mouth a few times, take a deep breath and spit it out. "Toby, do you ever feel like a polar bear, lost in a rainforest?"

Toby narrows his eyes thoughtfully. "What kind of rainforest?"

"Does it matter?"

"Absolutely, Harriet. Different rainforests have totally

different vegetation. It will dramatically affect how easy it is to be found again. Some have significantly more ground foliage and then it will be mainly cutting at plants with the paws." Toby waves his hands in front of his face to illustrate this.

There's silence again as I stare at him. "It's a metaphor, Toby. I'm speaking *metaphorically.*"

"Right. Gotcha." Toby thinks about it for a few minutes. "In that case, sure I do, Harriet."

My stomach flips over. He knows? "And then do you ever feel as if…" I pause, trying to think of how to put it. "As if no matter what we do, we're made of the wrong stuff and everyone can see it?"

Toby nods knowingly. "And we just want to get back again…"

"…to somewhere snowy, where the other polar bears must be…"

"…but we don't know how to…"

"…so we just wander around on our own."

Toby and I stare at each other for a few seconds and I can feel my entire body vibrating.

Not with romance. Just to make that clear. It's not a *romantic vibrating.* To make the point separately, Toby's nose chooses that moment to drip on to his scarf. But still: *he understands.*

"So what do we do?" I finally manage to blurt. "How do we get out, Toby?"

Perhaps there's a map I don't know about. Or – at the very least – a signpost.

Toby pulls a face, shrugs and wipes his nose with his finger. "Polar bears are awesome." He wipes his finger on his coat. "They're the largest land carnivores in the world, and did you know their skin is actually black and their hair is translucent, but looks white because it reflects light?"

I stare at him and my stomach is sinking already. So close and yet so far. "*Metaphorically*, Toby," I sigh. "We're still talking about metaphorical polar bears."

"I know. That's what I'm trying to say. We're awesome, Harriet." Toby picks up his flask and unscrews the lid. "We've got big paws so we can catch tropical fish out of rivers. And as we're genetically related to European brown bears, I think with a bit of practice we could climb trees too. Even the really tall ones."

"But..." And I pause. "We still don't *fit in*, Toby. Doesn't that bother you?"

"Nope." Toby takes a swig of soup.

I can feel myself starting to stammer. Toby knows, but he doesn't care? "B-b-but what about the others?" I start mumbling in confusion, almost to myself now.

"The frogs, the parrots, the... the tigers, the flying squirrels... What about them? They *know*, they see it, they don't want anything to do with us, they laugh at us..."

"In fairness, most of them end up getting eaten, Harriet. We've all got our bad points. The rainforest is an extremely harsh environment and shrinking in size. Just as the ice caps are. That's a much bigger issue."

"But—"

Toby puts the cap back on his flask and straightens out the blanket. "Just enjoy being a polar bear. Appreciate the size of our paws." He makes his hands into paws and waves them in front of his face again. "Plus," he adds, "we're deceptively fluffy and cute."

I stare at him, too surprised to say anything. Suddenly, cross-legged and bathed in the green light of his pocket torch, Toby looks otherworldly. Mysterious. Knowing. Almost... Yoda-like.

And then he sticks his finger up his nose and goes back to being Toby again.

We sit in silence: Toby fiddling with the channel on the radio and me picking distractedly at a leaf on the bush. There are so many things to think about and yet – somehow – I don't need to think about them. They're presenting themselves to me now, fully formed.

I clear my throat and start crawling out from under the bush. I finally know what it is I have to do. "Right," I tell Toby over my shoulder in my bossiest voice. "You're coming with me."

Toby looks at me with wide and delighted eyes. "I am? With you? When?"

"Now. Bring your green torch, Toby."

I'm going to need all the additional wisdom I can get.

65

I'd like to say that our ensuing journey is a profound one: filled with adventure and inspiration and self-discovery. That would be nice, wouldn't it? A little bit like *Pilgrim's Progress*, without the overwhelming religious analogy.

It's not.

"Are you sure you wouldn't like me to walk ten paces behind you?" Toby asks in consternation as we hurry down the pavement. "Would it make you more comfortable?"

"Toby, when does walking ten paces behind ever make someone more comfortable?"

"It depends on whether they see you or not. Although, I have to say it gets a bit tricky *measuring* the ten paces. It usually requires running up to them and then pacing away again. Which isn't as subtle as you might think."

I decide to ignore this. "Just walk next to me, Toby. Like a non-stalker."

"Golly." Toby seems overwhelmed. "This is a break with tradition, I have to say. If you change your mind, Harriet, just say the word and I'll duck behind a tree and pretend to be reading a newspaper or checking for woodworm, OK?"

"OK." I smile at him. Why have I always been so mean to Toby? He just wanted another polar bear to play with.

"Would you mind terribly if I attempted to hold your hand?" he adds, skipping next to me. "For just a short time? On this beautiful winter day?"

All right, I'm not feeling that sorry for him.

"Yes," I snap, stuffing mine in my pocket. "I would mind terribly, Toby."

Toby starts rummaging in his backpack. "I shall make a note of that," he tells me earnestly. He scribbles something in his notebook. "Perhaps in six months?"

I think of Nick's hand, the hand I'll never hold again. My stomach gives a sad little flip and I shake my head.

"Not a problem," Toby says cheerfully, making another note and putting his book away. "Seven months it is."

Nat's house seems even bigger now, although I'm pretty sure it's the same size. It's just my guilt making it loom like something out of a Tim Burton film.

"Stand back," I tell Toby quietly as we approach her front door. "Nat isn't happy with me. And, much like an angry *Camponotus saundersi*…"

"Commonly known as the Malaysian ant," Toby interjects.

"There's a good chance that when we get close, her head is going to literally explode."

Toby obediently stands a few metres back and the door opens. Nat's mum blinks at us a few times. She's now entirely pink: pink dressing gown, pink towel round her head, pink face mask. She even has a pink eye mask strapped to her head, like inflatable glasses.

"Harriet!" she says, delighted. "Are you here with gifts again? I finished the chocolates and arranged what I could salvage of the pink roses strewn around the driveway. Although the bits with the teeth marks obviously had to go in the bin."

Sugar cookies. I knew Nat preferred lilies.

"Is Nat here, please?"

"Still sulking somewhere, I believe, yes." Nat's mum glances behind me and waves. "And this must be your little stalker, Toby. I remember you from the school fête a few years ago. You were shuffling around the raffle on your belly with binoculars."

Toby steps forward, beaming. "That's me," he says, puffing out his chest proudly. "Although my Harriet-following skills have improved *immeasurably* since then. It's very nice to meet you properly, Mrs Nat's mum."

"It is indeed." She smiles at him, and then smiles at me, and then smiles at Toby again. And then – and I can't actually believe this – she winks at me. She'd better not be winking for the reason I think she's winking.

Ugh.

"Ahem." Nat's mum clears her throat and then gets a small hand-held microphone out of her pocket. "Excuse me," she explains to us, "but shouting up the stairs is causing unnecessary wrinkling in my forehead. So I've invested in an alternative." And then she clicks the little red button on the side. "Natalie?" she says into the microphone, and somewhere in the distance her voice starts bouncing around the stairs. "You have a couple of visitors."

Silence.

Nat's mum rolls her eyes and fiddles with the volume control. A loud screeching fills the house and she puts her hand over the top. "It's linked up to a speaker outside her bedroom," she whispers conspiratorially. "I put one under her bed too, although she hasn't found that one yet. Natalie? *Natalie?*" She listens for a few seconds, sighs and holds the microphone up again. "Don't make me turn it up to ten, young lady."

"All right, all right," I hear Nat shout, storming down the stairs.

Nat's mum turns the microphone off, winks at Toby and me, retreats into the living room and shuts the door. Leaving us to face Nat.

And – from the look on her face – I believe she's about to give the head-exploding Malaysian ants a run for their money.

66

"Well?" Nat says after a few seconds. "I'm surprised you're here again, Harriet. I thought you'd be busy auditioning for *A Midsummer Night's Dream*."

I blink a few times in surprise. "No. I'm not."

"You should be. I heard they're looking for an *ass*."

Oh.

Now why can't I think of quips like that when I need them? Does she sit and make them up beforehand or do they just pop out like that, fully formed? If she ever talks to me in a non-violent way again, I must remember to ask her.

Toby holds his head up very high and looks Nat dead in the eye. "Natalie Grey," he says in a stern voice. "Harriet has come here in great and glorious dignity – and, if I may say so, quite mesmerising beauty – to apologise to you. The very least you can do is stand there and listen politely. Otherwise you're nothing but a... a... a..." I can see him looking around desperately. His eyes fall on the ground next to the front door. "A

332

flowerpot head," he finishes triumphantly. "Full of lavender."

Toby clearly has the same problem I do. Nat lifts an unimpressed eyebrow.

"I don't want to apologise again," I say in a rush.

"Then what are you doing here? Are you going to give me more pointless gifts that I can enjoy breaking?"

"No. I just want you to come with me somewhere."

Nat's shocked into silence for a few seconds. "And why the hell would I do that?"

"Because neither of us is happy like this."

Nat makes a *hmph* sound. "Actually, being without you is extremely liberating, Harriet. I never knew how much time there would be in life when it's not being filled with documentaries about humpback whales migrating."

That's a low blow. She *liked* the humpback whale documentary. She said they were very "splashy".

"Please, Nat? Twenty minutes and if you still hate me then you can spend the rest of the night cutting my face out of all our photos."

"How do you know I haven't already done that?"

We glare at each other obstinately for a few seconds, neither of us willing to budge.

Toby clears his throat. "If you need somewhere to

put all the cut-out Harriet heads," he interjects, "I'd be happy to take them off your hands."

We both turn slowly to stare at him, but luckily my response is interrupted by the sound of the invisible Nat's mum tapping the top of the microphone. "Ahem," she says, like the disembodied voice of some kind of ancient goddess. "Go with them, Natalie."

"What?" Nat says to thin air.

"I'm not having you marching around the house with a face like a smacked bottom for the rest of the week. Go with them."

"*No.*"

"All right." The voice of the goddess clears her throat. "It's on six, Natalie." A screech starts filling the house.

"*Mum.*"

"Seven." The screech gets louder. Nat starts chewing on her bottom lip.

"At eight, Natalie, your ears are going to start hurting."

Nat puts her hand over her face. "Please, Mum—"

"Nine. Ringing in your ears for the rest of the day. Don't make me go to ten. I will."

"Fine!" Nat shouts, glaring behind her and grabbing her handbag. She violently forces her feet into a pair of shoes next to the door. "Fine, all of you. Happy now? I'm coming." She stalks out of the door and slams it behind her.

But not before we hear the faint sound of disembodied laughter.

I lead the rest of the way.

I have to: nobody else knows where we're going. And even if they did know where we were going, they wouldn't know how to get there. I'm the only one with that magical knowledge, thanks to a party eight years ago that Nat missed because she was having her tonsils out. The first and last party I ever went to without her. Although I haven't exactly been *wading* through solo invitations.

"Right," I say nervously as we get to a large front gate and I click the latch. "Just let me do all the talking."

"Harriet," Nat says crossly as we walk up the garden path. "Where the hell are we? And when do you ever *not* do all the talking?"

I know I'm supposed to be making peace with her, but with comments like that she is making it very difficult.

"You think I don't know what friendship is, Nat," I say, lifting up the knocker and letting it fall noisily. "But you're wrong. And I know how to be honest too." I lift it again and let it fall. "I just forgot for a little while, that's all. And now I'm going to prove it to you."

Slowly, with an ominous creak and a struggle – and some mild swearing – the front door opens.

And there, with a very surprised look on her face, is Alexa.

67

If you guessed this is where I was coming then your mind clearly works just like mine does. In a linear and sensible and yet simultaneously creative and poetic fashion.

Nat and Toby's minds, however, obviously don't. Their mouths have fallen open in perfect coordination with Alexa's.

"This," Nat says clearly behind me, "tops the list of most stupid things you've ever done, Harriet. That's a pretty huge achievement."

"*Harriet,*" Toby stage-whispers, "*did you know Alexa Roberts lives here? What were the chances?*"

I clear my throat. Alexa's face is going through emotions the way Annabel flicks through channels on advert breaks: shock, followed by incredulity, and then a long moment spent on anger and a brief glimpse of embarrassment. And for a few fragments of time I almost see… respect. Respect for my audacity. On second thoughts, no. It's not respect.

337

It's a reaction to the smell of Toby's powerful aftershave: the wind's blowing it straight into the house.

"Alexa," I say and I take a deep breath. I'm not absolutely certain what I'm going to say, even though I've been thinking about it all the way here. I just know that – whatever it is – it has to be perfect and it has to fix everything.

No pressure then.

"Harriet," Alexa says, beaming at us. "Natalie. Toby. What a pleasant surprise. Would you like to come in for a cup of Darjeeling tea? My mum's just bought a new box of Bakewell tarts and there's plenty to go round."

My deep breath rushes out of me all in one go. "Huh?" I say in confusion. "What? Seriously?"

Nat puts her head in her hands.

"Sure," Alexa says, folding her arms in front of her. "We can all sit in the living room and discuss the likelihood of a white Christmas."

"Really?"

The beam disappears. "*No*, not *really,* you moron. I have no idea what you're doing here and I don't care. Get off my doorstep before I set the dogs on you."

Toby takes a few steps backwards. Admittedly, I can't hear any dogs, but that doesn't mean there aren't any; they might just be really quiet ones.

I bite my bottom lip hard. "Not until I've said what I need to say."

Alexa's frown deepens and she starts making a whistling sound. "Rex? Fang? Come here, boys. It's geeks for tea."

Nat breathes out loudly and tugs at my arm. "OK, Harriet. You've made your point, you're risking your own safety to defend me, you're very brave, I love you again, now let's drop it and go home, all right?"

"No." I fold my arms, partly to look determined and partly because my hands are shaking with nerves. "I'm not going anywhere. Not until I've told her."

"Told me what?" Alexa stops whistling and her eyes narrow. "You're standing there like the three little pigs on my doorstep so that you can tell me *what*?"

There's a long silence while I look at her, my brain making whirring sounds. *The Three Little Pigs.* And their three little houses. One made out of straw, one made out of wood and one made out of brick. That's it.

I'm going to tell Alexa that if we're the three little pigs, then it's OK because there are three of us, and we're not in a house of straw, we're in a house of brick. So she can huff and puff as much as she likes, but she can't blow us down.

And if she has a problem with this analogy – I do, actually, because in Tudor times houses were made out of straw and *they* didn't seem to have a problem with the elements – then I'll switch to *The Three Bears* and tell her it doesn't matter how much of our porridge she eats and how many of our beds she sleeps in: we've finally found the strength to run her back into the woods.

And then I'll turn to *The Three Brothers*, and I'll just keep going with the fairytale triumvirate analogies until she understands that we're not frightened of her any more. And she can't hurt us again, however hard she tries. Because we won't let her.

I prepare myself to launch an attack verbally way below my range, but abruptly stop. I don't need to say any of it. I know. Nat knows. And Toby knows. We're here and that's enough. But there is something I do need to say.

"We're sorry about your hair." I point to Alexa's head. "That's what we came to say. What we did was horrible, malicious and wrong, and we are sorry."

Alexa lifts her eyebrows. "You came all the way over here to tell me you're sorry about my hair?"

"Yes." I turn to Nat, who looks totally speechless. "Aren't we, Nat?"

"I'm sorry too," Toby interjects. "Despite having nothing to do with it in a *literal* sense, as leader of this gang I feel I should take responsibility for its actions."

Nat and I look at each other. We'll just let Toby have that one.

Nat scowls and her cheeks go pink. I know she's been feeling bad about it too. She's just not mean enough to think it was acceptable behaviour. "Yeah," Nat says finally, her shoulders relaxing. "I lost my temper, Alexa, and I shouldn't have. I'm sorry." She pauses. "But if you do anything like that to Harriet again," she mutters so that only I can hear her, "I'll give you a buzz cut."

Alexa touches her hair. "Luckily my face shape can pull off just about anything. Are we done now?"

"Yes," I say slowly, looking at her hard. "We are done now."

And I really, really mean it.

"Then please feel free to go to hell. All of you." Alexa looks at the three of us. "Geeks," she adds, almost as an afterthought.

And closes the door on us.

68

We dance all the way home. Although we wait until we're out of Alexa's driveway first obviously. We're not on a suicide mission.

"*Did you see that?*" Toby keeps shouting, wiggling his hips. He's opened his jacket up and is accompanying our triumphant movements with the electric keyboard on his T-shirt. "Take *that*, Alexa! *WHAM!* We came all the way to your house and *everything*!"

I twirl round in a happy little circle with my hands over my head. It's all over. If the big bad wolf wants to get us, she's going to have to climb down the chimney. Where we're going to keep a big cauldron of hot water, just in case.

It feels *amazing*. Even Nat does a little triumphant shoulder wriggle when she thinks nobody's looking.

"You know," she says breathlessly when we've all finally stopped glorying in the moment, "that felt really good. Alexa's never going to say sorry for anything, which makes us the good guys, right?"

"Well, we know we're not the bad guys," Toby says earnestly. "If we were, we'd be wearing black with little skulls and we'd probably have moustaches."

"I still can't believe you cut her hair off."

"I *know*. What was I thinking?"

"Where did you even get the scissors?"

"The art room. Everything went a bit blurry for a few minutes and the next thing I knew I had a ponytail in my hand. I've felt horrible about it for days."

"Nat," I say seriously, slowing my skipping down a little. "I am sorry. For everything. For lying to you. For stealing your dream. And I know that you'll probably hate me forever, but…"

Nat rolls her eyes. "I was never going to hate you *forever*, Harriet. Just a couple of days."

"But you said…"

"We were *fighting*. What did you want me to say? *I'll hate you for about thirty-six hours until I've calmed down a bit?*"

Oh.

"Yeah, that would have been nice, actually," I tell her, slightly huffily. "Just a heads-up could have been really handy. I was in the depths of despair."

Nat laughs. "Drama queen as always. Although if you had a temper like mine, I probably would have kept the modelling secret too. I am *terrifying*." She looks proudly at her nails and blows on them. "Unpredictable and absolutely *terrifying*."

"So we're…" I venture.

"Yeah." Nat shrugs and grins at me. "Whatever."

I'm just about to throw myself into her not-even-slightly open arms when my phone rings and Toby holds his hands up.

"It's not me," he points out. "Just in case anyone's wondering. I'm not ringing you, Harriet. Although I could because I've totally learnt your number off by heart."

"Wilbur?" I say, grabbing it out of my pocket.

"Hello, my little Crunchie-nut," Wilbur says happily. "I'd love to sit and chat about all sorts of girly fun, but I want to go home, so here's the details for this thing Yuka wants you to do. It's tomorrow morning, Petal-moo; an interview for a fashion special on *WakeUp UK*. They need you there nice and early so you'll still get to school on time." He pauses. "If your school starts at 10am obviously."

I look at Nat, who's pretending she can't hear the entire conversation. Wilbur's voice carries like a Sports Day whistle.

"I can't do it, Wilbur." Nat's eyes go very round,

but we've only just resurrected our friendship: I can't risk it. "You're just going to have to tell Yuka to sue me. Remind her that I'm underage, please, and my stepmother's a really, really great lawyer."

I can feel it already. Nat and I will be like the dolphins at Sea World again, jumping in perfect harmony. Living in synergy; one stream of consciousness, with never a cross word between us. Two minds in one bod—

The phone gets snatched out of my hand.

"Wilbur? Hello. This is Nat. I'm the girl who cried in your reception on Saturday morning. Harriet says it's a fantastic and exciting opportunity and she'll be there. Text her the time and address. Thanks." And she hangs up.

I stare at her for a few seconds. *Nat's* the girl who was crying in the agency?

"Nat? What the hell are you doing?" I finally blurt.

"What I would have done at the beginning, if you'd let me."

69

Statistics aren't important, they're just numbers. Irrelevant, arbitrary numbers. So obviously I don't spend the evening on the internet, researching how many people watch *WakeUp UK* every morning.

(3,400,000.)

And I don't find out the demographic of the viewers.

(Extremely widespread: students getting ready for school, families having breakfast, workers as they get ready to leave the house.)

And I *definitely* don't find out roughly how many people watch the internet videos of the interviews.

(300,000 for a guy talking about trimming the edges of your lawn neatly.)

Most importantly, the thing I most absolutely don't do is skip breakfast because I'm locked in the toilet, breathing in and out of a paper bag, and then spend the entire taxi journey to the studio tearing the bag to shreds and scattering it all over my lap.

Why would I do that? I'm not the old, anxious

346

Harriet any more. I'm cool. I'm calm. I'm taking all of this in my stride.

Obviously.

"Harriet?" Dad says finally. *Everyone* has decided to come with me this time: the taxi is so full that the driver has started making grumpy sounds about what his insurance covers. Annabel's taken the front seat and Dad, Nat, Toby and I are all crammed in the back, trying to put our feet in places that don't already have feet in them. "Are you under the impression that you're some kind of hamster or possibly bird?"

I look at the papery mess on my trousers. It's true: if I was suddenly rendered much, much smaller, it would make excellent bedding.

"I'm making an ancient style of puzzle," I tell him loftily. "When I have time, I will consider putting it all back together again."

"Would you like me to make a start on it?" Toby asks eagerly. I tried to evade him, but after he explained how many buses he was going to have to catch to follow me, I relented. It's easier if he just stalks me in the same taxi.

"No. But thanks."

"I'm going to need to get out again I'm afraid," Annabel says from the front. "I need to pee."

"*Again?*" Dad sighs. "Honey, do you need a catheter?"

"No, it's fine, Richard. I'll just urinate all over this nice man's seats and then we'll just walk the rest of the way. Hang on, isn't this your favourite jumper, darling? Maybe I can use it to mop up the mess."

Dad's face goes pale. "*Stop the taxi.*" He looks at all of us. "Never lend a pregnant woman cashmere."

"I was going to anyway," the taxi driver tells us, pressing the little green light so that we can hear him through the speakers. "We're here."

The taxi turns a corner and we all fall silent. Partly because it's a little overwhelming arriving at an international television studio at 6.30am. And partly because Wilbur's waiting for us. Wearing a bright pink top hat and silver jumpsuit.

"Is it me?" Annabel says as the taxi pulls to a stop and Wilbur takes his hat off and bows. "Or does that man just get weirder and weirder?"

Once we've disembarked, Wilbur adjusts the pink hat slightly and then sends everyone to sit in another part of the studio while I go with him to "get beautiful". He looks at the frizz-ball masquerading as my hair. "Although, Baby-baby Panda," he adds sadly, "it looks like we're going to have to start from scratch again, doesn't it?"

Just in case I was under some illusion that I may have transformed even *slightly* in the last week, it's nice to be set straight.

"I can't control it," I explain in a small voice as he shepherds me down some skinny corridors towards a closed door.

"I can see that, Apple-blossom," he sighs, narrowing his eyes at the top of my head. "Any chance that it's controlling *you*?" He looks at my outfit. "Glad to see you're styling it out, though. Are these your pyjamas, Bunny?"

I ignore him. I'm getting quite used to doing that now. They're not my pyjamas, for the record. It's a snowman-themed T-shirt and baggy patterned trousers from the Moroccan shop in town. These are the only clean clothes I have left.

"So what do we do first?" I ask nervously. "Do I have any lines to learn?"

"Even better than that, my special Sugar-peanut. I've got *this*." And he holds out a small piece of plastic.

"A hearing aid?"

"I'm wiring you up, darling. With five million viewers, we reckon you might need some help."

Five million? The internet lied to me?

I look at the little plastic thing with a mixture of relief and horror. "You're going to tell me what to say?"

Wilbur throws back his head and laughs. "*I'm* not, Monkey-tiger. Can you *imagine*? I just don't think my vocabulary would fit in your little mouth, darling. No, Yuka Ito is. Word for word."

Oh, God. She's here? "And all I have to do is repeat it?"

"And all you have to do is repeat it," Wilbur confirms. He giggles again. "You see? I should *so* have been a model."

I look at the earpiece apprehensively. OK, I can do this. Say whatever it is Yuka wants me to say and then get back to my normal life. School. Trigonometry. History club. Walking to school, instead of getting a taxi via Shepherd's Bush and five million people.

"Now," Wilbur says, "let's get you ready and then we can get you both on to the sofa."

My brain twangs. *Both?*

"But if Yuka's sitting next to me," I point out, "how can she…"

"Oh, Yuka's not sitting next to you, Sweet-pudding," Wilbur laughs, throwing open the closed door. "Nick is."

My brain is now pinging in frantic little elasticated

movements around the inside of my head.

Nick looks up, grins at me and then goes back to doodling on a notepad.

Would people please stop doing this to me?

"Did I forget to mention he was being interviewed too?" Wilbur adds, looking carefully at my face and then winking. "Oops."

70

Does anybody – *anybody* – have any idea how hard it is to concentrate on getting ready to talk in front of five million people with an unexpected *Nick* sitting a few metres away?

Well, let me tell you: it's like trying to tune a digital radio while Mount Vesuvius erupts in the background.

"Why is he *here*?" I whisper under my breath as a nice lady called Jessica does my hair and make-up. I've already been put into a blue dress that I would never, ever have picked for myself. Mainly because it doesn't have cartoon characters on it.

"He's the male face of Baylee, Plumptious," Wilbur whispers back as if I didn't already know this. "Maximum brand exposure." He looks to the ceiling as if he's just seen an angel. "Yuka's a total publicity *legend*."

"Hmm." Nick's lazing around on the sofa – flicking his pen in the air and catching it again – as if national television is something he does all the time. Which,

actually, it might be. Today he is wearing a warm grey jumper and a pair of dark blue jeans. His hair is all sort of quiffed up at the front and now and then he puts his finger in his mouth and bites the—

"Hey, Manners," he says, looking up.

I look away quickly. *Sugar cookies.* "Y-yes?" I stammer, trying to look as nonchalant as possible.

He gestures towards the coffee table. "It's low, but if you really squidge, you might be able to do it."

Is that all he's going to say? After we held hands and everything? "I have grown out of my table-hiding days as it happens," I tell him in a cold voice. "It was a childhood phase, that is all."

"That's a shame. If we lived somewhere with lots of earthquakes, you'd be a really good person to know."

I glare at him. For somebody so gorgeous, he really knows how to be annoying. "Actually, there have been nineteen earthquakes in the UK in the last ten years," I snap. "Which makes me a good person to know right now."

"It does," he agrees, grinning at me and going back to his doodle.

I grind my teeth and feel my cheeks get hot. What's that supposed to mean? That I'm a good person to know, but only nineteen times in ten years? That's not a very good ratio.

"Now then, my little Squabbling-beans," Wilbur interrupts. He pushes a little bit of plastic in my ear, pulls the wire under my collar and pops another bit of plastic in a pocket at the back of my dress. "We don't have time for all this adorable Darcy and Lizzie tension, Kitten-cheeks. Let's get you on air so that your stepmother can stop texting me at three-minute intervals, Harriet. She's extremely anxious that we get you to school on time today."

I nod. I am too, actually. I don't want something to go horribly wrong later in life because I'm supposed to know about metaphysical poets and don't.

I notice that the little green light on my hearing aid has been switched on. I look at Nick. "Do you have one too?"

Nick and Wilbur both laugh.

"Harriet," a cold voice in my ear says. "This is Yuka Ito."

I look around, trying to locate her. "Don't look around trying to locate me," she snaps. "I'm in the production-control room."

"Can you see me?"

"No. I just know that's what you're doing. Are you ready?"

"I'm ready," I say as clearly as I can. Nick is standing just behind me, yawning and rubbing his face with the sleeve of his grey jumper. How come Yuka Ito isn't shouting in his ear like the little caterpillar in *Alice in Wonderland?*

"Just say what I tell you to," Yuka says, "and everything will go as planned. And please, Harriet…"

"Yes?"

"*Try* and behave yourself this time."

71

I'd always assumed that on TV, when it looks like the presenters are in a living room, they're actually, you know, *in a living room*. With a nice painting, a fireplace and maybe a few bookshelves for perusing while the cameras weren't rolling.

But it's just a stage with a few sofas, and a big open black space full of wires and intense-looking people. Frankly, I can't help but feel a little cheated.

"Good morning, sweetie," the chirpy blonde presenter says as I perch nervously on the edge of one of the sofas. "I'm Jane. I bet this is early for you, isn't it?"

I nod, even though I'm not quite sure what Jane's talking about. It's 7.30am – precisely the time I'm normally shouting at Dad to get out of the shower.

"And I'm Patrick," a slightly older man says, leaning forward to shake my hand, and then leaning a little further to do the same to Nick. "Don't be nervous, guys. This is just a bit of fun, right?"

356

"You know," Nick says in his slow drawl, "I just can't remember when I've had more." Patrick nods enthusiastically.

Yuka clears her throat in my ear. "Tell Nick that if he doesn't stop being facetious, he's doing his next show in a dress."

I lean forward and pass the message on.

"Awesome," Nick says, laughing. "Tell her to make sure it has sequins on it this time."

I keep looking anxiously into the dark space, but I can't see Nat, or Dad, or Annabel, Wilbur or even Toby. What was the point in stuffing themselves into that taxi if nobody's here now? Where's my stalker when I need him?

I look at Nick with my eyes wide. "Remember," he whispers under his breath. "No biggy."

I breathe out and can feel the panic starting to leave again. It's only six minutes. Just six minutes of saying whatever Yuka wants me to say, and then I can go to school and be normal again.

"Getting ready to go live," one of the cameramen shouts. "In ten, nine, eight..."

I look around the dark again.

"Seven, six, five..."

Where are they?

"Four, three, two…"

And suddenly – with the softest of shuffles – the five of them scoot into the room at the back. My entire body relaxes as if somebody's just cut all of the cords holding me upright. Nat holds her thumbs up and Dad points dramatically to Annabel's lower stomach, mimes going to the toilet and shrugs. Wilbur gives a little dancing move and then shoots me with the imaginary gun of his fingers. Toby simply stands there and grins at me.

"One," Jane says. And I'm live on air.

72

I jump a little bit and then – to cover it up – cunningly pretend I'm checking out the bounciness of the sofa.

"As part of our fashion special," Jane continues as if she hasn't noticed that I'm bouncing up and down on national television, "we have with us this morning Harriet Manners, the fifteen-year-old schoolgirl who made headlines across the world as the newest face of fashion powerhouse Baylee. How are you, Harriet?"

"I'm fantastic, thanks, Jane," Yuka says in my ear.

"I'm fantastic, thanks, Jane," I repeat like a robot.

"And we also have Nick Hidaka, the sixteen-year-old male face of the brand. How are you, Nick?"

"I'm barely awake, thanks, Jane." And then he grins at her so that his dimples pop in and out. "But I'll do my very best."

Are you *kidding* me? And *I'm* the one being spoon-fed lines?

Jane blinks a few times. "Amazing. Now, Nick, am I right in thinking that this wouldn't be your first big campaign? You've done Armani, Gucci, Hilfiger…"

"Apparently so."

"…And now Baylee. I remember there was a bit of controversy when you were first cast. Tell me, what's it like to work with your Aunty Yuka? Extra pressure or is it nice keeping it in the family?"

Nick laughs. "Well, let's just say if I screw it up, it's going to make for an uncomfortable Christmas dinner."

What?

My whole head has gone numb. Yuka is Nick's *aunt*? Nick is Yuka's *nephew*? They're *related*? They're *family*? The same blood runs through their… well, you get the picture.

And nobody told me?

"…you've caused a bit of a commotion yourself already, Harriet." Patrick's leaning forward and I suddenly realise that while I'm silently freaking out, he's trying to engage me in conversation.

"*Listen*, Harriet," Yuka hisses in my ear. "Or at least pretend to."

"Ahmmm," I mumble, smiling at as many people as possible.

"Fifteen years old, plucked from obscurity less than a week ago." Jane looks at her notes. "You caught legendary designer Yuka Ito's eye straight away, I hear. Gosh. That doesn't happen that often, does it? Isn't that just a fairytale?"

I look at her blankly.

"Yes, Jane," Yuka whispers. "It's a fairytale come true for any girl."

"Yes, Jane," I say obediently. "It's a fairytale come true for any girl."

"And Yuka's even designing a special outfit for you in her next show."

This is news to me. I stare at Jane.

"She is," Yuka says and I repeat. "I'm extremely lucky."

"Truly amazing." Jane shakes her head as if she wants to jump across the sofa and slap me jealously across the face. "Who wouldn't want that at fifteen?" She laughs gaily. "Who am I kidding: who wouldn't want that at any age? And it says here you're her new muse. Wow. Tell me, Harriet, have you always wanted to model?"

"Ever since I was a child," Yuka says clearly in my ear. "I used to dress up in my mother's clothes and twirl around my bedroom in front of the mirror. I have always been captivated by fashion."

"Ever since I was a child," I say dutifully. "I used to

dress up… in… my… m-m-m—" I swallow. Dad gave all my mum's clothes to the charity shop when she died. There was nothing to dress up in. And when Annabel came along, the only thing available would have been a suit.

I briefly imagine a skinny little red-headed girl twirling around in a huge pinstripe suit complete with tie and clunky office shoes and have to stifle a giggle.

"Harriet," Yuka snaps. "Say it."

"…in my mother's clothes and twirl around the bedroom in front of the mirror," I continue, trying to straighten my face out and not cry at the same time. "I have always been captivated by fashion."

"And how have you managed to balance it with your schoolwork so far?" Jane asks. "It must be hard, combining the two?"

"Baylee always puts my schoolwork first," I chime after Yuka has spoken. "It's of key importance to them."

Apart from – you know – the bit where they made me take two days off to go to Russia. And this morning.

"And your favourite school subjects?" Patrick winks at the camera. "I think we can guess what they'd be!"

Maths. Physics. Chemistry.

"Textiles and art, of course," I say diligently after waiting a nanosecond for my cue.

"And what about your school friends? You must be a very popular girl now."

I think of Alexa's scowling face and the shouts of *Geek*. I think of thirty hands in the air. "Uh-huh," I say.

"*Uh-huh* was not what I just said," Yuka snaps.

"As the new muse of one of fashion's biggest players," Jane says in excitement, "is the fashion life everything you thought it would be?"

Yuka clears her throat and I wince slightly: it's really unpleasant having that sound shot straight into your head.

"Modelling is everything I dreamed it would be…" I repeat. "And I love fashion because it's really about individuality, and creativity… and… and self-belief… and self-exp…" I trail off into silence.

Jane leans forward. "Self-exp?" she prompts.

"Self-expression," I say in a small voice. Then I stare into the black space where my family are sitting. There's a commotion behind the camera and somewhere in my ear I can hear Yuka starting to panic.

What the hell am I doing?

I'm sitting here, in front of five million people, repeating someone else's lines about self-expression. I'm harping on about individuality in a dress somebody else put me in, with a haircut somebody else gave me, wearing make-up somebody else did. I'm talking about self-belief when I became a model because I didn't have any.

Have I learnt *nothing*?

I take the microphone out of my ear and abruptly sit on it. Underneath my bottom, I can hear the tinny sound of Yuka yelling.

"It's not true," I say, taking a deep breath.

Jane flinches and I can see Patrick furiously reading the autocue.

"I didn't dream about being a model," I say firmly, refusing to look at Nick. "I dreamed of being a palaeontologist. I didn't do any twirling when I was a child, my favourite subjects are maths and physics, nobody at school has ever liked me and I don't think this is going to help much."

"Well," Jane says, laughing nervously, "isn't that just…"

"And I don't love fashion," I say because I can't stop now; this suddenly feels like the most important thing I'll ever say. "It's just clothes."

There's a gasp from around the studio and even the microphone under my bottom has stopped vibrating.

"And self-belief and self-expression and individuality are really important," I continue, looking into the dark and talking too fast, "but if you're wearing what everyone tells you to wear and saying what everyone tells you to say and thinking the way everyone tells you to think then – well… you don't have any of those things, do you?"

Patrick is starting to look frightened and there's a pink patch forming on Jane's cheeks. "You don't like it?" she says, her forehead creasing in the middle. "You don't like modelling?"

I think about going to Russia, and jumping around in the snow, and walking down that catwalk, and the butterfly girls. I think about how much fun it can be and how I feel when I'm doing it. I think about Dad's excitement, Annabel's pride and Nat's selflessness. "Actually, I *do* like modelling," I say in surprise. "But I don't want to be somebody else to do it. I still want to be me, and if that means wearing a suit and doing my trigonometry homework ten days before it's due then that should be OK."

"But if you hate fashion—"

I shake my head because I've suddenly realised that's not true either. "You know, Jane, cavemen used to wear different skins and bones to differentiate themselves from each other and from other tribes."

"Erm…"

"So if fashion's a creative way of showing the world who you are and where you belong, that's a good thing, isn't it? But if who I am is a Winnie the Pooh jumper then I should be allowed to wear it." I pause and look into the dark where Toby is standing. "Or a T-shirt with electronic drums." I look at Dad and Annabel. "Or a robot T-shirt or a pinstripe suit." And then I look at Wilbur. "Or a pink top hat for no reason at all."

"But—"

"But they're still *just clothes.* They can't make you something you're not. They can only help to say who you are."

Stop talking, Harriet. Stop talking *right now.*

I think I've sort of forgotten I'm on television. I'm having my little epiphany on air, in front of five million people. But at least I'm not lying any more.

Patrick is sweating and one of the cameramen is making a winding motion with his finger. Nick leans forward. "I disagree," he says and I flinch. *Of course*

366

he does. He's Yuka's nephew.

Jane smiles at him. "You do?"

"Piglet is far superior. Harriet's made quite an error of judgement."

I gape at him. What is he talking about?

"*Piglet?*" I snap. "What has Piglet ever done of any importance?"

"Helped to pull Winnie out of Rabbit's door, for one thing."

Nick and I look at each other for a few seconds and something passes between us. Except – yet again – I'm not quite sure what that thing is.

"Well," Jane says finally, breaking the silence. "That was a very interesting insight into…" she thinks about it, "something, wasn't it?" She glances at Patrick and puts her finger to her ear. Does she have a microphone as well? Is anybody round here just saying what's in their own heads? "Sadly, that's all we have time for. Coming up after the break, how to compost the hair from your pet brush." Jane grins at the camera and picks up her script again.

"And *cut*," the cameraman shouts.

And I'm done. Finished. Actually, considering what I just said on live television, I think that's probably true in more than one sense.

"Sorry for ruining your interview," I say in a small voice to nobody in particular. Or, you know. Everybody.

And I pull the microphone out from under my bottom, whisper, "Sorry, Yuka," into it and run to the back of the room.

73

It's not hard to see where my family is, even in dim lighting.

Dad's doing his dance again. Toby's bobbing up and down on the balls of his feet and Nat's standing on a chair and clapping. Even Annabel's nodding her head to what looks suspiciously like an internal beat. Wilbur is sitting on the edge of a box with his head in his hands and his hat off.

"Whoop!" Nat shouts across the room.

"Whoop," agrees Toby gravely. "And again, what Nat said: whoop."

"My daughter!" Dad cries as soon as I get close. He punches the air, scruffs my hair up and then folds me into a bear hug in one seamless movement. "Feminist, pioneer, trailblazer, general bottom kicker."

Annabel nods. "Harriet Quimby would be proud," she says approvingly, leaning forward and touching my face.

"As would Harriet the tortoise," Dad adds, nodding

369

up and down. Annabel rolls her eyes. "What, Annabel? She *would*."

"I'm glad you guys liked it," I say, my face going pink with pleasure. "I think that might be it for my modelling career, though. I'm so sorry, Wilbur. I let you down."

Wilbur looks up with a pale face. "No, you didn't," he says in a quiet voice. "That was really brave, Harriet. Don't worry about Yuka. I'll deal with her."

"Nobody *deals* with Yuka," a sharp voice says from behind us and we all spin round. Yuka Ito is standing in the middle of yet another spotlight, totally in black lace, but this time with bright red lips.

OK, does she just carry the spotlight around with her or does she just stop when she gets to one?

Yuka looks straight at me. "I do not appreciate being sat on, Harriet. Don't do it again."

"I'm sorry," I mumble. "This time I'm definitely fired, right?"

"Why would you be fired? If I had known you would say that, I wouldn't have given you an earpiece in the first place."

My mouth falls open. "But wasn't it just a PR..."

"Of course not. If I believed that fashion was about being the same as everyone else, would I dress like a

370

negative of Miss Havisham every single day for thirty years?"

"I guess not."

"Then this conversation is over. You'll sign your next contract with me tomorrow morning."

Yuka turns around and starts walking back towards the door.

"On one condition," I hear myself say in a clear voice. She stops and turns slowly back around to face me. "I'm not missing any more school. If you want me, you'll have to do evenings, mornings and weekends. Like a…" I think about it briefly. "A paper round."

Yuka narrows her eyes. "Did you just compare working for me to doing a *paper round*?"

I nod. "Yes."

She shuts her eyes for a few seconds and then opens them again. The corner of her mouth twitches. "Condition accepted. I'm hiring you for another season so you keep me on my toes. After that, I'll probably ditch you for somebody younger." She glances in the air. "Nick?"

Nick steps out of the dark where he's been standing, unseen. My whole stomach squeezes shut. "Yes, Aunty Yuka?" he says with a cheeky grin.

"Call me *that* again and you can collect your P45."

"Yes, Aunty Yuka?"

Yuka sighs. "Get your own taxi home, Nicholas. Like your father, you're far too irritating to sit with." And she turns around again and abruptly stalks out of the room.

I giggle slightly, feeling about six years old, and then turn back round to introduce Nick to the people I love most in the world. Except I can't.

Because they've all sugar cookied off.

74

"Well," I say after an embarrassed silence. There's still a door swinging, and if I listen *very* hard, I can hear the distant sound of my loved ones betraying me. "Everyone was here a minute ago." I cough a couple of times.

"*I'm* still here," Wilbur points out, standing up slowly and putting his top hat back on. "And wouldn't you know it, my little Chuckle-bum, Nick is here too. What a *coincidence*."

My cheeks are bright pink and when I glance at Nick, I notice with a spark of surprise that his cheeks are starting to… It must be a trick of the light. It's very dark in here.

"Well," I say, squeezing out the most unnatural laugh I've ever heard. "I guess we do work for the same person."

"And why is that, do you think?" Wilbur shifts his pose so that his chin's on his hand, like Rodin's *The Thinker* statue. "Nick? Any idea?"

373

Nick coughs too. "Nope. No idea at all."

Wilbur gives him a stern look. "So what was the point in doing all that Jane Austen stuff if she doesn't know about it, Poodle-bottom?"

The blush drains out of my body so quickly my head feels like it might float away. "W-what?" I manage to stammer.

"Nothing." Nick glares at Wilbur. "Have you been sniffing glitter again?"

"Harriet, my Baby-baby Panda," Wilbur says, rolling his eyes and sticking his tongue out at Nick. "*I* didn't discover you, honey, Nick did. Yuka recruited him to find the female face for the collection and then you fell into that hat stall... And the rest, as they say, is geography."

"History," I correct automatically.

"Yes," Wilbur agrees gravely. "His story indeed. *Nick* pointed you out to me, *Nick* gave your photos to Yuka and *Nick* said you'd be perfect for the campaign in Russia. With – as it just so happened – *him*."

I can't really breathe any more. Nick is the reason I'm here?

"But the table..." I say in confusion. "The pavement..."

"The table was a coincidence," Nick sighs, visibly

giving up. "You just happened to crawl under there. How was I to know you'd dive under it? Normal people don't do that and wannabe models definitely don't." He laughs. "And the pavement... I came to get you. I knew you'd freak out."

"But..." My head still feels like a helium balloon. "*Why?*"

Nick looks blank. "Because you always freak out."

I shake my head. My voice feels like I've swallowed it. "I mean, why do you care if I freak out?"

There's a long silence.

"Well," Wilbur finally bursts, "I can take a shot in the dark, if you want."

"*Seriously*," Nick snaps, making his fingers into a gun shape. "I'm going to take a shot in the dark in a minute and it *will make contact.*"

Wilbur looks charmed. "Isn't he adorable?" he says fondly. "My duty as Fairy Godmother is complete, anyhoo, and I believe it's time to spread my magic dust elsewhere. So many pumpkins after all; so little time." And Wilbur makes a few skipping steps backwards, takes a little bow and disappears with a dramatic flourish behind the door.

I'm going to pretend – simply for the sake of this moment – that I can't hear whispering on the other side of it.

There's a long silence. "I like you," Nick says finally. He's still speaking slowly, but the laziness that is always there seems to have disappeared. My whole body feels like it has a light bulb in it.

He likes me?

Lion Boy likes me?

"But... *Why?*" I manage to stutter.

Nick shrugs. "You're different."

I frown at him. "Good different or bad different?"

He grins. "Good," he says. "And bad. But even the bad bits are good different and they always make me laugh."

"That makes no rational sense at all," I tell him, crossing my arms. "There are 6,840,507,003 different people in the world. You clearly just haven't met that many."

"I've met enough," he says, twinkling at me and taking a step forward. His cheeks have gone pink now as well. I didn't know it could happen to boys.

A human heart is supposed to beat between sixty and ninety times a minute, while resting. A hedgehog's heart beats up to 300 times a minute when standing still. Honestly, I think I might be turning into a hedgehog.

Oh, God. Is he going to kiss me? It's my first kiss. My

first… *anything.*

I haven't brushed my teeth for hours and hours.

"Are you sure you don't want to meet a few more before—" I start and then I hear the door behind me open.

"Harriet? It's Toby." I turn round and only his fluffy head is visible. "I just want to reassure you that I am fine with this development. Fifty-three per cent of all marriages in the UK end in divorce and so statistics are actually on my side."

"Shut up, Toby," Nat says and I see a hand reach round and yank Toby back behind the door. Then the hand reappears, gives me a thumbs up and disappears again.

I look at Nick and clear my throat. I'm not a hedgehog any more. I'm a rabbit: 325 beats per minute.

Nick takes another step.

Now I'm a mouse: 500 beats a minute.

Another step.

A hummingbird: 1,260 beats.

And as he leans forward, all I can think is the following realisation: *nobody really metamorphoses.* Cinderella is always Cinderella, just in a nicer dress. The Ugly Duckling was always a swan, just a smaller version. And I bet the tadpole and the caterpillar still feel the same, even when they're jumping and flying, swimming and floating.

Just like I am now.

And in the fraction of time before Nick kisses me and every other thought in my head explodes, I realise: I didn't need to transform after all.

My name is Harriet Manners and I am a geek.

And maybe that's not so bad after all.

Acknowledgements

Thanks to Dad – a constant source of inspiration, encouragement and laughter – and Mum, for "doing the voices" at bedtime. Thanks to my little sister, Tara, for a lifetime of believing I'm better than I am; to Grandma and Grandad, for their never-ending wisdom and support and supplies of Jaffa Cakes; to Aunty Judith, who read the first few chapters and gave me the confidence to keep going. Thanks also to Hel, for reminding me to "write what I know". It shortened the process significantly.

Thanks to my agent, Kate Shaw, who rescued Harriet and has fought patiently and valiantly for both of us ever since; to Pippa Le Quesne, a wise guiding hand not unlike a literary Gandalf; to Lizzie Clifford, the most brilliant and sensitive editor a writer could ask for. Thanks also to the entire team at HarperCollins, for embracing geeks so warmly and wholeheartedly.

Finally, there is one person without whom this book would not exist: my very own "Alexa". You gave me a reason to write *Geek Girl*, and I will always be grateful.

Thank you. x